WICKED DECEPTION

M.V. KASI

Copyright © M.v. Kasi
All Rights Reserved.

To all of us.

May we emerge stronger with hope and compassion.

Contents

Contents

CHAPTER ONE

"I've been waiting to talk to the prettiest woman in the bar."

Narmada felt annoyed by the man's overly flirtatious smile and words. He was handsome and seemed to like her. But his presence grated on her nerves, and she wanted him gone.

"I'm about to leave," she said. She felt disappointed that she would have to leave the bar lounge and go back to her hotel room upstairs.

The man's smile got wider and he looked overly confident. "Are you staying in this hotel? I'll join you."

Irritation spiked inside her. "Sorry, I'm not interested," she said bluntly.

But the man didn't seem deterred. "I know you are interested. I'm Italian, and all Italian men are very good lovers."

Her skin crawled at the suggestive words.

"Come on, beautiful lady. Let's share the rest of the champagne bottle."

So it was him who had sent the bottle of champagne. Before Narmada could ask him to leave her alone and tell him she wasn't obligated to join him to finish the rest of the champagne, another voice cut through.

"Get out," a deep masculine voice ordered.

Narmada turned to see who it was, and her breath caught in her throat as her eyes clashed with the intense gaze of the darkly, handsome stranger.

It was him, the man she had been watching a while ago. She hadn't expected him to notice her, let alone come to her rescue.

The man named Marco didn't argue. He must have sensed the danger emitting from the darkly handsome stranger. Muttering under his breath, the man named Marco left.

Narmada didn't realize she still held her breath. Slowly, she exhaled, only to suck in another deep one.

Up close, the darkly handsome stranger was truly breathtaking. With piercing dark eyes, a bold nose, high cheekbones with a small scar on the left cheek, and a full bottom lip—it was hard to tear her eyes away from his striking face.

"Join me at my table," he ordered.

Her first instinct was to turn down his order. She had no idea how to deal with men or dating, let alone a man like the one in front of her. He appeared to be a man who was used to giving out orders and getting what he wanted.

"I..." Before she could say anything out loud, he began walking back to his table.

Even though he had ordered her to his table, he was giving her a choice. She could walk away or come up with a polite excuse and leave.

She followed behind him in a hypnotic daze.

He held the chair for her as though he knew she would come. With her heart thudding, she sat down while he took the seat opposite to her.

He was watching her again. Her cheeks heated at the impact of his dark, heavy gaze.

"A-are you from Milan?" she asked, trying to push away her nervousness.

Most Italians had dark hair, and their skin held a golden tan like the man in front of her. But it didn't necessarily mean he was an Italian.

"No." He didn't offer any more information.

Her cheeks heated all the more. Maybe he was a well-known celebrity or a millionaire who didn't want to reveal his identity. She didn't mind because she didn't want to tell him about herself either. She wanted to keep their meeting a secret.

But suddenly, she had another thought. Something that made her sick to her the stomach.

"Are you married?" she asked.

"No."

She felt embarrassed as well as relieved. Even though she was strongly attracted to the man, she would never consider messing around with a married man, even for a simple date.

She saw his intense eyes lower to her left hand, where she was nervously turning her wedding ring around her finger as a habit.

"I-I'm widowed," she quickly explained. "My husband passed away three years ago."

His eyes rose again and locked with hers. He didn't say anything. Not even the polite 'I'm sorry' that most people would say when they found about someone's husband or a loved one passing away.

Apart from the smoldering gaze he directed at her that heated her body and made her feel alive, he didn't talk or say anything.

"Sir, champagne." It was a waiter.

Narmada noticed that it was the same waiter who had delivered the champagne bottle to her table. He was holding another unopened champagne bottle in the ice bucket.

"Did you like the champagne I sent to your table before?" the darkly handsome stranger asked. "Or would you like a different drink?"

Narmada was stunned knowing that it was him who had sent the champagne bottle to her. He was her gentleman admirer. Although he didn't exactly look like a gentleman with his dangerous aura, she felt an exciting pleasure knowing he had sent her the bottle of champagne.

"T-this one is fine," she replied. She tried to hide her nervousness, but her stomach continued to flutter and her voice came out breathlessly.

The darkly handsome stranger's single nod had the waiter pouring the champagne into their glasses.

It would be her third drink, although she hadn't finished the champagne glass at her table. She made a note not to drink more than a glass. She didn't want to be drunk. She wanted to savor every moment of the night.

Her heart began thudding when he raised the champagne flute and his mouth twisted into a small smile. "To unknown beginnings."

Excitement raced through her as she toasted back. "To unknown beginnings," she repeated softly.

The champagne felt sweeter and more intense this time. The tiny bubbles exploded on her tongue, and once again, the smooth liquid slid down her throat leaving a trail of heat and fire.

She smiled, feeling happy and free after a very long time. It felt as though the invisible shackles from the past three years while grieving and living under constant scrutiny suddenly broke away.

The man paused for a moment seeing her smile. His eyes flared and emitted sparks while he stared at her lips.

Seeing the heat in his eyes, a heavy tension gripped her harder. She felt a raw need inside her that she had never experienced before. She wanted to lean over and touch him. She wanted to run her fingers on his hard jawline and trace his full bottom lip. She wanted and craved the intimacy that came with a touch.

"Would you like to order dinner?" he asked. His voice sounded gruff as though he sensed her urgent need and felt the same way.

She was hardly hungry. Not with the need coursing through her veins. She shook her head, unable to form words.

"Then let's go," he ordered.

She held her breath. "Where?" she managed to ask.

His eyes turned darker with intensity. "My room."

A loud ringing noise cut through Narmada's mind, jerking her awake.

As soon as she opened her eyes, she realized she was inside her bedroom and not in an upscale hotel bar lounge in Milan. Although she could see the reality, her heart continued to pound with the remnants of the dream.

It was a recurring dream she had been having for a month. But the dream usually ended with a passionate conclusion, unlike that morning when it was cut short due to her alarm.

"Dammit."

But even as she cursed, Narmada's face flushed in anticipation of dreaming about her darkly handsome stranger again soon.

The phone continued to ring and vibrate loudly, forcing her to groan softly and roll to the side of her bed. She realized it wasn't her alarm on the phone, and someone was calling her. It was her friend Supriya.

Pushing away the heavy remnants of her sleep, Narmada answered the call. "Hello?"

"I'm so sorry, Narmada. I know you must be on your way to the meeting, but I just received input from the sales team about a change in the quarterly number. Can you add the updated numbers before presenting to the board members?"

Narmada frowned. Supriya was not only her best friend, but also the CIO of Genesis, the company Narmada owned.

"Sure. Send me the numbers, Supriya. I'll look through it and add it before the meeting."

Narmada twisted on the bed slightly to reach for her laptop to finish the task right then. Her hands brushed the small picture frame on the nightstand. It was her wedding photo taken nearly six years ago.

Seeing her late husband's smiling face right after dreaming about another man should feel a little odd. But Narmada didn't feel that way. She knew Vaibhav would understand. Vaibhav had not only been her husband, he had also been her best friend since the age of ten.

Pushing away the thoughts of her late husband and the darkly handsome stranger, Narmada focused on her work. "Give me the updated numbers, Supriya," she said while turning on her laptop.

Narmada knew the ins and outs of the company she had built with Vaibhav nearly ten years ago. It only took five minutes to understand the change in the numbers Supriya had sent and apply it to the presentation she had made for the quarterly board meeting.

Shutting down the laptop, Narmada glanced at the clock to check how much time she had left to begin her daily morning routine. When she saw the time, her heart jolted in shock.

"Oh shit."

The clock showed eight o'clock in the morning. Her alarm must have rung several times and stopped nearly an hour-and-a-half ago at six thirty, which was her usual time to wake up.

"Supriya, I'll speak to you later after the board meeting." Ending the call, Narmada sprang out of bed and ran towards the bathroom

Dammit. I'm going to be late to the quarterly board meeting.

Narmada had never been late to a meeting before, much less to an important meeting. The recurring dream from that morning was going to delay her.

Suddenly an image of piercing eyes on a darkly handsome face flashed in her mind making her heart thump in anticipation.

"Stop distracting me," she muttered.

Ever since her passionate encounter with the handsome stranger, she wasn't able to get him out of her mind. It had been thirty days ago, but she still recalled each and every moment she had spent with him that night.

She hadn't even known his name or who he was or where he was from. She had been tempted many times over the month to find out the information by calling the hotel, but she stopped herself.

She couldn't afford to take the risk. If anyone found out about that night, she would lose everything.

Taking a deep breath, she hurried through her morning routine and took a quick shower.

She barely had time to check the mirror to see how she looked. She hoped whatever minimal makeup she applied wasn't smeared. Luckily, her clothes were perfect since she always wore business suits to work.

Glancing at the clock again, she realized she had no time to call her grandfather whom she usually called in the mornings. But knowing her grandfather would understand and wouldn't mind, she grabbed her car keys, laptop bag and morning coffee and hurried out of her house.

***

"Good morning, Narmada."

Narmada smiled at the executive assistant seated behind a desk that had Genesis Corporation written on it along with the logo. "Good morning, Nikita. Beautiful earrings."

The younger woman blushed with pleasure. "Thank you, Narmada. Viren gifted it for our first anniversary."

Narmada would have normally conversed a little longer, but she couldn't prolong the conversation like she usually did because of the meeting. All of her employees had easy access to her, and she maintained a good relationship with everyone. Most of the employees had been with the company for a long time and the environment was like that of a family enterprise.

"I'll talk to you later, Nikita."

The younger woman nodded with a smile. But Suddenly, Nikita's smile dimmed. "Oh, I forgot to mention that Mr. Mohan is also attending the meeting today, Narmada. He and the rest of the board are already in the conference room."

Shit.

"Thank you for letting me know, Nikita." Narmada cringed inside even as she smiled and hurried through the corridor towards the conference room.

Her father-in-law was attending the board meeting, which meant he would do everything possible to undermine her position as CEO of the company she had built with his son.

Her father-in-law felt it was his right to criticize her despite the good profits the company made each year. He had never forgiven his son for marrying the driver's granddaughter. It didn't matter that she was good at what she did and grew the company to its highest potential. In his mind, she had trapped his gullible son into marrying her.

Narmada would have usually ignored her father-in-law like she did during her childhood. But since the older man was an early investor and held a good number of shares and a position on the board, she continued to tolerate his rude and often obnoxious taunting.

Taking a deep breath to brace herself for his attack, she pushed open the door. She was five minutes late.

There was a soft buzz of conversation, and she smiled pleasantly at the familiar faces inside the room.

"Ah, look," a familiar voice taunted. "The gold-digging whore who trapped my son and drove him to an early death is finally here."

Narmada didn't react to her father-in-law's mean and vicious words. But the rest of the board members looked visibly uncomfortable and shifted in their seats.

Controlling herself from showing her anger and humiliation, Narmada took a seat at the table. "Sorry, I'm late. Traffic," she explained to the room in general. "We can start now."

She opened her laptop to present. But just as she predicted, her father-in-law didn't let go of his insulting taunts.

"I changed the agenda of the meeting," he said. Satisfaction oozed out of his words.

Keeping a neutral look on her face, Narmada faced him. Along with hatred and meanness, something else flashed in the older man's eyes.

Victory.

Narmada didn't understand the reason for it. But she knew her father-in-law was determined to make the quarterly board meeting uncomfortable for her.

"I always knew you were a whore. And now, you have proved it." He pushed a small yellow folder towards her.

A cold, slimy shiver slid down Narmada's spine. She wanted to ignore the folder her father-in-law pushed towards her, but everyone's focus was on her. Trying to maintain the unshakeable mask she usually kept on her face, she opened the folder.

They were two photographs. Suddenly, her heart began to thud sickly as she slowly pulled them out.

Shock gripped her when she saw the first image. The image was quite blurred, but to her eyes, it was crystal clear. It was a picture taken of a man and woman locked in a passionate kiss.

Both the man and woman were wearing dark business suits, and the man's fingers dug into the woman's long hair while she clutched his tie as they kissed in a dimly-lit room with a city's night view as a backdrop from a high-rise building. The picture was taken at an angle where their faces were not clearly visible as the man's head was tilted slightly.

"Go on. Look at the other photo too."

Narmada wanted to shut out her father-in-law's words. But clamping down the sick feeling inside her stomach, she looked at the other photo.

Shock ripped through her once again. The second picture was blurred as well. The couple was lying on a bed, and the woman's arms were tightly gripping the naked broad and muscular back of the man. Although the faces couldn't be seen in this one as well, the bright blue sapphire wedding ring on the woman's finger made the identity obvious.

Oh God.

The morning coffee she had grabbed earlier as her breakfast threatened to shoot up from her churning stomach.

"I knew you wouldn't keep your legs closed for long because of your whorish tendencies. I'm glad because you are done. You will not be a part of this company anymore."

Oh God. No. Please no.

Narmada shut her eyes to fight the tears that threatened to break her down. She sucked in deep breaths to control herself. But her father-in-law wasn't done.

"I invoke the chastity clause which my dear daughter-in-law broke by spreading her legs to a man."

There was shocked silence followed by murmurs from the other board members.

The chastity clause was made by her father-in-law three years ago when his son died by suicide. Narmada was blamed for it.

"If you allow a man's touch, you will lose the company."

Narmada hadn't fought back at the time due to her shock and grief of losing her best friend. Even though she was humiliated by such a clause, she had agreed to it due to the guilt she felt for not being able to save Vaibhav.

But now, Vaibhav's dream of protecting the company they built together was going to be destroyed.

How did this happen? Did the darkly handsome stranger in Milan know we were being followed and spied on? Why would there be cameras in the hotel room?

Even as her mind swam in shock while she tried to make sense, she noticed the sudden shift in the air. The room had fallen silent. Soft footsteps sounded loud in the silent room along with the sound of the conference room door shutting with a click.

"Just in time." Narmada's father-in-law's voice was excited. "Ladies and gentleman... I'm proud to announce that Fortune Group, one of the biggest conglomerates is acquiring our company. This is Yash Varma, the CEO of Fortune Group and our new majority shareholder."

There were shocked gasps all around.

Blinking her eyes rapidly to get rid of the blurred vision caused by tears, Narmada looked up.

Her breath was knocked from her chest when her eyes met with a piercing, dark gaze of a tall man.

Watching her intently with a cold, ruthless gaze was the new owner of her company.

The darkly handsome stranger she had spent a passionate night with nearly a month ago.

CHAPTER TWO

Everything froze inside Narmada.

Her breaths. Her heartbeats. And even her ability to think.

Her father-in-law was making the introductions. He was introducing the board members to the new owner of the company. Her company.

Narmada blinked again to see if she was caught in a dream. She had been dreaming of the man in front of her for the last thirty days. She had even been dreaming of him early that morning too. The dark, piercing eyes, the strong jaw, the small scar on the man's left cheekbone were all too familiar. She had seen him from up close, and touched and kissed his face for those features to be branded into her mind.

But it wasn't a dream right then.

She was now caught in a terrible nightmare where the darkly handsome stranger who had been haunting her passionate dreams and also her thoughts was standing in front of her and destroying her future.

Oh God.

Why? Why did he do this to me?

The sheer amount of the man's deception stole her breath away. She controlled the burning urge to stand up and scream. She wanted to attack him and demand answers of why he had betrayed her so cruelly.

But she knew the answers already—money, power and greed.

Almost everyone in the room was introduced to him, except for her. But instead of ignoring her like her father-in-law did, Yash Varma continued to look at her.

His body was rigid, and his gaze was cold and piercing.

"Mrs. Mohan," he said in a deep voice that haunted her dreams often.

But unlike those other times, her body now reacted differently to his deep voice. Instead of craving his voice and touch, burning anger along with a strong sense of betrayal and hatred erupted in her stomach.

The feeling was so strong that she had to dig her nails into her palms to stop herself from going to him and slapping him hard. She sucked in deep breaths to control her feeling and dragged her eyes away from him.

Her father-in-law was watching her with satisfaction, waiting for her to break down completely and make a scene.

But she refused to let him have the satisfaction of witnessing her breakdown.

Even though all her hard work and dreams lay shattered due to a man's deception, she held herself together. Gathering every ounce of strength, she kept her face carefully blank.

Her father-in-law smiled viciously. "You are no longer the CEO or a board member of this company," he stated. "You may gather your things and get out of the building."

Ten years of pouring her heart and soul into building the company from scratch was ending in such a cruel way. Narmada got up from her chair to leave, but a deep voice stopped her.

"No, I want Mrs. Mohan to stay. I want her to continue as the CEO."

Her father-in-law looked outraged. "What! Why do you need her?"

There was cold silence. "I don't like my decisions questioned, Mr. Mohan. Ever. But I'll let it go this time. I need Mrs. Mohan's presence for the transition during the merger as well as for running this company."

Narmada's father-in-law visibly seethed, knowing Yash Varma was right. Narmada was the best person and the only one who could help with the transition of the company she had built.

"Fine," Rajesh Mohan said grudgingly. "But as soon as the transition is done, fire her and get a new and more qualified CEO."

Cold silence followed the older man's suggestion. For the first time, Narmada saw uncertainty along with a flicker of fear in her father-in-law's face as he confronted the cold, ruthless gaze of Yash Varma's.

Narmada wasn't grateful for being allowed to stay as the CEO of Genesis. She felt trapped and resentful that she was made to feel like a disposable object in her own company. To be used and thrown away later.

Just like Yash Varma used you a month ago. He slept with you that night, knowing he was going to use you and throw you out of your company.

She couldn't hold it anymore. The deception, the shock and the sheer helplessness she felt with the situation rose up as bile inside her.

Without asking to be excused, she grabbed the folder with the pictures and walked out of the conference room. She held her chin high and kept her back straight until the conference room door closed behind her. And then, she rushed to her office room.

She ran inside and went into the private bathroom and emptied her churning stomach into the small bathroom sink.

There was nothing remaining in her stomach, but her body continued to heave violently over the sink. Her eyes watered, and sobs rose from deep inside as her eyes fell on the folder with the pictures inside.

He used me. He knew who I was and used my loneliness against me.

And like a fool, I fell for his trap and dreamed about him.

A broken sob escaped her.

No. I won't cry.

Pushing away the hurt, she took several deep breaths. She turned on the tap and rinsed her mouth with cold water before splashing her face.

Then, taking a few more deep breaths, she straightened her business suit and adjusted her hair. Her eyes fell on the folder. She wanted to destroy the pictures inside, tear them into pieces and burn them into ashes. But she knew it was of no use. There must be several copies of the pictures and possibly a video proof as well.

Bile rose inside her stomach again at the thought of her father-in-law and his lawyers watching her having unrestrained, passionate sex with a man who was deceiving her to steal her company.

No. Don't think of it. You have to be strong.

Taking in a few more shuddering breaths, she picked up the folder with slightly trembling hands. She wanted to keep the pictures as a reminder never to trust anyone again.

As soon as she stepped out of the bathroom, she saw the worried face of Supriya.

"Narmada, are you okay?" her best friend asked. "I just heard some rumors floating around about Genesis getting acquired."

Narmada nodded. "It is true."

There was shock on her friend's face. "What? How did this happen?"

Narmada wasn't in a position to explain right then. "I'll call you later and explain, Supriya," she said.

That was if Supriya didn't figure it out herself soon. The moment Supriya would see Yash Varma, she'd know.

Pushing away that thought, Narmada picked up her handbag from her office desk. "I'm not feeling well. I'm going home. Call me if there is an emergency at work."

Her friend looked worried. "I'll drop you home."

Narmada shook her head. "No. It's okay. I'll take the cab. It's easier."

With a worried frown, Supriya nodded. "All right. Text me after you reach home."

"I will."

Continuing to keep a composed look on her face, Narmada strode out of her office room. She instructed her executive assistant, "Pooja, please cancel all of my meetings for today. I'll let you know by tonight whether or not I can keep tomorrow's appointments."

The younger woman looked surprised and worried. "Sure, Narmada."

Supriya accompanied Narmada as they walked along the corridor towards the elevators. Just when Narmada pressed the button on the elevator panel, a deep voice called out.

"Mrs. Mohan, I'd like to speak to you for a moment."

Narmada's heart jerked violently, listening to the familiar deep voice. She turned, and her eyes clashed with Yash Varma's dark, piercing gaze.

Vaguely, she heard Supriya gasping out in shock.

Narmada locked her gaze with the man who deceived her while he watched her with an unreadable look.

"I don't want to talk to you, *Mr. Varma*." His name came out as a curse from her mouth.

There was no change in his expression. "You don't have much choice, Mrs. Mohan. You are my CEO, and I want your presence in my office. Right now."

Narmada wanted to slap him right then. She wanted to attack the perfectly cold and controlled look on his darkly handsome face. It took an inhuman effort to control herself from reacting.

Clenching her fists, she bit out her words. "Then fire me. Because there is no way in hell I would ever work for you!"

His eyes flashed at her challenge, making him look dangerous.

Ignoring him and ignoring the warning signals of challenging a man like him, she turned back to face the elevators.

The heat of his piercing gaze burned on her back, but she continued to ignore him.

Luckily, the elevator doors opened right then, and she stepped inside. When she turned to face the front of the elevator, their eyes clashed again. But this time, a shiver ran through her at the raw intensity of his gaze.

She was reminded of the heated memories of the night when he held her, enthralled with his gaze and touch while he took her to passionate heights again and again.

"You are so damn beautiful."

"Come for me."

Suddenly, her tight composure wavered as heat gripped her body at the memories of his deep voice.

She hated her body's reaction and weakness caused by years of loneliness.

Before the elevator doors shut, she put in every ounce of hatred she could into the look she directed towards the man who cost her everything—her pride, her future and her trust.

I hate you.

I wish I had never set my eyes on you.

CHAPTER THREE

One month ago...

Milan, Italy

"Come on, Narmada. It's high time you let your hair down. Literally!"

Narmada smiled as her slightly intoxicated friend giggled at her own joke.

Narmada and Supriya were at a crowded upscale bar lounge for their pre-dinner drinks. The place was under the luxury hotel they were staying in during the two-day conference trip in Milan. Since they had come directly from the conference, they were still in their business suits. As usual, Narmada had her hair tied into a smooth knot like she did during work or business meetings.

"We're going to return to our regular lives tomorrow," Supriya reminded. "We better make every moment count!"

It was the last day of the conference, and they would be flying back home the next morning. Normally, Narmada would have preferred to catch up with her pending work, but Supriya insisted they make use of an offer that evening.

The hotel management had called them earlier to let them know that drinks would be complimentary for guests who had attended the conference. Although Narmada didn't drink much, she decided to avail the offer since Supriya was very excited.

"We need to take proper advantage of the free drinks!" Supriya said excitedly.

Narmada laughed. "You go ahead. I'm happy with my drink."

Supriya frowned, seeing Narmada's half-filled cocktail glass with lemonade and vodka.

"You barely drank it! Remember how much fun we used to have in college. You and Vaibhav could drink anyone under the table!"

Narmada felt a deep tug inside her heart at the mention of her late husband.

It had been three years since Vaibhav died, but she still felt his loss deeply. Unconsciously, she rotated the blue sapphire wedding ring on her finger.

"We were teenagers at that time, Supriya," Narmada reminded with a smile.

"So? We are only in our twenties now! That's hardly that old!"

Narmada might be in her twenties. But the life she led the last few years made her feel as though she were a hundred.

. "You promised to unwind on the last day!" Supriya remarked. "Once we go back, you'll be neck-deep in working twenty hours a day, seven days a week!"

Narmada laughed at her friend's exaggeration. "I don't work that long!"

"During our product releases, you always do!"

Narmada smiled. "So do you and everyone else in Genesis."

Supriya grinned. "Thanks to you, we hardly feel we are slogging."

Narmada smiled at her friend's compliment. Employees at Genesis loved their jobs. Narmada ensured the level of energy constantly remained high.

"All work and no play make Narmada a dull girl!"

Narmada was amused by her friend's playful words. She was just about to reply when a waiter came to their table.

"Excuse me, madam."

Narmada saw that the waiter was holding a small bucket filled with ice with a glossy bottle inside it. "Champagne from a gentleman admirer."

Supriya was excited. "Oooh."

Narmada was mildly annoyed. But not showing her annoyance, she smiled at the waiter. "Thank you, but I can't accept it. Tell the gentleman I'm sorry."

The waiter looked surprised, but he nodded and was about to leave when Supriya stopped him.

"Wait!" Supriya shouted before she grabbed the bottle and placed it on their table. "She changed her mind and accepts! Please open the bottle." Supriya then looked at Narmada. "Come on! I want to know who this man is."

Narmada laughed.

At Supriya's instructions, the waiter smiled and opened the bottle. Then pouring the champagne into two glasses, he kept the rest of it inside the ice bucket and left.

Supriya took a large sip and smiled widely. "Whoever it is, the man has excellent taste." She turned and began scanning the people in the bar. "If it's anyone under forty and single and hot-looking, you are having the rest of the champagne with that man!"

Narmada laughed. Her friend had been determined to fix her up on a date for the last two years, saying it was unnatural how Narmada had been clinging to the memories of her late husband. But Narmada managed to dodge Supriya's attempts by using work as an excuse.

"No more excuses!" her friend said sternly, reading Narmada's amused smile. "You promised to unwind and keep your laptop away until we land back in India."

"Did I?" Narmada teased her friend. "I don't recall it."

"You did! I made you promise earlier this evening!"

Narmada laughed in amusement.

Supriya turned and continued to scan the lounge. Suddenly, she gasped out aloud. "My God! I hope it's that man, Narmada! I can almost imagine what beautiful half-Italian babies you'd both make together. He's so hot! And he's looking this way too!"

Narmada was amused by her friend's words about babies. Supriya was trying to fall pregnant, and so her thoughts often ran around that topic.

A small painful tug pulled inside Narmada's heart as she recalled the time when she and Vaibhav had discussed starting a family. They had kept putting it off until later because all of their energy went into building their company. And when they finally decided to try, it was too late.

"Look at him, Narmada! You'll agree with me he's hot!"

At her friend's insistence, Narmada turned. Her eyes met with a handsome man with dark brown hair. He was watching her with a smile. When he saw her looking at him, his smile widened, displaying impressive bright white teeth.

Even though the man was quite handsome, Narmada didn't feel even a flicker of interest pass through her. She was glad.

Unlike what everyone thought, she wasn't unnatural or dead from inside. She felt Vaibhav's loss deeply, but she also had the natural urges of a normal woman. She often felt lonely and wanted to feel the closeness, passion and desire like any other woman.

The only reason she couldn't actively seek the company of a man was because being with a man would cost her everything.

The chastity clause.

Supriya and many others didn't know about the humiliating legal clause that her father-in-law had added into the company's shareholder agreement. Only a few board members and lawyers knew about the humiliating clause that Narmada was made to sign right after Vaibhav's death.

"He looks so... alpha," Supriya continued to gush. "Maybe he runs some kind of Italian mafia," she said with a giggle.

Narmada turned back to her friend and laughed. "I highly doubt it."

"But what do you think of him?" Supriya asked in excitement.

Narmada shrugged. "He looks okay, I guess."

Her friend looked shocked. "Just okay! That brooding look, those chiseled features... he looks like the king of alphas. That small scar on his cheek makes him look all the more dangerous. If I weren't happily married and in love with Shekhar, I would go after that man."

Narmada was confused. She didn't recall seeing a scar on the brown-haired man's face. He didn't look brooding or alpha either.

She followed her friend's gaze, but this time, her eyes moved slightly to the left.

When her eyes fell on the man who was sitting alone at a table and looking at his phone, she felt her breath catch.

The man did look like the king of the alphas.

He was wearing a dark business suit that couldn't hide his broad shoulders and powerful body. There was also a powerful aura around him. He was seated alone, but several servers hovered around his table, subtly waiting to assist him.

Maybe he is a celebrity.

No, he couldn't be a celebrity. He didn't have classical handsome features. He was darkly masculine to the point of looking dangerous. The small scar added to the dangerous aura, and certain ruthlessness exuded from him.

Narmada noticed that other women's eyes were drawn to him like hers.

As though sensing her gaze, the man raised his head, and his eyes met with hers. Narmada's stomach fluttered, and her heart began racing as her body came alive instantly.

She was shocked at her body's reaction. Heat radiated from her stomach and spread to other parts of her body, making them tingle deliciously.

The darkly handsome stranger raised a masculine eyebrow.

She wanted to turn away in embarrassment at being caught staring, but she couldn't. His eyes held her completely captive. She stared at him shamelessly while his eyes lazily swept over her face and over her body covered by a business suit.

"My goodness," Supriya said out aloud. "It's getting too hot in here. Whoo!"

Narmada's face burned, and she tore her eyes away from the darkly handsome stranger and turned back to look at her friend.

Her friend was grinning. "I knew it!"

"What?"

"That you are still human like the rest of us. You just needed the right man to evoke such feelings again."

Narmada forced out a small smile. "I don't feel anything," she lied.

Her heart rate was still dangerously high, and her stomach continued to flutter. The darkly handsome stranger had more or less stripped her with his gaze, and she loved every moment of it.

If his gaze can do this to you, imagine how his touch would feel.

Immediately, she pushed away that forbidden thought. She couldn't risk fantasizing about a stranger, not when she had so much to lose.

Supriya grinned with a knowing look. "A woman would have to be dead not to feel anything for that man. And I think he can make even a dead woman feel alive."

Narmada laughed. "Stop it. I don't think he sent the champagne bottle."

"So? Don't let that hot alpha get away. Share a drink with him and have a nice time. Maybe you'll find a lot in common too."

A strange ache tugged her heart. It had been years since she shared a drink with an attractive man. Despite not wanting to, she did feel lonely quite often.

What she wanted was a meaningful connection that would last forever like it did with Vaibhav, but she knew it was impossible to find it again.

"I'm not interested, Supriya," she said with a sigh.

But her friend wasn't ready to let it go. "I'll join you too if you want. I want to see that man up close too."

Narmada laughed. Before she could once again say no, Supriya's phone began to ring.

"You should take the call," Narmada said. The call might be from Supriya's family.

Supriya answered the call. "Hello?" Immediately she frowned. "Yes, I am. Don't tell me the flight is cancelled."

There was silence, and then there was excitement on Supriya's face. "Oh! Yes, sure. I would like to accept that offer. What time?" Once again, there was a frown. "But that's only two hours away! And what about my friend who is in my next seat?"

Narmada watched as Supriya looked disappointed. "Oh. Then, I'm not sure I'll take the offer. Yes, I'll confirm in the next thirty minutes. Bye."

Supriya ended the call and shook her head. "Looks like today is the day of upgrades," she said.

Narmada smiled, taking a small sip of her drink. "What do you mean?"

Supriya laughed. "Well, first the complimentary drinks in the lounge. Now, I got a call from the airlines asking if I would like an upgrade to first class with a stop in Paris for a day. The flight leaves in two hours."

Narmada smiled. "That's a cool offer."

"Yes! I know! But the offer was not extended to your ticket. So I'm turning it down."

Narmada frowned. "Why?" she asked. "It's okay if I can't join you. You should go, Supriya. I know you always wanted to visit Paris." Her friend's social media was littered with pictures of Paris.

Supriya looked uncertain. "Are you sure?"

"Yes! Go! I'll see you in the office on Monday. Enjoy the weekend in Paris."

Supriya laughed. "You are right. I think I'll take up the offer!"

Narmada smiled. "Let's go, then. I can help you pack."

Supriya shook her head. "Don't you dare! Stay here a little longer and make use of the complimentary drinks. And I want you to buy a drink for that hot alpha dude too! I'm going to ask you about it on Monday, and you better tell me you had drinks with him."

Narmada had no intention of doing it, but she nodded. "Sure." She decided to wait for her friend to leave and would follow behind her after a few moments. She would go back to her room and order room service for dinner.

"Go and get him, girl," Supriya cheered before giving her a hug and waving her goodbye.

As soon as Supriya left the bar lounge, Narmada decided to wait for five minutes before leaving as well. She picked up the thin champagne glass and took a long sip of the chilled, bubbly liquid.

"Ah, finally. I'm glad your friend left."

Narmada looked up and saw the handsome brown-haired man who had been smiling at her earlier. Strange disappointment hit her.

"Can I join you?" he asked. "I'm Marco. I've been waiting to talk to the prettiest woman in the bar."

Narmada felt annoyed by his overly flirtatious smile and words.

What is wrong with you?

He was handsome and seemed to like her, but his presence grated on her nerves, and she wanted him gone.

"I'm about to leave," she said.

The man's smile got wider, and he looked overly confident. "I'll join you. Are you staying in this hotel?"

Irritation spiked inside her. "Sorry, I'm not interested," she said bluntly.

But that man didn't seem deterred. "I know you are interested. I'm Italian, and all Italian men are very good lovers."

Narmada felt her skin crawl at his suggestive smile.

"Come on, beautiful lady. Let's share the rest of the champagne bottle."

So it was him who had sent the bottle of champagne. Before Narmada could ask him to leave her alone and tell him she wasn't obligated to join him, another voice cut through.

"Leave," a deep masculine voice ordered. "She's with me."

Narmada turned slightly, and she was shocked when her eyes clashed with the intense gaze of the darkly, handsome stranger she and her friend had been staring at.

"How can you ask me to leave? I—"

"Leave. Right now."

The man named Marco didn't argue further. He must have seen the intent gaze of the darkly handsome stranger and the danger emitting from it. Muttering under his breath, he left.

Narmada didn't realize she still held her breath because her gaze was still locked with the handsome stranger's. She slowly exhaled, only to suck in another deep breath.

Up close, the man was truly breathtaking. With piercing dark eyes, a bold nose, high cheekbones with a small scar on the left one, and a full bottom lip—it was hard to tear her eyes away from him.

"Join me at my table," he ordered softly.

Her first instinct was to turn down his order. It would be a sane thing to do.

She had no idea how to deal with men or dating, let alone a dominant man like the one in front of her. He appeared to be a man who was accustomed to giving out orders and getting what he wanted.

Would he let me say no to anything?

Do you want to say no to him?

She didn't know.

Narmada's eyes were once again drawn towards the darkly handsome stranger. He was watching her still with an unwavering look.

A strange recklessness coursed through her as their gazes locked.

Maybe it was the drink she had earlier, but whatever her friend was suggesting didn't seem like a bad idea. She knew she would be risking a lot by being with a man, even if it were to only to share a drink.

Narmada's stomach fluttered as the man's eyes smoldered as he watched her. Although he didn't smile and still had a dangerous aura around him, the hooded look in his eyes felt like an invitation to her.

"I..." Before she could say anything out loud, he began walking back to his table.

Even though he had ordered her to his table, he was giving her a choice. She could walk away or come up with a polite excuse and leave. But she followed behind him in a hypnotic daze.

He held the chair for her as though he knew she would come. Taking a deep breath, she sat down. He took the seat opposite to her.

He was watching her again. Her cheeks heated at the impact of his dark, heavy gaze.

"A-are you from Milan?" she asked, trying to push away her nervousness.

Most Italians had dark hair, and their skin held a golden tan like the man in front of her, but it didn't necessarily mean he was an Italian. He could easily be from her country.

"No." He didn't offer any more information.

Her cheeks heated all the more. Maybe he was a well-known celebrity or a millionaire who didn't want to reveal his identity. She didn't mind because she didn't want to tell him about herself either. She wanted to keep their meeting a secret.

But suddenly, she had another thought. Something that made her sick to her stomach.

"Are you married?" she asked.

"No."

She felt embarrassed as well as relieved. Even though she was strongly attracted to the man, she would never consider messing around with a married man, even for a simple drinks date.

She saw his intense eyes lower to her left hand, where she was nervously turning her wedding ring around her finger as a habit.

"I-I'm widowed," she quickly explained. "My husband passed away three years ago."

His eyes rose again and locked with hers. He didn't say anything. Not even the polite *'I'm sorry'* that most people would say when they found about someone's husband or a loved one passing away.

Uncertainty gripped her.

Maybe he isn't interested in me.

Apart from the smoldering gaze that heated her body and made her feel alive, he didn't talk or say anything.

"Sir, champagne."

It was a waiter. Narmada noticed that it was the same waiter who had delivered the champagne bottle to her table. He was holding another unopened champagne bottle in the ice bucket.

A single nod from the handsome stranger had the waiter pouring the champagne into two glasses.

It would be her third drink, although she hadn't finished the champagne glass at her table. She made a note not to drink more than a glass. She didn't want to be drunk. She wanted to savor every moment of that evening.

Her heart began thudding when he raised the champagne flute and his mouth twisted into a small smile. "To unknown beginnings."

Excitement raced through her as she toasted back. "To unknown beginnings," she repeated softly.

The champagne felt sweeter and more intense this time. The tiny bubbles exploded on her tongue, and once again the smooth liquid slid down her throat leaving a trail of heat and fire.

She smiled, feeling happy and free after a very long time. It felt as though the invisible shackles she felt for the past three years while grieving and living under constant scrutiny suddenly broke away.

The man paused for a moment seeing her smile. His eyes flickered while he stared at her lips.

But seeing the heat in his eyes, tension gripped her. Suddenly, she felt a raw need inside her that she had never experienced before. She wanted to lean over and touch the man. She wanted to run her fingers on his hard jawline and trace his fuller bottom lip. She wanted and craved the intimacy that came with a touch.

"Would you like to order dinner?" he asked. His voice sounded gruff as though he felt the same urgent need.

She shook her head, unable to form words. She was hardly hungry, not with the strange, urgent need coursing through her veins.

"Then let's go," he ordered.

She held her breath.

"Where?" she managed to ask.

"My room."

Narmada was stunned as she stared at the man in front of her.

She knew she should be offended by the blunt proposition, but she wasn't. Having loved just one man, she wasn't the kind to have casual hookups with men. But for the first time, she was tempted.

She knew the risks she would be taking by spending a night with a man she desired.

But you are in a different country.

Nobody would know.

She trusted Supriya with her life. She knew her friend would never tell anyone when she found out she spent a night with a stranger.

Even as she contemplated her decision, sparks and electricity buzzed around her as he came closer and waited by her side. Once again, he was giving her a choice. She could either ignore him or say she didn't want to join him inside his room.

Biting the corner of her lip, she stood up.

Fire scorched through her body when he placed his hand lightly against her back and led her out of the bar lounge.

I want to do this.

I need this. I need these memories when I go back to the rest of my lonely life.

No one would know.

Those words kept repeating inside her head.

The walk to his room was silent and filled with thick tension. Her heart continued to race in both nervousness and anticipation.

What kind of lover would he be?

A man like him wouldn't make love. He would have sex. Her thighs clenched at the thought.

She knew he wouldn't be sweet or romantic. Passion and danger radiated from him. He would be a demanding lover.

Will he find me lacking? Will he ask me to leave because he might find me unskilled?

She was in no way skilled when it came to lovemaking. But what she lacked in experience, she hoped her desire and need would make up for it.

Pushing away her insecurities, she decided to enjoy the thrill of the current moment.

They took the elevator to the topmost floor. Then stepping out, they walked in silence along a corridor. His room was at the corner. Swiping the keycard at the door, he led her inside a large suite.

There were two separate bedrooms and a living room. He led her into the bedroom, where one wall was made of glass that overlooked the beautiful city of Milan.

But she didn't get the chance to notice beyond a glance.

Before even the door to the bedroom shut behind her with a soft click, she felt the strong arm at her back moving up to her shoulder and pushing her until her back hit one of the bedroom walls.

Her heart threatened to burst out of her ribcage as he stood in front of her with barely a few inches between them. The burning intensity in his eyes made her skin break into goosebumps, and she struggled to breathe normally. Her breaths came out heavily as she returned his stare.

With slightly trembling hands, she did what she had been craving to do when she saw him. She touched him.

Raising her hand, she traced his hard jawline, shivering a little as his thick, prickly stubble tingled her finger tips.

His eyes closed briefly at her soft touch. But when he opened his eyes again, desire blazed in them. He dug his fingers into her hair and tugged until the pressure of his fingers loosened her smooth knot, and her hair cascaded down her back.

He tipped her face up and held her in a tight grip that left her with no choice but to look at him. Her eyes widened slightly in confusion seeing the angry determination along with desire on his face. But before she could think about it, his mouth covered hers.

His tongue plundered, and he kissed her with a ferocity that made her lose her mind. Her pulse thundered loudly in her ears, drowning out everything.

Her body melted against his, and she clung to him as she returned his kiss with equal ferocity. She could feel the heat radiating from him and felt his heartbeats racing like hers.

She gasped into his mouth when she felt his hand pushing away her suit jacket and cupping her breast. A moan escaped her as her breasts peaked and ached with arousal.

But suddenly, the heat of his tongue left hers when he dragged his mouth away from hers. He looked at her with harsh and heavy breaths. His already dark, intense eyes darkened even more with his arousal and looked completely black.

"I want you," he growled, his guttural voice sending a shiver of need inside her.

Her voice was stuck inside her throat. But she managed to speak. "I want you too," she whispered.

She gasped when he swung her up and carried her towards the bed and lowered her right next to it. He barely gave her time to catch her breath before he attacked her clothes. He pushed away her suit jacket and then yanked her knee-length skirt down. She was wearing a tank top inside her suit jacket which he tugged up and threw aside. She was left only in her underclothes.

Her breaths came out in loud exhales. With great difficulty, she controlled herself from crossing her hands across her body to cover herself. She didn't want him to think she was inexperienced.

His eyes blazed as his gaze slowly swept over her body.

"You are fucking gorgeous," he rasped before gripping her hair and dragging her close again for another carnal kiss.

Desire blazed through her, pushing away her shyness and uncertainties. Clutching his jacket, she kissed him back.

The kiss spun her world again, making her feel as though she was falling. She realized she was really falling when the soft mattress of the bed hit her back.

She opened her eyes and stared at him in a daze.

Holding her captive with his eyes, he shrugged away his suit jacket and then unbuttoned his shirt revealing his toned, muscled body. Her heart rate accelerated dangerously when he unbuckled his belt and opened his trousers. He then stepped out of his clothes until he was completely naked.

She raised herself on her elbows on the mattress and stared at him in awe.

With broad, powerful shoulders and sinewy muscles covering his body, he was magnificent. Biting her lip, she slowly lowered her eyes and saw his hard arousal. It looked big.

An unfamiliar throbbing anticipation along with nervousness pulsed through her core. Unconsciously, she licked her dry lips, only to see his arousal jerk.

Her eyes flew up to his, and she almost gasped when she saw the dark, predatory look on his face. But he didn't come to her right away. Dragging his gaze away from hers, he drew out something from the nightstand next to the bed. Her cheeks heated when she realized it was protection.

She hadn't even thought about it because she never used birth control before. She was glad that he was sensible enough to think of it.

He wore the protection in a smooth move and then looked up at her. He looked harshly savage and primal, ready to mate.

Her heartbeat thundered in her ears, and goosebumps peppered her skin as he more or less stalked closer. Instinct made her scoot back towards the headboard.

But he didn't allow her the escape. She gasped when his large hand circled her leg and dragged her close by the ankle until she was towards the edge of the bed. He leaned over her, caging her with his hands on either side of her head. The weight of his body was held away from her, but she could feel the heat radiating off him.

"Do you want me?" he asked again while darkness and sexual arousal swirled in his eyes.

She stared at him. He was a stranger. Although she felt a strange emotional connection to him, she knew it wasn't real. But the physical need and desire she felt for him was more than real.

"Yes, I want you," she whispered as liquid heat coursed through her.

Immediately, she saw dark satisfaction in his eyes.

With a low growl, his fingers dug into her hair again, and his mouth covered hers. She felt his other hand going behind her back and unclasping her bra before yanking it off her.

The lights were on. Under normal circumstances, she would have insisted on turning them off because she was conscious of her naked body. But she was too far gone to care about anything else but him and his touch.

Fire sizzled through her body as she felt the tips of her aroused breasts brushing against the hard muscles of his chest. She grabbed his bare shoulders to hold on while his kiss and touch spun her mind.

But his kiss didn't last long. His mouth left hers. Before she could pull him back, he slid down her body, and his mouth fell on her bare breast and latched on to it.

Red hot searing heat shot through her, and she cried out aloud. He sucked the aroused tip, using his tongue and teeth in a way that made her body shake. Clutching his head with both her hands, she arched towards him. "Oh God," she moaned.

The feelings coursing through her were too intense. His mouth moved to the other aroused tip, and he dragged his teeth around it before sucking it hard until her womb quivered deep inside.

Another shudder ripped through her body as heat and pleasure grew. His movements were tense and aggressive. He didn't just explore her. It felt as though he wanted to mark her.

The heat of his mouth was everywhere on her body. Gasping, she tried to hold on to his shoulders, but he moved easily as he wanted. He slid lower.

Biting and kissing her stomach, he moved between her legs before yanking her underwear and throwing it away. His dark eyes then met with her shocked ones.

"You don't have to—" she broke off in a gasp when he lifted her thighs and placed them on his broad shoulders. She barely braced herself when he kissed her between her legs the same way he kissed her mouth.

It was raw, deep and aggressive. His tongue stabbed into her sensitive folds while his lips sucked and his teeth scraped.

She screamed and shattered. She couldn't help it. Never had she felt such shockingly intense pleasure before. Hot tingles of fire shot through her bloodstream while she shook in her climax.

She shuddered hard, wanting more but also wanting to escape because the feelings were too intense. "Please," she gasped, unable to take anymore. But he held her still and continued the passionate assault.

She yanked his hair as his hot tongue continued to burn her from inside and out. "Oh God."

The fiery liquid wave spread, but it also built an empty ache between her thighs which she knew had to be filled by him.

"Please," she begged again.

His heated gaze met with hers from between her legs. Seeing her flushed face, his mouth left her core, and he loosened the grip on her thighs. And then, lowering her legs, he moved up her body again until his face was in level with hers.

He stared at her with tension rolling off his body.

Once again, she found him harsh and savage in his arousal. Wanting more, she touched him. She placed a hand on his tensed jaw and then moved her hand lower over his neck, then over his muscled chest, and then to his hard stomach. She was in awe of his savage beauty. Her fingers tingled as she touched his heated skin and muscles.

His breathing came out harshly as his eyes seared into hers. She was just about to move her hands lower from his hard stomach to the place that intrigued her, but his hand caught hers in a firm grip.

"No," he growled with clenched teeth. "Not yet."

She wanted to touch him and give him the same pleasure he was giving her, but he didn't allow her to. He captured both her hands and locked her wrists together above her head using just one of his hands.

And then, keeping his gaze on hers, in another primal move, his thick, muscular thigh spread her legs wider before he thrust deep into her.

Shocked, she cried out with her back arching. He was too big. She tried to struggle under him to get him to pull out a little, but he stayed still deep within her while gritting his teeth.

"Don't move," he rasped out harshly.

His breathing was harsh and ragged while his chest rose and fell against hers. Her breath was stuck inside her chest as she tried to figure out how to breathe with him so deep inside her.

His free hand cupped the back of her head. "Breathe," he ordered. His harsh voice softened a little while he looked into her eyes.

She did as he ordered. As soon as she let out an exhale, she felt much better. The pain felt distant, but a strange empty ache to feel more of him began to throb. She raised her hips slightly and gasped at the pleasurable tremor. "Oh!" she cried out with a shiver, automatically tightening around him inside.

His eyes fell shut, and he let out a deep groan. Wanting to feel more again, she repeated the move. But this time, his eyes opened.

His eyes flashed with a dark need that made her gasp. Before she could brace herself, the hand behind her head fisted into her hair. Then dropping his head to her neck, he began to thrust.

It was shockingly intense.

His heavy weight kept her pinned under him as he took her body. Choking whimpers escaped her mouth with each hard thrust. She almost passed out with the sheer pleasure caused by the intensity.

He kept her hands shackled in his and was relentless. Her body began craving the harsh intensity of his thrusts and the feel of him deep inside. Her hips rose, and she moaned and gasped with every harsh thrust as he took her body with a ferocity that shocked and excited her.

This is what I wanted when I saw him in the bar.

The rough, savage beauty and intense stares of the darkly handsome stranger promised to take her to unknown heights. She wanted him to take control and make her forget everything else.

Her orgasm was shockingly violent. She screamed, and her body shuddered hard. Heat and pleasure pulsed through her core and radiated all over, making her cry out with tears rolling down her cheeks at the intensity.

He didn't stop. His thrusts remained harsh as he watched her breaking apart in his arms.

He took her savagely until the heat inside her built up again. Before even she could come down from her earlier high, she shattered again, almost blacking out at the sheer intensity.

This time he joined her. With his head thrown back, he roared out loud and shuddered hard before collapsing on top of her.

She didn't know how long she went in and out of consciousness as her body shook along with his.

It took a long while for the tremors to stop. When she slowly began to regain her senses, she realized he was lying on top of her, breathing harshly into her ears.

His heavy weight pressed her deep into the mattress, but she didn't mind. She felt satisfied and blissful.

His grip on her wrists had loosened, so she pulled her hands free and held him close.

His body tensed slightly at that gesture, but he didn't move away.

She caressed his back and felt his muscles jump and shift under her soft touch. Shivering in delight at having such an effect on a man like him, her chest felt much lighter in wonder and also in blissful content.

Somehow, holding him in her arms felt right. Despite the circumstances and their raw sexual encounter being a one-night stand, she didn't feel ashamed or guilty. Happiness and wonder filled her from deep within.

For the first time after many years, she felt close to another human. And for the first time, the deep loneliness she felt over the years seemed to have disappeared. She smiled as she stared at the ceiling, continuing to caress his muscled back.

As though sensing her thoughts, he raised his head and his dark eyes fell on her face.

Her eyes were drawn to his. "Thank you," she said softly.

His face was unreadable, and he didn't ask her what she was thanking him for.

"Don't thank me yet," he said in a gravelly voice that made her body shiver from deep inside. "We are far from done."

Before she could say anything, his mouth covered hers in a deep kiss, shattering her thoughts.

For the rest of the night, he took her to pleasurable and unknown heights. He was demanding yet generous. She lost count of the number of times she shattered in his arms.

Hours later, when the daylight broke into the sky, they made love for the last time.

"Thank you," she whispered again, kissing him tenderly on his lips.

Even though her heart ached at the thought of never seeing him again, she didn't regret the passionate night spent with him. She would carry the memories of their night until the end of her days.

CHAPTER FOUR

Narmada stared out of her bedroom window with her jaw clenched.

Her body was flushed with anger, arousal and humiliation as she recalled the night she had spent in Milan with Yash Varma.

She hadn't known who he was. She thought she was spending a passionate night with a stranger who simply desired her. His dark, fiery passion had resonated deep within her, and she felt a connection that remained long after.

Lies. All lies.

He was only using her to cruelly deceive her later.

She took a deep, shuddering breath to control the hurt inside.

There wasn't a connection. He was just a hot stranger you met and satisfied your desires with. Nothing more.

She was determined to consider him as nothing more.

Then why are there tears in your eyes?

Angrily, she wiped away her tears of hurt. Yash Varma didn't deserve them. He was nobody to her. If anything, he was her enemy right then. He was the man she hated with every fiber of her being.

The loud sound of the phone ringing shattered the silence in the room.

Narmada wanted to ignore it, but she knew the call would most likely be from Supriya who must be concerned. Taking a deep breath, she answered the call.

"Narmada... are you okay?"

"I'm fine, Supriya."

There was a brief silence. "You don't have to talk to me about what happened. But I want you to know I'll always support you."

Some of the anger and pain inside Narmada's chest disappeared. She knew she could trust her friend with her life. But her wound was still raw, and she was still in too much shock. She wasn't prepared to discuss her night with Yash Varma to anyone, not even with Supriya, who had been her close friend since their college days.

"Thank you, Supriya. I'm lucky to have you as a friend."

Taking a deep breath, Narmada ignored her hurt and focused on the most important aspect—Genesis.

"Has the board sent out a message?" she asked Supriya.

"Not yet. But we just had an emergency meeting. Yash Varma's team more or less threatened us, saying we need to get used to acquisition and cooperate with the merger, or there would be consequences."

Narmada felt furious.

How dare he threaten my employees!

Most of the employees had been with the company from the beginning. She felt angry and guilty about leaving when the news of the shocking acquisition was announced. She knew she had to protect her employees from the bullying of a large corporation such as Fortune Group.

"There will be no such consequences," Narmada assured. "I'll be at the office tomorrow morning. I'll have an all-hands meeting to address everyone's concerns."

There was another silence. "Narmada, I understand if you don't want to come. You must be still in shock—"

"I'll come, Supriya. I'll see you tomorrow."

Narmada ended the call.

She did need time to process what had happened and also time to pull herself back up. But unfortunately, she couldn't afford that. Her employees needed her.

Closing her eyes, she fought the panic attack that was threatening to pull her down. She took deep breaths, inhaling in and out. But that didn't help.

She opened her eyes, and with slightly trembling hands, she reached for her phone. She dialed the number of a person who she knew would calm her down. The person would remind her of her worth and purpose in life.

The phone rang several times. It was late afternoon, and she thought it might not be answered. She was about to hang up when she heard a familiar voice answering the phone.

"What a surprise that the CEO of Genesis Corporation is calling me in the middle of her busy work day."

Despite the sudden upheaval in her life, a smile broke out on Narmada's face. "Hello, Grandpa. Did I disturb you?" She could hear the faint noises in the background which must have been the television.

Her grandfather laughed. "No. I was watching a movie. I couldn't hear the phone ringing in the bedroom."

She knew her grandfather spent his afternoons either napping or watching old movies. In the evenings when it cooled down, he went to meet his friends for a chat.

"When are you coming to visit me, Grandpa?" she asked. "I miss you."

She did miss him a lot. Her grandfather was the only family she had left. After her parents had died when she was barely an infant, he took her in. He brought her up singlehandedly as he was a widower even before she was born.

Her grandfather often teased her, saying that because she didn't have a woman's influence in her upbringing, she dressed and thought like a boy. Instead of choosing pretty dresses, she was comfortable in jeans and a t-shirt. And instead of playing with other girls from the neighborhood, she hung out with boys.

That's how she had become friends with Vaibhav. She met Vaibhav when she was ten. Her grandfather joined as Rajesh Mohan's driver. Before that, her grandfather had been working for Rajesh Mohan's close friend.

Her grandfather laughed. "I miss you too, my dear CEO. But whenever I visit you, you are always busy with work. You should come to visit me in the village for a break. You know it's beautiful this time of the year."

Narmada was tempted. She wanted to leave everything and run to the comforting embrace of her grandfather. And the village was indeed breathtakingly beautiful. Until she was ten, she grew up at a large estate near the village where her grandfather had worked for a family for nearly three decades. But soon, her grandfather took up a job in the city for the sake of her education.

Most of her life lessons were taught by her grandfather. He often taught her not to run away from problems and to fight for what she wanted.

And right then, it was because of those lessons she decided to stay on and fight her powerful enemy—Yash Varma.

Not just for herself, but also for her employees.

"I promise I'll come for a few days next month, Grandpa."

She hoped things would settle down by then, and Yash Varma would be gone from her life.

"Bye, Grandpa."

"Bye."

Ending the call, Narmada latched on the determination that flowed through her after speaking to her grandfather. She recalled another life lesson her grandfather taught her.

It was not to feel victimized and give up.

Even when Vaibhav had died in an accident which was actually suicide, her grandfather demanded that she be brave. He told her it wasn't her fault, and she needed to carry on with her life and dreams.

She had braved through losing her husband, who was her best friend. She had mourned his loss deeply and missed him a lot. But at no point did she feel she would give up on Vaibhav's and her dreams.

I won't give up, Vaibhav. I will save our company.

With that thought, she picked up her phone and made a call to her personal assistant.

"Pooja, I need your help with the acquisition papers."

Narmada gave detailed instructions to Pooja regarding who would have the papers and what exactly was needed.

While she waited, she took out her laptop and looked up information on Fortune Group.

She had already heard about them before. They were one of the biggest corporations in the world. They began as a real estate company and had diversified into the hospitality industry and IT software as well.

They were also known for their aggressive and risky acquisitions that often turned failing companies into profitable ones.

Narmada's jaw clenched.

Genesis isn't a failing company.

Before she could dig in anything personal, Narmada received the notification from Pooja with attached copies of the acquisition.

Narmada clicked on the attachment. The first thing she saw was the bold signature of Yash Varma at the bottom of the document. Her anger shot through her.

Taking a deep breath, she sat on her bed and settled in for the rest of the day.

Pushing aside her panic, anger and fear, she decided to read through every line of the fine print. She had to find out how Yash Varma managed to seize her company so easily and why.

Some way or the other, she intended to defeat her enemy and grab back control of her company.

CHAPTER FIVE

The next morning, Narmada walked into the Genesis building at an early hour like she usually did.

Although she didn't sleep well the previous night, she took extra care with her appearance that morning. She didn't let her worry show on her face. She covered the shadows under her eyes with makeup and wore red lipstick. She dressed in a black-colored business suit and paired it with high heels.

Feeling confident, she walked to the front lobby, where everything still looked the same.

She wondered with resentment if the name of her company would be changed soon too. Her heart tugged painfully as she recalled the time when she and Vaibhav had picked the name Genesis together after they put a lot of thought into it.

I won't let Yash Varma destroy our company.

The thought of facing her enemy that day made her feel a cocktail of emotions. Although anger and hatred topped her feelings, fear and uncertainty were a part too.

Yash Varma was a ruthless man who held the power to destroy her company.

No! I won't let him.

Taking a deep breath, she pushed away the fear. Instead, she focused on her schedule for that day. She had asked her personal assistant to set up a meeting with all the employees. Even though she didn't have enough information at that point, it was her duty to address all the employees' fears.

"Good morning, Narmada."

Narmada looked towards the front desk and was surprised to see the receptionist seated at her desk at eight in the morning. Most of her employees came to work around nine. Since she encouraged flexible working hours, there was no pressure for most employees to come very early or leave very late. The news about the change in ownership must have made everyone be on their toes.

"Good morning, Sejal."

The younger woman looked nervous. "Sir has asked me to inform you that you are to go to his office as soon as you arrive."

Narmada frowned slightly. "Sir? Which sir?" She wondered if it was one of her executives to talk about the acquisition.

"Mr. Yash Varma."

Narmada was stunned and then immediately furious. Controlling herself, she forced out a smile. "Thanks, Sejal. Which office room is Mr. Varma currently in?"

"The chairman's office."

Narmada's jaw clenched. Nodding at the younger woman, she strode to the elevator. Stepping in, she pressed the button to the topmost floor where the chairman's office was situated. It was surprising that her father-in-law gave up his office to Yash Varma.

Although her father-in-law rarely came to the office, he did sometimes have some closed-door meetings with a few shady-looking men. She had always hated that her father-in-law used her company to throw off suspicion on some of the shady deals he was constantly making.

The elevator came to a stop with a soft ping, and the doors opened.

Stepping out, she noticed that the corridor was empty. But just as she turned towards the corner office room, she saw a man with thick spectacles seated at the reception desk. Although the man was slightly older and looked more like a top executive, Narmada knew he must be Yash Varma's personal assistant.

"Good morning, Mrs. Mohan," the man said formally. "Mr. Varma is waiting for you inside."

How does he know who I am?

His boss must have told him while acquiring her company.

"Thank you," she gritted out and walked along the corridor.

She then stopped in front of a door and glared at the golden nameplate which had been updated.

Yash Varma

Chairman, Genesis Corporation

Although she wanted to barge into the office room angrily, she took deep breaths and knocked on the door.

"Come in," a deep voice commanded.

She pushed the door open with more force than necessary and strode in. Her anger spiked up when she saw Yash Varma seated in the luxurious leather chair behind a heavily carved desk.

He looked like a conquering king enjoying the spoils of war.

The kingdom he raided and grabbed was hers. And the most humiliating part about the war was that there was hardly any fight. Yash Varma bested his enemy using deception.

"You wanted to see me," she gritted out.

Her enemy's dark, intense eyes pierced into her. Despite her anger, a small shiver racked her body. Her cheeks began to heat as images of the intimate moments between them flashed into her mind, where he looked into her eyes in the same intense way while he was deep inside her.

Sucking in a deep breath, she pushed away her memories.

"Yes," his deep voice rumbled. "I wanted to talk to you about the next steps. Sit down."

Her outrage burst out along with her anger at his order. "I'm not going to sit down! If you are planning to dismantle my company, I'm not going to let you. There are close to a hundred employees and their families who will be affected. I won't—"

"Sit down, Narmada."

The dangerously calm tone sent another shiver up her spine. Breathing in and out and gritting her teeth to control herself, she sat in front of him.

Her anger at his deception was too raw, but she had to keep her cool and be sensible. Many people depended on her ability to negotiate a deal with the company's new owner. Her personal feelings should not affect them in any way.

Yash Varma watched her with an unreadable look. "There won't be any layoffs with this merger," he said. "But that doesn't mean I encourage inefficiency in my companies."

Despite her resolve, she was angry again. "My employees are not inefficient. They are one of the best. They always deliver on time, and they are all smart, intelligent and hardworking people, most of whom have been with the company for a long time."

He looked unaffected by her passionate outburst. "That's good," he said coolly. "I value loyalty as one of the biggest assets. But if any of them put up resistance towards the new management, they will be fired immediately."

He was coldly ruthless with no mercy or compassion. Narmada controlled the words she wanted to hurl at him. Clenching her teeth again, she nodded.

"That includes you too, Mrs. Mohan," he added. "Help me make this transition go smoothly, and you can run the company as you did before."

There was a decided threat in his tone, warning her about what would happen if she didn't follow his orders. As a reply to his threat, she wanted to slap him.

His eyes flashed dangerously again as he read her mind easily.

"Don't fight me, Narmada," he warned quietly. "No one has won over me. You won't win either. Whatever happened between us that night has led to this, but if you want to make your life and everyone's life around you easier, you need to follow my orders."

She wanted to scream at him that she would never follow his orders.

But she controlled herself again. Instead, taking another deep breath, she asked him what had been eating her from inside. "Did my father-in-law plan this?" she asked. "Did he send you to sleep with me that night in Milan?"

His eyes flashed. "No."

She laughed. It was a cold, bitter sound with no amusement. "So you magically knew that having sex with me would win you my company shares?"

"It doesn't matter when or how I knew," he said. "I own this company now, and you need to deal with it."

"Or what?" she asked. "You'll fire me? Or leak the sex tape to all the employees? Maybe you conveniently forgot you were there with me. If you shame me, I will drag you down along with me."

His eyes blazed at her threat. "I deleted the tape, and there are no copies of it. The two pictures I showed as proof are the only ones left." Then a small, cold, ruthless smile spread on his face. "And I don't give a damn if you reveal the identity of the man in the pictures as me," he added.

She knew he was right. Even if she decided to reveal the man's identity in the pictures as him, it would gain her nothing. Her father-in-law would most likely pat Yash Varma on the back for deceiving her and would still call her a gold-digging whore.

Her face heated once again with angry humiliation.

Yash Varma watched her again with an unreadable look. "I heard you set up an all-hands meeting with the employees at nine."

Narmada looked at the time. The meeting would start in fifteen minutes. "Yes."

"I'll join you," he said. "You can drive the meeting, but I'll be there next to you."

She wanted to oppose, but she didn't have the time to argue. Gritting her teeth again, she nodded.

"Is that all?" she asked.

"Yes. For now," he replied coolly.

Helpless anger shot through her. Without excusing herself, she got up from the chair and walked away. But until she shut the door behind her, she felt the heat of his gaze burning on her back.

She absolutely hated Yash Varma.

But what she hated even more was the shiver that racked her body at his stare.

***

The all-hands meeting went smoothly.

The atmosphere began with tensed uncertainty among the employees, but after listening to Narmada as she stated there wouldn't be any changes to the upper management or to the rest of the organization's structure, the employees relaxed.

Seeing Yash Varma standing silently next to her while she spoke also reduced their fears. Although Narmada hated his presence next to her, she had to grudgingly acknowledge that it was much needed right then.

"Thank you, everyone," she concluded with a smile, keeping her face carefully devoid of anger and anxiety.

Soon, the employees exited the large hall.

Narmada could hear their murmurs. During her address, she hadn't revealed why her shares had been taken away and there was a new owner. But it was a matter of time before office gossip made its rounds, and everyone found out about the chastity clause which had caused her to lose her shares and partnership.

It would be humiliating, but there was nothing she could do.

Chin up. Focus on the goal.

Ignoring Yash Varma's presence next to her, she walked away with her head held high. She went towards her office.

As soon as she stepped inside her office room, she shut the door and went to her desk. And then, she sat down and closed her eyes.

I won't let you down, Vaibhav. I'm going to win back our company.

Once again, she repeated the words in her mind that kept alive her determination to fight.

It was only ten in the morning, but thanks to the encounter with Yash Varma that morning, she felt as though she had been fighting in a boxing ring for hours. She was mentally exhausted.

There was a knock on the door.

"Narmada?"

"Come in, Supriya."

The door opened, and Narmada saw her friend's familiar face. Her friend was also carrying a hot, steaming cup of coffee.

With a small smile, Supriya came in and sat across her. Unlike the chairman's office, the CEO's office was comparatively smaller and much more practical. It had a window with an outside view, but the rest of the office was a simple desk and three chairs. Her laptop was connected to a large monitor, and the desk remained clear with only a photo frame on top. It was a picture of Vaibhav and her along with the small team when they started the company five years ago. Supriya was a part of it as well.

Narmada reached out for the coffee gratefully. "Thank you. I really needed this."

Her friend smiled at her. "You did well in the all-hands meeting. It shut down the rumors and eased people's worries when you said that the company shares would skyrocket to Fortune Group's share value."

Narmada knew the positive financial aspect wouldn't shut down the other rumors. Nothing could because there was truth to those rumors.

Taking a deep breath, she took a sip of the hot, steaming and slightly bitter liquid to let the caffeine enter her blood stream. Not that she needed to be more alert. Ever since she saw Yash Varma in the boardroom the previous morning, her body had been in constant alert mode.

"Don't you think it is surprising that the new owner doesn't want to change anything?" Supriya asked.

Most large corporations that made acquisitions made significant changes to the acquired companies.

"Our company is running on profits," Narmada replied. "Fortune Group will not want to change it." At least, not yet.

Supriya nodded, but there was a worried gleam in her eyes. "Do you think it was a coincidence that you met him in Milan a month ago?"

"No. He knew who I was." *And like a dumb fly, I fell into his trap.*

Supriya frowned. "It's just so surreal, Narmada. Why would he come on to you knowing he would acquire the company a month later? And how did he get hold of the majority shares when you have a thirty-five percent share?"

Narmada knew that although her friend was curious, she wouldn't push for answers. But Narmada decided to tell her friend everything.

"I lost my shares to him," she said.

There was a stunned look on Supriya's face. "What? What do you mean by lost?"

"I slept with him that night."

Supriya looked shocked, but her friend didn't judge her. She frowned in confusion instead.

"So what if you slept with him? You aren't married, and neither is he. It's nobody else's business what you do on your personal time."

Narmada sighed. "It's not that simple."

Narmada told her friend about the chastity clause. "According to the chastity clause, if I sleep with a man, I lose my shares of the company and also my fifty-percent stake of the inheritance. Yash Varma provided picture proofs."

Narmada didn't care about the inheritance. She had never wanted Vaibhav's family money. She only cared about holding on to her company shares.

Supriya was shocked. "What! That's so sick and unfair! How could your father-in-law insist on such a clause? And why did you agree to sign it!"

Narmada fell silent. "He thinks I cheated on Vaibhav because of which Vaibhav deliberately ran his car into a tree."

"What! Oh my God! Doesn't he know that Vaibhav—"

"No, he doesn't."

Supriya looked stunned. "My God, Narmada. I know you loved Vaibhav. But you can't just let his secrets kill your future. Your father-in-law is a sick-minded man. I also feel it's your father-in-law who had sent Yash Varma to trap you."

Narmada had thought that too initially. But somehow, she knew the man who deceived her was telling her the truth when he said her father-in-law hadn't sent him. And Yash Varma hardly looked like the kind of man who would allow others to dictate to him.

Then why? With his money, he could have easily hired or paid someone else to lure her into the trap. Why did he personally get involved and sleep with her to get hold of her company?

Narmada badly needed answers.

It wasn't a simple case of acquisition or merger. Her gut instinct screamed that there was much more to it.

But what?

"Is there a way to revert the clause?" Supriya asked with a frown. "Prove that it wasn't you in those pictures and that those pictures or videos were forged?"

Narmada considered that option too. Yash Varma had told her there were no copies of the pictures available. But she didn't trust him. She would never trust him.

"No, I can't revert the clause. The only option I have is to buy back those shares from him."

Supriya's face fell. "I can't believe he deceived you this way. I feel ashamed that I thought he would make a good match for you."

Narmada shook her head. "None of this is your fault, Supriya. Don't ever think it. Yash Varma would have found a way to deceive me."

Her friend nodded, looking unconvinced.

Taking a deep breath, Narmada sat back in her chair. "I went through the acquisition papers last night," she said. "Yash Varma had bought twenty-five percent of the shares from the investors before even he met me. He had pre-planned this, and there was nothing you or anyone did to change the course."

If anyone were to be blamed, Narmada would blame herself. Her loneliness and constant need for a connection with another human led her to be easy prey for a ruthless hunter like Yash Varma. All he had to do was look at her and ask her to come up to his room, and she followed behind him without much thought.

No. Don't think of that night.

Pushing away her memories of the night, she let out a trembling smile at her friend. "I wasn't lying when I said that being acquired by Fortune Group is advantageous for employees. The stock value would skyrocket, and there are endless possibilities to get new clients and projects within the Fortune Group. I want us to work on any immediate opportunities."

Supriya nodded. "Sure. I'll meet the team and discuss it in detail. I'll update you later this afternoon."

Narmada knew her friend would once again slip into the CIO mode and not be stressing and worried about what had happened in Milan.

"Thanks, Supriya."

Her friend smiled. "I'll see you later," she said and left to get back to work.

Narmada wished she could slip into her work mode too. She had spent the night obsessively going over the acquisition papers to look for loopholes. Even though she hadn't found any, her mind refused to accept reality.

She picked up her phone and searched through her contacts. When she found the one she was looking for, she dialed the number.

It was answered in two rings. "Good morning, Mrs. Mohan."

"Good morning, Ravi. How are you?" she asked.

"I'm doing good, Mrs. Mohan. How are you? It's a pleasant surprise you are calling me after so many years. Is everything all right?"

No. Everything isn't all right.

If things were normal, she wouldn't be calling a private investigator. Taking a deep breath, she stated the purpose of her call. "Ravi, I need your help in finding out information on a man."

There was silence. The last time she had spoken to the private investigator was to ask him to follow her husband and ensure his safety. But Vaibhav had found out, and he insisted he was doing okay and didn't need anyone following him. Six months later, Vaibhav crashed his car against a tree.

"Sure, Mrs. Mohan. Just email me whatever information you have about that man."

"I will send those details right away from my personal email."

"Sure, Mrs. Mohan. I will start working on it and keep you posted."

After ending the call, Narmada felt slightly better. She needed to know her enemy better to understand what she was dealing with.

A nagging feeling continued to persist inside her that there was much more to the corporate takeover.

The previous night, she tried to look up information on Yash Varma on the internet. But she didn't find much. The man was very private. Except for being the chairman of Fortune Group, there was nothing else about Yash Varma on the web.

Frustrated, she decided to wait for the investigator to get back with the information she wanted.

***

Narmada spent the rest of the day catching up with her work. She continued to attend meetings and take calls. It was late afternoon when she got a call from her personal assistant.

"Mr. Varma wants to meet with you in his office, Narmada."

"Thank you, Pooja."

Narmada didn't want to go. But she knew she could not rebel outright in the open where her employees could sense there was something wrong between their CEO and the new chairman of the company.

Taking a deep breath, she grabbed her cell phone and went straight to her enemy.

This time, she didn't wait for Yash Varma's executive assistant's permission. She decided to barge in. Giving a curt nod to the older man, she strode angrily through the corridor and pushed the heavy door of the chairman's office open.

Yash Varma was speaking on the phone, but his eyes fell on her as soon as she stepped into his office.

There was no change in his expression or demeanor, and he continued with his conversation while watching her with an unreadable look.

"I'll tell you when you can come by," he told someone on the phone. "The three of us can meet and discuss the details of the sale."

His eyes swept over her as she stood with her hands clenched into fists at her sides.

"Call me if anything changes," he said.

He ended the call but continued to watch her silently.

Despite the cool air conditioning, Narmada felt as though the air in the room had turned heavy with tension. A small shiver racked her as his dark gaze swept over her.

Pushing away the effect of his gaze, she raised her chin slightly. "You summoned?" There was a hint of angry sarcasm in her voice.

He continued to watch her with an unnervingly intense look. "As the CEO of this company, I want you to report to me each day with updates."

His order shocked her.

"What? I don't report to anyone on a daily basis." She only gave quarterly updates to the board members regarding the profits and sales.

"Start doing it from now on, Mrs. Mohan, because that's how it is going to be. I want you to align with how Fortune Group operates."

Anger shot through her.

She didn't understand why she felt so volatile when it came to the man in front of her. Despite having dealt with many rude and obnoxious men like her father-in-law before, she had never lost her calm. She had always been a peaceful person. But the man in front of her made her feel things she never felt before.

"Is that all... sir?" she asked sarcastically. "May I leave now?"

His eyes flashed again, whether in anger or annoyance, she didn't know. She didn't care at that point.

"Yes, you may leave."

She turned to leave, but she stopped and faced him. She had planned to speak with him the next day when she didn't feel emotionally exhausted. But being in his presence pushed away her mental exhaustion, and she was ready to fight again.

"What if I contest the clause?" she challenged. "I could say I was drugged and I wasn't in my senses when we slept together. I drank the champagne you sent to my table that night. I even had some of it at your table."

There was a dark flash in his eyes. "I don't have to drug women to get what I want," he said coolly. "Whatever happened between us that night was by your choice."

She clenched her jaw because he was right.

With his dark, handsome and regal looks, many women would crave his attention. She had been one of them too. She had even begged and reveled in his dominant attention.

Pushing away those thoughts, she glared at him. "I read through the acquisition papers. You bought twenty-five percent shares from four of our investors who had signed exclusive agreements. They can't sell their shares outside without first offering the shares to the family first. So, those twenty-five percent shares you purchased is illegal. With my shares, you'll only have a thirty-five percent stake in the company, which isn't a big majority."

His mouth twisted slightly in the semblance of a smile. It was a cold smile, the kind that would create panic and fear in his opponent.

"The two investors did offer the shares to the Mohan family first," he said. "They offered their shares to Rajesh Mohan, and he declined."

Anger burst inside her. She wasn't shocked by her father-in-law's role in her deception.

"I won't let you steal Genesis," she vowed softly.

He didn't seem affected by her threat. "It's already my company now. Give up, Narmada. There is nothing you can do."

Helpless anger coursed through her because she knew he was right. "No. I won't give up. I will pursue this legally as soon as I gather information that the stocks were purchased by wrongful means."

He didn't appear worried. "We both know how long that case would take to resolve and how the verdict could be easily manipulated. And meanwhile, the company's reputation would be dragged through the mud, and I'll be forced to break it into pieces and sell it to someone else."

Narmada gritted her teeth at the picture he painted while issuing her a warning. Once again, she knew he was right. Even if she contested the clause and the sale of the shares from the four investors, it would take many years to resolve the case in court. And with Yash Varma's unlimited money and power, he could easily influence the verdict.

Her shoulders drooped slightly with defeat. But immediately, she straightened them again, refusing to give up. Slowly, with her heart thudding, she decided to use another tactic. She decided to negotiate.

"I am willing to buy back my thirty-five percent shares for double the price. You can keep the twenty-five percent." Narmada didn't know how she would manage to get all that money, but she had to try. She was desperate to hold on to her company.

His answer was immediate. "No."

"Why not?" she demanded. "You are a businessman. In barely a month, you would be doubling the amount of money you spent on the shares. And I'm even letting you keep the twenty-five percent in case you still want to keep a stake in my company."

He sat back in his chair. The predatory look was more intense on his face. "That's quite generous of you to make the offer, considering you don't have enough personal wealth to buy back your shares. But no."

Narmada's face heated in embarrassment at his remark. She had been working as the CEO of a successful company, but she hadn't made any investments to amass personal wealth. All of the money she had earned, she ended up reinvesting into her company to make it more successful. The few savings she had, she put that amount into a bank account for her grandfather to use, which he hadn't touched either.

"Banks will loan me the amount," she said, a hint of desperation entering her voice. "I will pay you in installments. I'll do anything you want. Just give me back my shares."

She hated the desperation in her voice, but at that point, she was willing to do anything to get her company back.

His smile got darker. "Your offer to do anything I want is quite intriguing, Mrs. Mohan. I might take up the offer, but I still won't sell you the shares."

Narmada's face heated in anger at his suggestive remark.

She truly hated the man in front of her. She had never hated anyone the way she hated him right then. He had humiliated her in more than one way and took away her pride and respect.

"Go to hell!" she hissed out and stormed out of his office.

CHAPTER SIX

Yash watched as Narmada Mohan stormed out of his office angrily.

He knew he could have easily left instructions through his personal assistant or got updates from her through email. But he had ordered her to come to his office because he wanted to prove to himself that he didn't have a burning need to see her and be near her.

The meeting didn't go quite as he expected.

While she was talking after storming into his office, it had taken an inhuman amount of control on his part not to drag her close and kiss her until her soft lips were swollen and the red lipstick she wore was completely gone. He had wanted to do more than just kissing. He wanted to pick her up and push her on top of his desk and get rid of their clothes before driving deep into her until she clung to him like she had done during their night in Milan.

"Fuck!"

Letting out the curse viciously, Yash rubbed his palm on his face. His body was painfully aroused, and he tried to bring it under control.

He couldn't afford distractions. Even though he didn't want to acknowledge it to himself, he knew he was getting dangerously obsessed by the beautiful widow who was only supposed to be a means to an end of his revenge plan.

It had been over thirty-one days since they had spent a passionate night together. Since then, he had spent thirty-one damn nights recalling every moment he had touched her, kissed her and seen her face in the throes of passion when he was deep inside her.

It wasn't supposed to be that way.

Seduce the widow, grab control of the company where she owned thirty-five percent of the shares and move on to the next step of the plan.

He was done with the seduction part and had also grabbed control of the company, but he wasn't able to forget the widow. Dark, hungry desire to possess her body, heart and soul haunted him constantly.

Maybe it was because he hadn't expected their night to be any different from the ones he usually spent with other beautiful women. Narmada Mohan had left a lasting and searing impression on him.

He had wanted to be disgusted by her. Her cheating had led to her husband's suicide. And according to her father-in-law, Narmada Mohan was money-hungry and man-hungry. But none of it mattered when he had seen her a month ago.

***

One month ago...
Milan, Italy

"We are so honored you joined us, Mr. Varma. Your success story is truly inspiring."

Yash normally didn't attend large business conferences. He usually had one of his top executives represent the company. But this time, he was attending a conference for a reason.

A beautiful reason who was currently standing at a distance talking to a small group of people.

Narmada Mohan.

Yash's gaze swept over her in a cold, clinical way. She was wearing a business suit that hid the shape of her body and revealed only the lower part of her shapely legs. Despite trying to hide behind her clothes and lack of makeup, the woman was quite beautiful.

But she wasn't his usual type.

He never chose women from business circles or anyone who worked for him. He always preferred beautiful women who wore expensive, shapely designer clothes and flaunted their beauty. And most importantly, he wanted his women to be available and cater to his demanding needs in between his hectic work schedule.

He knew it was chauvinistic and arrogant of him to have that demand. But ever since he made his first million at the age of nineteen, he never had to pursue a woman or make any attempt to draw their attention. Women always came to him, and he made his pick based on his demands.

So, the beautiful CEO of a company who led a busy life was far from his ideal choice.

But he wasn't there at the conference to pursue her. At least not for himself.

"I hope you can attend the dinner event after the conference, Mr. Varma," the man continued. "We have some exclusive shows for our select

VIP guests. There's also special champagne from one of the best vineyards, which will be served during dinner."

"I have other plans, Mr. Rogers," he told the event head. "However, I'd like to purchase a few bottles of the champagne."

The man nodded eagerly. "Whatever you wish, Mr. Varma. We will send out this year's newsletter with Fortune Group logo as the primary attendees."

Yash nodded once and dismissed the man.

He continued to observe his beautiful prey discreetly while the conversation he had two weeks ago with his two brothers ran through his mind.

"Rajesh Mohan," Aryan stated as he handed the investigative folders put together by the private investigation company. "He was the one who had insisted on getting the power of attorney, saying it would make things easier."

Yash flipped through the folder. Forty percent of Rajesh Mohan's assets were held in his daughter's name. But the most valuable asset was the company that Rajesh Mohan's late son started seven years ago with a partner whom he married eventually. His son died three years ago and left all of his shares to his widow.

"Buying out majority stakeholder's shares and acquiring the power of attorney rights should finish the older man," Bhargav stated calmly.

Yash didn't say anything. He continued to read the file, paying close attention to the details. The investigator had done a thorough job even though he was given just two weeks. The investigator had even put together the older man's will and legal clauses document of the company shares.

One such document caught Yash's attention—the chastity clause. The history behind the clause was written in a brief write- up. Rajesh Mohan blamed his son's wife's cheating ways to be his son's cause of death. The woman had an affair with her husband's good friend.

Yash didn't care about the woman or her deeds. Opening another folder, he flipped through Rajesh Mohan's family member's pictures.

The older man looked shrewd and cunning as he gazed at the camera in the pictures. His wife looked subdued as did his daughter. Yash's eyes didn't linger on Rajesh Mohan's daughter's pictures even though he knew she held the key to accomplish his task. Instead, his gaze landed on the pictures of the couple—Rajesh Mohan's son and daughter-in-law—especially the daughter-in-law.

The young couple was smiling in all pictures. The first picture was taken when they were eighteen years old. They weren't married then and had only been very close friends. Genuine affection radiated from both their faces. The affection remained in the second picture as well which was taken on their wedding day. But it was in the third and especially the fourth picture where the couple's smiles looked forced.

Did Narmada Mohan begin cheating on her husband by then?

Yash assessed the woman's pretty face. Despite the minimal makeup, there was innate sensuality in her eyes and lips. And she didn't look like a woman who was content with her life either.

"Do you think Narmada Mohan will sell her shares to us?" Bhargav asked. "She is one of the majority shareholders."

Yash continued to look at the picture of Narmada Mohan. "No, she won't sell us her shares. She founded the company along with Rajesh Mohan's son."

Aryan frowned. "Then she is going to be hard to convince then, even if we offer her above-market price."

A small smile escaped Yash. Strangely, he felt a spark of anticipation like he did when he went after the most difficult business deals.

"She doesn't have to sell," he replied. "Because after a month, the shares won't remain hers."

Yash had set out a plan to trap Narmada Mohan, but he wasn't supposed to be the one executing it.

He had initially been disgusted by the fact that Narmada Mohan cheated on her husband, which led to his suicide. But something about her drew him towards her. While he planned her downfall, he had also set out another investigation to focus entirely on her. And what he found out about her background had shocked him.

No wonder I feel drawn to her.

So, instead of being in New York running his empire, he was in Milan, overseeing a task which he could have easily gotten an update the minute after it was completed.

This damn plan better work.

Yash turned slightly to look at the man named Marco, who was discreetly following and watching Narmada Mohan. Although the man had approached her many times, she seemed distracted and had barely glanced at him. She was talking to her CIO and a few other people who most likely would be her future clients.

Narmada Mohan's life revolved around her company, Genesis. After the death of her husband, she began to make big investments and expanded her company to a decent-sized corporation from a small startup. Acquiring her company would be quite profitable.

But Yash wasn't interested in Genesis to make a profit. It was only a stepping stone to something bigger.

"I just called the hotel management, Yash. They have confirmed the table reservation." It was Yash's personal assistant.

Suresh Raman had been his personal assistant for the last ten years. Over the years, Yash had offered him many executive job positions in Fortune Group, but the older man insisted on being his personal assistant.

Yash trusted him, and the older man had earned the trust many times over the years.

"Did she receive a call, Mr. Raman?"

"Yes, Yash. Although Mrs. Mohan hasn't confirmed."

Yash had asked Mr. Raman to arrange for someone to call Narmada Mohan, letting her know of a complimentary drinks offer at her hotel bar lounge that evening.

It was critical that she agree to the offer for his plan to work.

Yash knew there were chances Narmada Mohan would choose to dine out, forgoing the generous offer. But he took the calculated risk.

"What about Supriya Katri's ticket?" Yash enquired.

"Mrs. Katri will receive a call later in the evening letting her know about her ticket being upgraded to first-class with a stopover at Paris."

"Good."

Everything was going according to the plan, except for a small change.

"Mr. Raman, book a table for me as well in the bar lounge.

The older man looked slightly surprised. They were supposed to fly out to NewYork that night to attend an important business meeting the next day.

"Sure, Yash."

Yash knew he was taking a huge risk by deviating slightly from the well-laid plan. If Narmada Mohan saw him in the bar lounge, there were chances she would recognize him after a month when she sees him again.

But he wanted to stay. And he wanted to see through the execution of the plan that night.

***

Five hours later, Yash's calculated risk paid off. He was seated at a table that was a short distance away from the table reserved for Narmada Mohan and her friend.

He watched her while she laughed and spoke to her friend who was also her CIO. Both women hadn't changed their clothes and were still in their business suits. But something was different about Narmada Mohan.

Unlike in the conference where she had a reserved smile and stiff formal posture, she was now relaxed. Yash found her easy smile entirely familiar and fascinating.

"Sir, would you like the champagne sent now?" a waiter asked.

Yash raised a chin towards Narmada's table. "Yes, send a bottle to the lady and say it's from an admirer."

The waited nodded with a smile. "I'll do that right away, sir."

Yash watched as the waiter delivered the bottle. Although Narmada didn't seem that keen to accept the gift, her friend accepted it enthusiastically.

Yash's eyes fell on the man seated at another table.

The man was useless. Yash had hired him to catch Narmada Mohan's attention. But the man was failing miserably. Narmada was barely paying him attention.

Until now.

Yash watched as Narmada Mohan's friend said something after which Narmada's gaze searched and fell on Marco.

Suddenly, Yash felt a strange burning sensation inside his chest as Narmada and Marco locked glances. Yash had the sudden urge to pick up the other man and throw him out of the bar.

Frowning at the strange feeling, Yash looked away from them.

What the fuck is wrong with me?

Angry and irritated at his irrational feeling, he pulled up his phone and typed a text.

Mr. Raman, have the jet readied for tonight.

Now that the man Yash had hired to seduce Narmada Mohan had caught her attention, he decided to fly back to New York.

Even as he typed the message, the burning sensation inside his chest grew. He also felt a strong pull which was different from everything he had felt before.

Frowning slightly, he looked up.

A shockingly strong bolt of desire hit him as his gaze clashed with Narmada Mohan's. She was watching him with a fascinated gaze.

When he raised an eyebrow, her eyes widened even more. He saw her face flush in a familiar way that indicated an attraction.

She looked away hurriedly, but it didn't stop the sparks that flew because of their locked gazes. If anything, the desire he felt grew stronger.

He watched as things played out according to his plan.

Narmada Mohan's friend received a call. After the call ended, Supriya Katri told Narmada about the flight upgrade option. The woman felt guilty, but Narmada asked her friend to take up the upgrade offer. Feeling excited, the woman hugged Narmada and left the table.

That's when the man Yash had hired to seduce Narmada made his move. Marco went to her table.

The burning sensation inside Yash's chest grew stronger, making him finally realize what it was.

A dark, burning jealousy.

Yash wanted his beautiful pawn, and he didn't want the other man going anywhere near her.

Clenching his jaw, he typed another short message.

Cancel jet.

Even though Yash knew he would be risking a lot, he got up and went to the woman who was only supposed to be a pawn.

Marco was unsuccessfully trying to convince Narmada to leave with him. "Come on, beautiful lady. Let's share the rest of the champagne bottle."

The fool sounded like a B-grade actor, which was exactly what he was.

"Get out," Yash ordered.

Narmada Mohan turned, and when her eyes clashed with his, she looked shocked.

The man named Marco began to protest. And he wasn't very bright either. He almost revealed the fact that it was Yash who had hired him to seduce Narmada.

"How can you ask me to leave? I—"

Yash cut him off midway. "Leave. Right now."

Finally, the man got the message when he saw the dark look on Yash's face. Marco left the table without arguing.

Yash stared at the beautiful woman who was watching him with shocked, uncertain eyes.

She has excellent instincts.

He could sense her strong attraction along with her hesitation. Yash knew she felt the same strong pull as he did, but her gut instinct was warning her of danger.

He decided to give her a choice.

"Join me at my table," he ordered before leaving her table and going towards his.

Yash had always believed in luck. Although he and his brothers put a shit-ton of hard work to amass a fortune, luck and taking calculated risks played a vital role in their success as well.

He knew that his risk would pay off. The desire between him and Narmada was too strong to ignore.

He held the chair out for her. A moment later, Narmada sat on it. Taking the seat opposite her, he looked at her. He saw her beautiful face flushed due to attraction as well as nervousness.

"A-are you from Milan?" she asked, trying to cover her nervousness.

"No." He didn't offer any more information. The pulse beating rapidly at her throat made him want to taste her nervousness.

Her cheeks heated all the more at his stare.

Then suddenly, her eyes widened, and her face paled a little. "Are you married?" she asked.

"No."

She looked visibly relieved.

Yash found that very intriguing. If she cheated on her husband, why would she give a damn about him being married or not?

His eyes lowered to her left hand, where she was nervously turning the wedding ring around her finger.

Her husband had died three years ago, but she was still wearing his ring.

Did that mean she loved her husband?

Once again, a burning feeling rose inside his chest. He knew her wedding ring would be critical for that night. But he had an irrational urge to grab her hand and take the wedding ring out and fling it far away before he did what he wanted with her.

"I-I'm widowed," she quickly explained as though sensing his dark possessive thoughts. "My husband passed away three years ago."

He locked his eyes to hers but didn't say anything. Her words dragged him back to his rational senses, reminding himself of who she was and what he had to do.

He knew Vaibhav Mohan had crashed his car deliberately against a tree. And it was right after the man's death that Narmada was made to sign the chastity clause document by Rajesh Mohan.

A clause that would be Narmada's downfall.

"Sir, champagne."

It was the waiter. Yash nodded, and the waiter poured the champagne into two glasses.

Raising the champagne flute, Yash twisted his mouth in a smile. "To unknown beginnings," he toasted.

"To unknown beginnings," Narmada repeated softly with a smile.

Yash barely tasted the expensive champagne. He was struck hard by Narmada's smile. It lit up her face and made her look breathtakingly beautiful and familiar.

He had the sudden urge to crush her lips with his to capture her smile.

He wanted to taste her. She would taste lightly of the champagne she was drinking, but he wanted to taste her essence. He wanted to peel away her clothes and kiss her everywhere until he drew her essence deep into him even when she was gone from his life.

Fuck.

The dark, urgent need he felt for her pissed him off.

"Would you like to order dinner?" he asked. His voice sounded gruff with desire.

Narmada shook her head.

"Then let's go," he ordered.

Her eyes widened. "Where?" she whispered.

Keeping his gaze locked to her, he replied. "My room."

She looked shocked at his blunt proposition.

He deliberately didn't offer her soft words of comfort. Although he would deceive her in the future, he wanted this part of their interaction to be honest.

He wanted her. And he wanted her on his terms.

Standing up, he waited. He watched as she bit her lip in nervousness while she stared back at him. He knew she could sense his dark need.

He thought she would shy away based on the nervousness on her face, but deep satisfaction coursed through him as she stood up and came closer.

He placed his hand against her small back and led her out of the bar lounge.

The walk to the room he had booked under a different man's name was silent and filled with thick tension as harsh, impatient desire coursed through his bloodstream. He wanted to drag Narmada into his arms and kiss her right in the lobby, not giving a damn about anyone.

He sucked in a tensed, impatient breath. He reminded himself why he was doing it. He needed the proof of their encounter on camera.

They took the elevator to the topmost floor, where the room was located at the corner. And by the time they entered the suite and the bedroom, his body was vibrating with a raw hunger he had never felt before.

He held her and pushed her against one of the bedroom walls before covering the distance between them.

Their eyes locked.

As he stared at her, he felt a different kind of burning. Staring into her beautiful eyes, he knew it wasn't just desire or the need for revenge. She awoke a part of him deep inside that no one had ever reached before.

Just when he was burning with the unknown feelings, she touched him.

It was a simple touch on his face, tracing his jaw lightly. But the simple contact sizzled his skin, burning him inside out. His eyes closed shut at the depth of the craving he felt towards her.

This is just desire.

She is only a pawn, nothing more.

You are only imagining things.

Fuck her and get her out of your system. Your final goal is more important.

He opened his eyes, determined to get her out of his system. A soft gasp escaped her mouth at seeing the dark, hungry look on his face. Even though he saw nervousness along with desire in her face, he didn't stop. He dug his fingers into her upswept hair and tugged until the pressure of his fingers cascaded her beautiful hair down her back.

Tipping her face up, he held her in a tight grip. Her beautiful face with soft eyes and trembling lips increased his burning hunger.

Pushing aside everything else, his mouth captured hers, determined to satisfy the dark, burning hunger he had for her. At the end of the night, he wanted his hunger completely sated, just so he wouldn't think of her again.

***

Present...

"Fuck!"

Yash couldn't get Narmada Mohan out of his system.

He recalled every passionate moment of that night in Milan when he had taken her repeatedly to satisfy the burning need he felt for her. Even though his body climaxed with each passionate joining, it only increased his hunger.

What was supposed to be simply a one-night stand turned into much more.

Her unexpected sweet smiles, the look of wonder on her face, the small gestures when she had touched his face or when she held him close in her arms during sex—all of it got to him.

It was as though she saw something wonderful in their torrid sexual encounter.

I want that look of wonder on her face again.

"Fuck," he cursed out again.

Feeling agitated, he dialed a number on his phone. As soon as it was answered, he barked out, "What happened? Did they agree?"

"Not yet," a deep, calm voice replied. "But they will soon."

Yash felt an uncharacteristic impatience. "I wanted it done by now, Bhargav. We are offering twice the amount of money."

"It's under government control now, Yash. It's not as straightforward. But yes, if our offer doesn't move things by next week, we'll apply pressure through other ways."

Yash knew his brother was right. Buying a government-controlled estate wasn't as straightforward. Although they had money, they were still building local influence and connections.

Those facts didn't stop him from feeling frustrated.

"I'm going with the next plan of action. Rajesh Mohan will expedite our process."

There was a momentary silence on the phone line. "Don't you think it's too soon?" Bhargav asked. "Rajesh Mohan might get suspicious. And didn't you speak with Aryan a few minutes ago, asking him not to make a move too soon?"

Yash was the oldest of three brothers. Bhargav was the second and Aryan was the youngest. Among the three brothers, Yash was known to operate in a cold, ruthless way and strike the enemy without much added drama.

"No, it isn't too soon," Yash replied. "The man is already on a high with the money he got with the takeover. Greed will make him agree to the next strike too."

There was another silence.

Yash frowned at the silence. He knew his brother was taken aback by the rash decision. Yash was the one who had always taught his two brothers to patiently wait until the enemy lost the battle before even the war began.

But now, he was changing the rules of the war because he didn't want his obsession with Narmada Mohan threatening his plans.

Pushing away the thought of his beautiful pawn, Yash focused on the plan. "What about you?" he asked. "Have you established contact?"

"Yes," Bhargav replied. "She will most likely accept the offer and start next week."

Yash knew that unlike him, Bhargav and Aryan would have to go slow for their plan to work without any glitches

"Good. Remember, we need to go for the final strike without warning the other two."

"Yes, I remember. But what about Narmada Mohan?"

Yash didn't like hearing her name from his brother. "What do you mean?"

"Won't she create trouble and warn Rajesh Mohan?"

Yash knew there was a possibility. But if Narmada hadn't revealed the truth until then, the chances were quite low she would in the future. She also knew revealing the truth would only make Rajesh Mohan use it to humiliate her further.

"She won't. I'll take care of her."

"How?" Bhargav asked. "She hates you, and she has already contacted her legal team to find a loophole in the clause."

Yash had found that out the previous day. He knew Narmada wouldn't give up so easily on the company she built from scratch. She was working with the legal team and had requested them to invalidate the chastity clause.

But he had warned his beautiful pawn by painting a picture of what would happen if she pursued a lawsuit or fought against him. The warning he had issued earlier not to pursue the legal route ended half the battle before it began. His beautiful pawn looked furious and upset, but he had seen the look of resignation in her eyes because she knew he could influence the legal system.

Yash's mouth twisted. "She might hate me, but there is nothing she can do. Even if she tries, she won't win against me. Aryan called me a while ago. He is checking her digital footprint. In case there is something suspicious, I've asked him to reach out to me."

Aryan was computer savvy. Among the three brothers, Aryan was the only one who chose to go for higher studies and graduated from a top Ivy League school. Yash and Bhargav dropped out of school at a young age to make their first million at the age of nineteen.

"All right," said Bhargav. "I'll call you back when I hear about the estate sale."

Ending the call, Yash stared out of the office window.

Although he was the one who had insisted on jumping ahead with the next part of his plan, he wasn't remotely excited or even interested in pursuing it. Because the next part of the plan didn't include Narmada Mohan. If anything, the plan would make her hate him even more.

But no matter what the consequence, he would go ahead with the next part of his plan.

Pulling out his phone, he called his personal assistant. "Mr. Raman, arrange for a dinner meeting at Rajesh Mohan's guesthouse tonight."

CHAPTER SEVEN

"What do you mean there isn't anything more on Yash Varma?" Narmada asked in frustration. "Dig deeper, Ravi. I'm sure there will be information. And how can there be no pictures of the family?"

Narmada was at her home speaking to the investigator on the phone. So far, the call had been frustrating.

"I will try, Mrs. Mohan. But the Varmas have used their money and influence to fiercely guard their privacy. It's only because of my contacts that I was able to get this information."

Narmada flipped through the document he had sent earlier. "Just keep trying. And call me when you find something more."

With that instruction, Narmada ended the call in frustration.

She stared at the pictures that the investigator had sent. But the pictures appeared to be more or less downloaded from the internet from some business magazines she had read before.

Yash Varma had a typical rags-to-riches story. He grew up in New York in a poor neighborhood along with his mother and his two younger brothers. His brothers were also his business partners. He did not complete his formal education since he quit school at the age of fourteen to work in construction jobs. He began taking in small renovation contracts and reinvested that money in real estate to buy and renovate more homes.

By the time Yash Varma was nineteen, most of his investments had increased several times over, and he became a millionaire. Since then, Fortune Group grew from a small real estate company to a formidable corporation with real estate and construction projects worldwide.

Although Yash Varma took care of the primary business, his two brothers diversified the business and took care of the hospitality industry and the software solutions business.

Genesis was a software company. Then why was Yash Varma tackling the acquisition rather than his youngest brother Aryan Varma?

Narmada recalled the conversation she had heard when she had barged into his office two days ago. He was speaking to someone on the phone which didn't sound like a work-related call.

Was it a family member?

Or a girlfriend?

Her heart jerked at the thought. Even though she hated him with a burning passion, the fact that he might have a girlfriend filled her stomach with a sour feeling.

She shook her head, pushing away the feeling. Instead, she focused on finding out more about her enemy.

"Who the hell are you?" she murmured while looking at Yash Varma's picture that was featured in a business magazine.

The dark intensity of his eyes was captured well in the image. He looked utterly cold and ruthless.

Narmada knew a person had to be ruthless to be able to rise from poverty and turn into a billionaire within ten years. But somehow, she felt there was more to the takeover of Genesis.

"I won't let you win, Yash Varma," she whispered.

Narmada continued to stare at the darkly handsome picture.

Even though she hated the man now, looking at his pictures reminded her of the night they had spent together. In between their several bouts of passionate lovemaking, they were moments of softness. During those times, she had softly kissed and explored the dark, brooding and handsome features that endlessly fascinated her. He had watched her with an unreadable look.

He probably thought I was a desperate fool begging for simple human touch.

Did he hate my touch and tolerate it for the sake of acquisition?

Her cheeks heated in humiliation at that thought.

No! He couldn't have been faking it.

In fact, there had been no need to spend the entire night with her. The two pictures he had used to implicate her were taken within the first thirty minutes of being in the hotel suite.

Then why did he spend the rest of the night with me?

Was he playing some sort of twisted mind game?

Her mind spun with confusion and anger, trying to figure out Yash Varma's motive.

She frantically went through the investigative folder again to look for clues, but found none. She was about to search for more information on the internet, but her phone began ringing.

She wanted to ignore it, but looking at the number flashing on the phone screen, she decided to answer.

It was Vaibhav's sister. "Hello, Divya. How are you?"

There was a choked sob on the line. "Narmada... Papa is trying to get me married."

Narmada frowned. Divya was only twenty-two years old. But it technically wasn't too young to get married because Narmada herself got married to Vaibhav at the age of twenty-one. But what concerned Narmada was that Divya wouldn't be crying if her father was getting her married to the man Divya loved.

"Have you told your father and mother yet about Rahul?" Narmada asked.

"How can I?" the younger woman asked. "You know very well Papa won't agree."

Narmada knew it was true. She and Vaibhav had to elope to get married because Rajesh Mohan would not agree to allow his only son and heir married to his driver's granddaughter.

Narmada recalled the threats her father-in-law had issued at that time. But luckily, even though Vaibhav had never stood up to his father before, he had stood up for her right then. Rajesh Mohan had no choice but to accept his son's decision in marriage.

"You must let your father know, Divya. Tell him you love Rahul."

"I can't!" the younger woman cried out in anguish. "When my brother married you, you were worth a lot because of Genesis. My father agreed to the marriage when my brother threatened he would give away his shares to you and step away from the company. I don't have any such leverage, Narmada. Rahul doesn't even have a job yet!"

Narmada didn't know what to say. She knew her sister-in-law was right about her not having leverage currently. Rajesh Mohan cared a lot about whether or not the people his children married belonged to the same wealthy class or not.

"Narmada... if... if Papa forces me to marry someone else... I'm going to kill myself."

Narmada felt a chill passing through her as she listened to familiar words.

"I can't take this anymore, Narmada. I want to let go."

Vaibhav's last words resonated in Narmada's mind.

"Don't ever say that, Divya! I'll speak to your parents. Just give me some time."

Divya began to cry. "I'm not strong like you, Narmada. I heard Papa telling Mamma that he took away your shares and sold the company to someone else. Papa can be stubborn and really mean. He won't let me marry Rahul. I love Rahul and cannot live without him."

Narmada tried to maintain calm even though panic ripped through her because of her sister-in-law's suicide threat.

"Divya, you need to stay strong. There is nothing that cannot be resolved. Your father might not like me, but I'll do my best to get you married to the man you love."

"Promise?" the other girl whispered.

Although Narmada had no damn idea what she would do, she was determined to help. "Yes, I promise. I will help you."

Soon after the call ended, Narmada couldn't get back to her laptop. Her heart continued to thud sickly even though Divya had promised not to do anything hasty. Memories of Vaibhav and their marriage flashed in her mind.

Vaibhav had been her best friend since the age of ten. Although Vaibhav was moody and withdrawn at times, the rest of the time he was sweet, cheerful and brilliant.

It was only after their marriage that she got to see the extent of Vaibhav's mood swings. She had asked him to seek professional help, but he said he couldn't because of his father. Vaibhav didn't want his father to find out his secret. Narmada knew Rajesh Mohan would not be supportive of his son. In fact, the older man was capable of abusing his son and calling him names if he found out the truth.

But Narmada hadn't given up. She had begged and pleaded Vaibhav to at least take medications, which thankfully Vaibhav did for a few years. But it was only towards the end when he had stopped taking the medications due to a reason. Narmada had found out only after Vaibhav's accident that he had stopped taking his medications.

Even though Supriya repeatedly said it wasn't anyone's fault, Narmada still blamed herself for not having helped Vaibhav enough.

I miss you, Vaibhav.

Narmada missed her best friend. When Vaibhav was alive, they spoke for hours at length, sharing their mutual dreams and planning a bright future. But now, not only was Vaibhav gone, their shared dream was slipping away from her.

I'll keep your promise, Vaibhav. I won't let Yash Varma destroy it.

CHAPTER EIGHT

Despite the promise Narmada made to her late husband, two weeks passed since the takeover of Genesis, and she had done nothing to get her company back.

In fact her enemy was sabotaging her company.

"We were told we can't renew the license with Ikon Tech, Narmada." Supriya looked worried. "We barely have two months' time until the license and the contracts would expire."

Narmada controlled from showing her anger. "I'm sure there was a miscommunication. I'll speak with Yash Varma and have it cleared."

Supriya nodded.

Narmada walked out of the meeting room and went straight up the top floor. She was breathing hard and fast at the sheer anger she felt.

In fact, she constantly felt angry and miserable over the last two weeks.

She hated that she continued to work for Yash Varma. For the past two weeks, she was forced to sit across from him each day in his office and discuss the day-to-day operations with him. She felt suffocated and could barely sit through the meetings while he watched her with his unreadable look.

She couldn't sleep well due to worry about what else was going to happen to the company she built. She was worried that the man who deceived her and stole her company would do something that would risk the livelihood of her employees and the credibility of her company.

I won't let him get away with it!

"Good morning, Mrs. Varma."

Narmada nodded her head at Yash Varma's PA in greeting. She wasn't in a position to chit chat.

The older man didn't stop her or ask her any questions. He knew she was meeting his boss for the daily briefing meeting.

Narmada pushed the door open and strode in angrily. Yash Varma was typing something on his laptop. But when the door opened without a knock, he looked up.

"What do you mean we can't work with Ikon Tech anymore?" she demanded. "They have been strategic partners to Genesis for the last six years."

Yash Varma sat back in his chair with an unreadable look. He didn't react to her outburst.

It only made her angrier.

"You are deliberately sabotaging my company," Narmada accused. "You said there wouldn't be any layoffs or change in management, but you are using other means to destroy Genesis. If you think I'll simply sit back and watch you destroy my company, you are wrong!"

"It's my company now," he reminded.

Her cheeks heated in anger and humiliation at his reminder.

"I'm still the CEO and responsible for the well-being of Genesis!" she gritted out.

It took great control on her side not to slap him and beat him on his chest to demand why he had deceived her and what his true intentions were. It wasn't just about Genesis.

The investigator wasn't able to find anything more. Even though she didn't have much money to spend, she had asked him to hire additional resources and dig out whatever dirt they could on Yash Varma. She was desperate to get back her company and remove the man she hated permanently from her life.

"I'm buying Ikon Tech," Yash Varma coolly replied.

That shocked her. "What?"

"As you said, Ikon Tech has been a strategic partner for Genesis. It makes more sense for it to be a part of the company. Next in line are ProTech and Adsoft."

Narmada didn't know how to react.

On one hand, what he said made good business sense, but on the other hand, it only added to her confusion. Why did he care about Genesis, a company that was barely ten percent of what Fortune Group's net worth was?

Her confusion led to more anger. "You can't just keep acquiring companies that are strategic partners to Genesis!"

"Why not?" he asked coolly. "I can afford it, and it's a good business decision."

She gritted her teeth knowing it was true. She didn't want to be grateful or appreciate the move. She was sure there was some ulterior motive. The ruthless man wouldn't do anything unless there was something in it for him.

Feeling angry and confused, she glared at him. "Is that all?" she asked.

He was quiet, and his eyes moved slowly over her face and then to her body before returning back to lock his gaze with hers. Her body heated and her face felt flushed due to anger and awareness.

"Is there something you would like to tell me?" he asked.

His question caught her off guard.

Did he find out about the investigation? Did the legal team reach out to him to let him know she was asking them to find a loophole in the acquisition?

She knew he was a man with unlimited powers. There was every chance he would react badly by striking back at her in a way she couldn't recover.

A shiver ran through her body. "W-what do you mean?" she asked in return.

His eyes hooded as he watched her closely. "I've noticed that you have lost weight. You also look angry and tired most of the time. Are they consequences of what we did?"

For a moment, Narmada's mind was blank. She knew she had lost weight because she hadn't been eating well, and there were dark circles under her eyes due to sleepless nights that she couldn't hide much with makeup. Anger and tiredness were consequences of his takeover.

But slowly, she realized what he actually meant when his eyes lowered to her stomach again.

Oh my God.

"That's impossible!" she whispered in shock and horror.

His eyes flickered while his face remained unmoved. "I would say it is quite possible, Mrs. Mohan. Considering we had sex multiple times."

Her face burned as she recalled the hot, urgent and passionate lovemaking of that night.

"No! I cannot be pregnant! You... you... used protection that night.

"That doesn't necessarily mean it is completely safe. Unless of course, you were on some form of protection too."

Her face paled at his words. She hadn't been on any form of birth control that night. She had never used any protection even prior to Vaibhav's death.

Seeing her shocked, pale face, Yash Varma understood. "I'll call a doctor and have the tests done," he said grimly.

"No! That's not needed. I know I'm not pregnant." She had her period in between. But it was only light spotting that could occur even if someone was stressed. Or pregnant.

"Your words don't mean much, Narmada. I need concrete proof that you are not carrying my child."

Her face burned even as panic gripped her. Pushing away the panic, she focused on her anger. "I'm not carrying your child! And even if I do, I'm not going to ask anything from you. So rest assured, your fortune is safe from me and my child, Mr. Varma."

He looked unmoved by her passionate outburst. When he spoke, it was in a dangerously calm tone. "What makes you think I wouldn't want my child?" he asked.

Fear ripped through her seeing his dark, possessive look.

"If there is a child," he continued in the same tone. "Then rest assured, I will want what belongs to me. So get the tests done and let me know for sure. Or I will ensure we confirm through my way."

Fear and panic grew as his softly worded threat made it even worse. Not responding to him, she walked away with her legs trembling.

I'm not pregnant.

It's impossible.

I can't be carrying Yash Varma's child.

I hate him.

Oh God. But what if I am pregnant with his child?

She blindly went back to her office room. But she didn't settle down for work. Grabbing her purse, she stepped out of her office again.

"Pooja, please postpone the rest of my morning's meetings. I will be back in a couple of hours."

Pooja nodded. "Sure, Narmada."

Thanking the younger woman, Narmada began to head out. She was near the elevators when Supriya called out to her.

"Narmada, wait!"

Narmada thought her friend needed to ask her something related to work. But Supriya shocked her.

"Yash Varma called and asked me to join you. He said you were going to a doctor. Are you all right?"

Narmada's face heated in anger and embarrassment. "I'm fine, Supriya."

Her friend frowned. "Then why are you going to a doctor?"

Narmada gritted her teeth angrily at Yash Varma's interference. But seeing the worry on her friend's face, she had to tell the truth.

"I'm going to the doctor for a pregnancy test."

There was a stunned look on Supriya's face.

"I don't think I am pregnant, but... he... he wants me to confirm."

"Oh." Supriya visibly pulled herself together. "I'll come with you. I'll drive."

Narmada wanted to say it wasn't needed. But she didn't. Her legs and stomach still trembled with worry about the pregnancy test. She didn't know if she would be in the right frame of mind while driving to the doctor.

"All right."

***

They drove to the gynecologist's clinic that Narmada went for her yearly checkups.

Narmada had known the doctor for a long time. So, the doctor appeared surprised when Narmada asked for a pregnancy test.

Narmada's cheeks heated because the doctor knew Vaibhav had died in a car crash three years ago.

"Sure, Narmada. I'll ask the nurse to prepare for a blood test. Meanwhile, if you would like, you can do a quick check with a home pregnancy kit."

"Yes, I would like that. Thank you."

With her heart thudding, Narmada took the small kit and went into the bathroom. She followed the doctor's instructions, and took the test and waited for the results to appear.

Her heart thudded loudly in her ears as she saw a line appear. She held her breath and waited for a few more moments. When the other line didn't appear, she stared at it for a while.

Not pregnant.

Narmada knew she should feel relieved, but she could only stare at the result. Strangely, she felt a loss.

What is wrong with me!

She took a deep breath to pull herself together.

Then washing her hands, she stepped out. Supriya was waiting outside.

And when Supriya saw her face, her friend became. "What does the result say?"

"Not pregnant."

Supriya looked relieved. "Oh, thank God! Don't worry, Narmada. These pregnancy tests are quite accurate too."

Narmada nodded.

They went back to the doctor and gave the blood sample.

"I can send the results in a few hours. I'll call to confirm, Narmada."

Narmada nodded. "Thank you, Doctor Swati."

As they stepped out of the clinic, Narmada asked Supriya to drive them back to work.

Supriya looked at her with concern. "Are you sure, Narmada? I can drop you home, and you can take meeting calls from home."

"I'm fine."

They drove back to work.

Narmada continued with the rest of the day, taking calls and attending meetings in conference rooms. Luckily, none of the meetings had Yash Varma attending them.

She didn't want to face him.

But at the end of the day when she received a call from the doctor, she took a printout of the report and went to the top floor.

"I would like to meet Mr. Varma."

The personal assistant looked at her. "Yash has a meeting in another ten minutes."

"This is urgent, Mr. Raman. And I'm not going to take more than five minutes."

The man looked at her from behind his spectacles. Whatever he must have seen on her face must have convinced him. "All right, Mrs. Mohan. You can go in. I'll call Yash to let him know."

"Thank you, Mr. Raman." Nodding curtly at the personal assistant, Narmada strode to the room.

As soon as her knock received a deep command to enter, she strode in. And then, when she was right in front of the office desk, she slammed the paper containing the results of her pregnancy test on top of the desk.

"I'm not pregnant," she said angrily. "So you don't have to worry anymore or threaten me with lawsuits. And just so you know, even if I were pregnant, I wouldn't have come to you for paternal support or ask you for anything. You are the last man I would want in my life, let alone as my child's father. I wish I never met you, and I would be happy if I never see you again."

Yash Varma was silent through her outburst, but his eyes flashed dangerously.

She didn't care if she had offended him. She wanted to do more than just offend him. But she couldn't do much apart from pushing back his threats by insulting him.

Throwing him a hate-filled glare, she turned away and walked out of the room.

CHAPTER NINE

The next morning, Narmada decided to visit her grandfather.

"Yes, I'm fine, Supriya," Narmada said over the phone. "Don't worry about me. I'm going to the village to surprise my grandfather."

"Oh. That's good! When are you returning?" Supriya asked.

"I'm planning to stay there for a day and a half. I'll return on Sunday evening. Don't worry about me and enjoy your weekend. I'm sure Shekhar has planned something special."

Her friend laughed happily. "Yes, he has. But you know we love having you over anytime. So don't hesitate to come in case your plans change."

Narmada smiled. "Yes, I will. Enjoy your weekend."

As soon as she ended the call, she continued to get ready.

The reason she was planning the surprise visit was because she missed her grandfather and wanted to see him. She also badly needed time away from home to sort things out.

She had barely slept the previous night. Apart from the worry of losing her company, another reason had kept her up all night. The reason was quite shocking even to her.

She couldn't sleep because she was mourning the negative pregnancy test result.

When Yash Varma had mentioned the possibility of her falling pregnant because of their night, her first reaction had been shock and panic. She didn't want to be pregnant with his child because she hated him and didn't want to be tied to him in any way.

But when her pregnancy test came out negative, all she felt was losing the chance of having a baby. The fact that the child would have been Yash Varma's hadn't made a difference. She would have loved her child with all of her heart regardless of who the child's father was.

She and Vaibhav had always wanted a child to cherish and nurture. Being the only child, she had wanted two children as a way to compensate for never having grown with a big family.

Even after she had found out the truth about Vaibhav, they still made plans to have a child. They had consulted multiple doctors because Vaibhav was more concerned about passing on his genes of what he termed as a 'mental disorder'. But the doctors had assured there wouldn't be any complications, and Narmada could easily conceive when it was time.

But the time had never come, and Vaibhav met with an accident. And with Vaibhav's sudden death, she had known her dream would never be fulfilled.

But despite her brutal reality, the craving to have a child to call her own hadn't entirely disappeared.

No. Don't think about the pregnancy test results or Yash Varma.

She definitely shouldn't be thinking about the man she hated. If she were to have a peaceful weekend, all thoughts of her enemy needed to be removed from her mind.

Letting out a deep sigh, she straightened the simple white cotton dress she was wearing. The weather in the village would be slightly warmer and more humid, and cotton dresses were the most comfortable.

She didn't wear many accessories. She put on her regular ear studs and wore a gold chain with a pendant that Vaibhav had gifted her on their first wedding anniversary.

She smiled, looking at the pendant which had both their initials together with an eternity symbol. She missed her best friend.

She and Vaibhav had been inseparable until his untimely death. Although she had gone through a lot dealing with his issues, she cherished their happy memories together.

She wondered what Vaibhav would have said seeing her life thrown into chaos.

Would he forgive her for losing their company because she spent a passionate night with a stranger? Or would he understand that she had it out of loneliness and for wanting to feel alive?

She knew he would understand her. When it came to her, he had always been very understanding.

If only I could have understood him better and saved him.

Pushing away those thoughts, she focused on the present. There was nothing she could do to change the past.

Grabbing her car keys and overnight bag, she went to her car.

Just when she had driven for five minutes, she received a call. It was her sister-in-law.

The moment Narmada answered the call, the younger woman's panicked voice came out from the car's speakers.

"Narmada! Where are you?" Divya asked.

"I'm driving to the village to visit my grandfather."

"No! You can't go, Narmada. I need you here. Please help me!"

Narmada frowned. "Calm down, Divya. Tell me what happened."

Divya was sobbing. "My father just told me that the man he is forcing me to marry is coming with his family to meet me."

Narmada frowned. "When are they coming?" she asked.

"Later this morning!"

Narmada cursed her father-in-law. He had already bullied his late son on nearly all aspects of his son's life. And now, he was bullying his daughter into an unwanted marriage.

"Don't worry, Divya. I'm coming."

There was sobbing. "Please hurry."

"I promise I'll be there in forty minutes."

Ending the call, Narmada let out a deep exhale. And then, she took a U-turn and went towards her in-laws' home.

It had been nearly three years since she had been there.

After Vaibhav's death, Rajesh Mohan had made it very clear that she was not invited to his home. Although she was reasonably close and friendly to her mother-in-law and sister-in-law, she still chose not to go there. She met the other two women outside or invited them both to her home.

Why does this have to happen now?

She was already in a messed-up state of mind herself. But now, she had to deal with stopping her sister-in-law from being forced to marry a man she didn't love.

But no matter what the state of mind, she was determined that Vaibhav's sister did not suffer the same anxieties that led to her brother's death.

***

The traffic wasn't heavy since it was the weekend. Narmada was able to reach her in-laws' home in thirty minutes.

Hoping she wasn't late and the prospective bridegroom and his family hadn't arrived yet, she hurried inside. The maids and help recognized her, and they looked shocked. But they didn't stop her. Forcing out a smile, she hurried up the stairs to her sister-in-law's room.

She knocked on the door. But there was no response.

She knocked again. "Divya? It's me, Narmada. Please open the door."

Suddenly, her heart began to thud. When she didn't hear any sounds coming from inside, memories flashed in her mind. She recalled the time when she had found Vaibhav passed out inside the guest bedroom after taking sleeping pills overdose.

"Divya!" She began to bang on the door loudly. She didn't care if her in-laws heard the racket. She wanted their help in case their daughter was inside fighting between life and death.

A few nerve-racking moments later, there were sounds from inside the room, and the door was opened.

Narmada heaved a sigh of relief when she saw the tear-stained face of her sister-in-law.

Narmada more or less barged into the room and began checking for empty pill bottles or something that should cause alarm. When she didn't find anything, she faced her sister-in-law.

"Are you okay?" she asked.

The younger girl let out a choked cry. "No. I'm not okay, but I haven't done anything yet."

The word 'yet' sat heavily between them.

Narmada went to her and placed a comforting hand on her. "I know things are hard right now, but trying to harm yourself is not a solution. I promise to sort this out—"

Narmada was interrupted by an angry man's voice.

"How dare you come here!" Rajesh Mohan shouted. "Get out of my house!"

Narmada turned to see two people inside the doorway. Rajesh Mohan and his wife. His wife was silent and looked helpless while her husband was yelling.

Narmada stood her ground. "I came here to support Divya. She called me this morning."

But Rajesh Mohan was having none of it. "I don't care if she called. And I also don't care if she doesn't want to marry the man I picked for her. She needs to do what she is ordered to do and what is good for the family."

Narmada felt frustrated by her father-in-law's greed and selfishness which would come at the cost of his daughter's life.

"What are you waiting here for!" he yelled. "Get out, or I'll have you thrown out by the servants."

Before Narmada could reason, another voice cut into the heated yelling.

It was her father-in-law's driver. "Sir... a car has arrived."

Immediately, there was a change in Rajesh Mohan's face. "It must be the groom and his family."

He looked at his daughter and barked out instructions. "Get ready in five minutes. Don't oppose me, or I will keep you shut in the house until you do as I say!"

He then glared at Narmada. "There isn't time to throw you out. You better act as though everything is normal. If you cause any trouble, there will be hell to pay."

Narmada didn't care for her father-in-law's threats. Right from the day he had found out about his son wanting to marry her, he had been issuing threats. She hadn't cared about the threats at that time, and neither did she care about them right then.

She turned to Divya, who looked as though she were about to shatter. "Let's get ready," she said gently.

As soon as Rajesh Mohan strode away angrily to receive the guests, his wife shut the door. "Please don't oppose your father," the older woman told her daughter.

Divya looked upset. "I don't want this marriage, Mamma."

The older woman didn't look shocked, but she had a look of resignation. "There is nothing you or I can do, Divya. Just get ready and come down."

Narmada was frustrated by her mother-in-law not standing up to her daughter. But she wasn't surprised by the older woman's passiveness. Rajesh Mohan controlled and bullied his entire family including his wife and two children. Vaibhav could never stand up to his father either, which pushed him further into depression.

"I'll help her get ready, Ma," Narmada told her mother-in-law.

The older woman nodded and left.

"How can you say that, Narmada?" Divya cried out. "You know I love Rahul."

Narmada placed a comforting hand on her sister-in-law's shoulder. "I'll make sure you won't be forced into an unwanted marriage, Divya. But you need to approach this carefully. Just come down and meet the prospective groom. You can speak to him and tell him you don't want to marry him."

There was a hint of doubt and fear. "But Papa will—"

"Don't say anything in front of your father. You can speak to that man in private."

Divya looked hopeful. "Okay."

Narmada badly wished the prospective groom and his family would understand.

She helped her sister-in-law get ready. Since the younger girl enjoyed dressing up, it was an easy task. Divya wore a rich, embroidered dress with matching jewellery and applied makeup to remove the traces of tears.

"You look good," Narmada said with a smile. "Now just appear confident."

The younger girl nodded.

The two of them went downstairs. Narmada could hear her father-in-law's voice while he spoke. She couldn't hear a lot of people. She hoped the prospective groom didn't come with a big group of family members because it might be embarrassing for him to explain after Divya spoke with him.

"Two months is not too short a time, Mr. Varma. We will definitely make the necessary arrangements."

Narmada froze hearing the name from her father-in-law.

Her heart began to thud sickly as she neared the living room where her father-in-law was seated with the prospective groom.

"I'll ask Mr. Raman to get in touch with you regarding the arrangements," a deep voice replied.

Oh my God.

Narmada recognized that voice clearly. That voice had been haunting her dreams for over a month, and lately, it was featured in her nightmares.

"There she is! Divya, come here." Rajesh Mohan had an eager smile on his face. "Mr. Varma, this is my daughter Divya."

When Yash Varma turned to look, his eyes met with Narmada's shocked face.

"You are the last man I would want in my life, let alone as my child's father. I wish I never met you, and I would be happy if I never see you again."

The words Narmada had shouted at him the previous evening sat heavily in between them.

Her heart began to thud seeing him again so soon and under such shocking circumstances.

Yash Varma didn't seem surprised to see her. His eyes swept over her. She was standing next to Divya, who was wearing an expensive dress with diamond jewellery and matching earrings. In contrast, she was still in the simple white dress she had worn earlier that morning, expecting to visit her grandfather.

His eyes lingered on the sapphire pendant that matched her wedding ring.

A shiver passed through her as his eyes flashed, looking at the pendant. He looked as though he wanted to yank it from her neck and throw it away.

Oh God.

I must be imagining things.

Not even in her wildest dreams did she imagine Yash Varma to be the prospective groom for her sister-in-law.

What is happening?

"Divya, this is Mr. Yash Varma. He has asked for your hand in marriage, and I have agreed. We have set your wedding date in two months.

Listening to Rajesh Mohan's mandate to his daughter, Narmada forcibly tore her eyes away from Yash Varma's intense gaze and looked at her father-in-law.

"Papa... Divya would first like to speak privately with Mr. Varma," she said.

Rajesh Mohan threw her an angry glare. "There's no need," he gritted.

Narmada could feel Divya trembling next to her. Extending her hand, Narmada gently squeezed Divya's hand asking her to speak up.

Luckily, Divya finally spoke up. "N-narmada is right, Papa. I-I do want to talk to... Mr. Varma."

Narmada looked at Yash Varma, who was still watching her with an unreadable gaze.

"I'm sure Mr. Varma would want to speak with his prospective bride alone as well," Narmada said with a hint of challenge in her tone.

Yash Varma didn't say anything in response. Their eyes remain locked in a silent war.

An angry voice cut into their locked gazes.

"Divya!" Rajesh Mohan barked out. "Take Mr. Yash Varma outside and talk to him in the garden."

Narmada dragged her eyes away. "I'll join them," she said.

"No! You will stay right here. Divya will talk her future husband alone."

Narmada's heart thudded sickly, hearing Yash Varma referred to as her sister-in-law's future husband.

Divya clutched Narmada's hand in a death-like tight grip. Giving her sister-in-law another reassuring squeeze, Narmada forced out a smile. "Go, Divya. Talk to Mr. Varma alone."

The younger woman nodded nervously and went towards the patio that led to the outside garden. Yash Varma got up from the couch in a smooth move and followed behind his prospective bride.

Meanwhile, Narmada couldn't do anything except watch them going out.

An angry voice snapped at her. "You will not sabotage my daughter's marriage!" Rajesh Mohan thundered.

Narmada turned to see her father-in-law's furious face. Although he looked as though he was personally about to shove her out of his house, she stood up to him.

"Please don't do this," she said. "Yash Varma is a ruthless man. I'm not saying this because he took away my company shares. I'm saying this because I know he is not the kind to care for your daughter's happiness."

"Keep quiet!" Rajesh Mohan snapped. "No one has asked for your opinion. Unlike you, he is not after my money. He is rich and powerful and is worth a hundred times over than I am."

Narmada latched on to that point. "That alone should worry us, Papa," she insisted. "He is a billionaire. Why would he suddenly want to marry a woman he has never met?"

There was a mean look on Rajesh Mohan's face. "He wants to marry my daughter because, unlike you, my daughter is not the lower-class help's child. She comes from a decent family and has a proper upbringing. Most rich and powerful men want simple girls from good families. Not gold-digging whores like you, who want to marry upper-class men to increase their status in life."

Narmada ignored the insults thrown at her and stood her ground. She wasn't ashamed of her background. If anything, she was proud of her grandfather and her humble roots.

Pushing aside the insults, she continued to try to convince her father-in-law. "Yash Varma is a dangerous man who is after something. This isn't a case of a rich man wanting to marry a simple girl from a good family."

"I don't care!" Rajesh Mohan snapped. "As long as I have access to his money and power, I am willing to give away my daughter. Now get out of my house before they return. Don't think that I haven't noticed your whorish stares trying to lure him towards you. I also know about your daily closed-door meetings with him in his office. But luckily, men like Yash Varma know how to differentiate between low-class whores like you and decent women whom they can marry and take to their mothers."

Strangely, the last part of the insult hurt her. But she pushed away the feeling.

I don't care what men like Yash Varma think about me.

She tried a different tactic. "Why didn't he come with his family?" she asked. "He has a mother and two brothers. Where are they?"

Rajesh Mohan dismissed her question. "They live in New York. They will come on the engagement day. Now stop bothering me with questions and get out of my house!"

Narmada wanted to leave the house as well. She wanted to go as far away from Yash Varma as possible. But she knew she couldn't. Not when her sister-in-law needed her and was in a fragile state of mind.

"I'll leave only when I speak with Divya," she said calmly.

"Get out now!" her father-in-law roared.

This time Narmada's mother-in-law intervened. "Rajesh, please. Let her stay. Divya wants Narmada here. If Narmada leaves, Divya will have a panic attack."

Narmada knew her sister-in-law had panic attacks similar to what Vaibhav used to have through his childhood and also through adulthood until his death. Her father-in-law had witnessed quite a few as well.

There was a disgusted look on Rajesh Mohan's face. "Damn you!" he cursed his wife. "You gave me such weak, defective children. Let's hope that useless daughter of yours won't have an attack before the wedding. Or Yash Varma will break the alliance right away. I have already made too many promises and investments claiming he would be our son-in-law."

Narmada wasn't shocked by her father-in-law's lack of sensitivity. She had witnessed it several times when he directed it towards both his children and his wife. She wasn't also surprised that he was using Yash Varma's name to make several business investments. She only hoped they weren't too risky or with shady, dangerous people.

Rajesh Mohan glared at her. "You can stay," he gritted out to her. "But keep your mouth shut."

Narmada nodded while she kept her gaze turned towards the garden patio. She couldn't see Divya or Yash Varma.

Was he threatening Divya as well?

Why is he doing this?

Finally, after what seemed like a long time, even though the huge clock on the wall said it was only fifteen minutes, they returned.

Divya looked pale and nervous, but she didn't appear to be close to a breakdown. She came and stood next to Narmada. Yash Varma had an unreadable look as always. His eyes fell on Narmada, and something dangerous flashed in them.

Did Divya tell Yash Varma about not wanting to marry him?

Did he think I am behind Divya's decision?

Will he withdraw the proposal?

Narmada's mind spun with questions she had no answers to at that point.

"Your daughter is very charming, Mr. Mohan," Yash Varma drawled. "She has a very good sense of humor."

"Oh yes. Divya gets that from me. My daughter is very talented too."

Narmada cringed on behalf of her father-in-law, who clearly wasn't getting darkly sarcastic vibes from Yash Varma.

Divya must have raised the topic of not wanting to marry. And Yash Varma was deliberately dismissing it as a joke.

"Mr. Varma, my wife and I were discussing the wedding just now," Rajesh Mohan said eagerly. "We are very excited to have you as our son-in-law in two months."

Narmada heard Divya's shocked gasp before she ran away from the living room.

"My daughter is feeling shy, Mr. Varma," Rajesh Mohan said with a forced smile that barely hid his anger and disgust towards his daughter. "She feels honored that someone like you has asked to marry her."

There was a dry smile on Yash Varma's face. "I see."

Narmada threw an angry glare at him. *You are a heartless monster!*

How could he not care, seeing that Divya was obviously upset?

Narmada clenched her teeth. "Excuse me. I'll go speak with Divya," she said.

As she went up to Divya's room, she made a vow to herself.

There is no way I will allow Divya to get married to that heartless monster.

***

It was late evening by the time Narmada returned home.

She had spent all day with her sister-in-law who had been alternately afraid, nervous and also shockingly in awe of Yash Varma.

"He is so handsome, Narmada. Most women must want him. And according to Papa, he is very rich too. Why does he want to marry me? Doesn't he have a girlfriend already?"

Narmada was irritated listening to the praise directed to the man she loathed with a passion.

But her sister-in-law was right. Yash Varma was rich and handsome. He also had a dark magnetic aura that drew many women's eyes towards him. Even she had been drawn to him instantly as well when she saw him in Milan.

Then why does he want to marry someone he never met?

In the fifteen minutes that Yash Varma and Divya were alone, Divya had apparently told him about not wanting to marry so soon because she wanted to pursue a career first.

"He asked me what my future plans were, and I told him. H-he didn't seem to care much about my answers even though he was the one to ask me questions. I didn't speak about Rahul because I don't want Papa to know yet."

Narmada knew Yash Varma wouldn't care about her sister-in-law's willingness to marry him. He had already made up his mind to marry her. And Narmada's gut instinct told her that a man like Yash Varma wouldn't do anything without an agenda. He wanted something from the Mohan family.

But what? And why?

She knew she would have to find out the answers soon before her sister-in-law was forced to marry him. And based on what she had heard so far, the marriage was going to take place within two months, which didn't leave her with much time.

She badly wanted to discuss the possibilities with someone. Supriya had invited her over to her place that weekend. But Narmada didn't want to disturb her friend. She knew her friend had a special weekend planned with her husband.

So, she called her instead in a brief phone call and told her what had happened.

Supriya was shocked. "Oh my God! Why would he want to marry Divya all of a sudden?"

Narmada let out a sigh at her friend's question. "I don't know. The worst part is my father-in-law thinks it's entirely normal."

Supriya let out a scoff. "Apart from greed and bullying, Rajesh Mohan isn't exactly known for being caring and considerate."

Narmada knew her friend was right.

"Doesn't Divya have twenty-five percent stake in Genesis shares?" Supriya asked.

"Yes, but Yash Varma already has a majority in shares. He doesn't need the additional twenty-five percent."

"Maybe he is greedy or wants to start establishing a base here by marrying your sister-in-law."

Narmada highly doubted it was a simple case of greed. Something was off. He was after something bigger, and it had a lot to do with Rajesh Mohan.

"How are you going to stop him, Narmada?" Supriya asked.

"I don't know. All I know is I have to stop him somehow."

The man might be powerful, but he wasn't invincible. She would somehow stop him.

"All right, Supriya. I'll speak to you later. Sorry to be disturbing you on your special weekend."

"Don't be silly. Of course, you didn't disturb me."

Narmada felt grateful for her friend's understanding.

After the call ended, Narmada couldn't stop thinking about that day's shocking turn of events. She spent the rest of the day desperately searching for information on Yash Varma.

She looked him up on the internet obsessively. She left a message to the investigator asking for more updates. She also left instructions to have someone follow Yash Varma and report back to her on who he was meeting.

It was close to midnight when a dull headache began to form around her forehead. The stress, lack of sleep and having to face both her father-in-law and her enemy at the same time were finally getting to her.

As soon as she lay down on her bed and closed her eyes, Yash Varma's ruthless face flashed in her mind. Even as her body trembled in anger and fear and also something she didn't want to acknowledge to herself, she made a vow.

I hate you. I will do anything to stop this marriage.

CHAPTER TEN

"Congratulations, bro. Heard you got yourself engaged."

It was well after midnight, and Yash was seated by the pool on the penthouse balcony. He had been drinking alone for the last two hours while looking at the city lights before his two brothers joined him.

Just before they had arrived, he had to briefly shut down the security cameras in the building to stop anyone from tracing his brothers' visit.

"So when is the happy day?" Aryan continued to tease.

Yash didn't react to his youngest brother's teasing. "I gave two months' time," he replied.

"Did Rajesh Mohan suspect anything?" Bhargav asked.

"No."

The older man's greed was stronger than his logical brain. And just like Yash had predicted, Rajesh Mohan had already begun bragging in his social circles about landing a rich son-in-law. He also made promises and signed agreements in a few risky business deals using Fortune Group's name as security. The man was pathetically stupid.

Unlike his daughter-in-law.

Yash took another sip of his whiskey at the thought of Narmada Mohan. He knew that his beautiful pawn could sense right away that there was more to the marriage proposal. She had glared at him in an angry challenge, making it obvious she was going to cause trouble.

Yash knew that the anger and hate in Narmada Mohan's beautiful eyes shouldn't be impacting him. But it did. The strong pull he felt towards her each time she was nearby only got stronger. And even when she wasn't nearby, the way she still invaded his mind most of the time made him furious.

He absolutely hated it.

The obsession with her was reaching dangerous levels, making him think and even act irrationally.

One of the most irrational behaviors was on the previous day when the report of Narmada's pregnancy came back negative. He had felt strangely disappointed. Even though he knew it would ruin all the plans, a part of him had wanted fate to bind Narmada Mohan to him in the most primitive way.

Fuck!

"How did Rajesh Mohan's daughter react to the news?" Bhargav asked.

Yash shrugged. "She tried to hint she wasn't ready to marry. But she didn't mention anything about her boyfriend."

Yash had barely acknowledged or noticed the woman he was going to marry. All his attention had been on Narmada, who had been watching him with a hate-filled look.

Aryan frowned. "According to the investigation, Divya Mohan hasn't met her boyfriend recently, but she is speaking to him quite often. She is also friends with that bastard Girish Shetty's daughter."

Yash didn't care that Rajesh Mohan's daughter often spoke to her boyfriend. During their brief walk in the gardens, he discovered she had no strength or determination to stand up for herself. Whatever her father would dictate, she would eventually be forced to do it, even if she absolutely hated it.

Unlike Narmada Mohan.

Yash knew his beautiful pawn would fight tooth and nail to win back her company.

"What about Rajesh Mohan's daughter-in-law?" Aryan asked.

Yash knew both his brothers could sense the dangerous obsession Yash was developing towards one of their pawns.

"What about her?" he asked.

"Would she threaten to tell your future bride about what happened in Milan?"

Yash knew there was a high possibility. "Rajesh Mohan doesn't care about his daughter's or his daughter-in-law's opinions."

Aryan frowned. "Yes, but if Narmada Mohan gets a hint of who we are, she could risk our plans. We already know she has hired an investigator. The man is still trying to dig out information about us. He has reached out to someone in New York for additional help."

Yash wasn't shocked by Narmada's move of hiring another investigator. She wasn't the kind to give up easily just because her initial investigation didn't give her the information she wanted. The woman was not only just smart in business, she often fought hard to defeat her adversaries. And he wasn't just her adversary, but he was also her biggest enemy.

"I think you should be careful with her, bro," Aryan insisted.

"I'll take care of her," Yash replied. "Has our investigating team found anything from her grandfather?"

"Not yet. The old man isn't willing to reveal much. He doesn't seem the kind to get swayed by money."

Narmada's grandfather had worked as Rajesh Mohan's driver for over fifteen years before retiring three years ago. But the man didn't reveal anything about his employer.

Yash didn't think Rajesh Mohan was the type to inspire loyalty in anyone. There must be some other reason why the older man refused to talk about the past.

"Plant someone in the village and ask them to get closer to him," Yash instructed.

Aryan nodded.

Yash looked at his two brothers. "It's better if we are not seen meeting each other until my wedding."

Both his brothers nodded in agreement. They knew that they couldn't risk their plan if any of the investigators digging up information on them found out they were in the same city.

"What about Ma?" Aryan asked. "Her cruise is going to be done in three weeks."

Yash nodded. "I'll meet Ma when she returns."

Yash and his brothers often travelled for business. And since their mother chose to stay independently in a gated senior community where she had many friends, it was easier to manage their ruse of the three of them not being in New York for a long period of time.

"We should increase the security around Ma too," Bhargav suggested. "Just in case a nosy investigator manages to dig up her address or follow her to the school."

"Add two more people," Yash instructed. "Hire women so it's easier for them to blend in a school environment without anyone being suspicious."

Yash's mother was a school teacher. She had been teaching for nearly two decades and loved her job. Although all three of her sons were successful and billionaires, she still chose to continue the profession which she loved.

"Are you sure you don't want Ma attending your wedding? Not only will Ma be hurt, it will raise suspicion with Rajesh Mohan."

Yash knew his mother would be hurt. "Yes, I don't want Ma to attend the wedding. It will risk both your plans. Rajesh Mohan wouldn't care much as long as I marry his daughter."

And Yash wasn't keen on his mother meeting the woman he didn't intend to stay married to for long. As soon as he and his brothers achieved their goals, he intended to divorce Divya Mohan so she could marry her boyfriend.

The next few hours, Yash continued to discuss the rest of the plans with his brothers. Everything was going according to what they had planned and anticipated.

By the time Yash's brothers left, it was close to four in the morning.

"Let's not risk meeting again for a while," Yash reminded his brothers.

The three of them grew up close. And even when their lives got busy, they always met at least once a week no matter which part of the world they were in. But now, until the final execution of their plan, they would have to stay away from each other.

Aryan shook his head with annoyance. "I can't believe Narmada Mohan has hired someone to have you followed. That woman is dangerous, bro. You should be careful."

Yash didn't react to his brother's warning. "I'll handle her."

Bhargav didn't seem surprised that Yash was going to be followed on Narmada's instructions. "I'll keep you updated on the sale. I'm expecting a call from the agent tomorrow."

Although Yash wasn't entirely satisfied by the speed of the progress, he nodded. "That's good."

Bidding goodnight to his brothers, Yash closed the penthouse door and went back to the bar area.

He knew he would have a hell of a hangover with the number of drinks he already had. But he continued to drink while his beautiful pawn invaded his thoughts.

His thoughts weren't centered on what she was doing to ruin his plans. His thoughts went back to the night they spent together in Milan.

"Can I ask you something?" a soft feminine voice asked breathlessly while desperately trying to breathe in some air.

Narmada Mohan was lying naked next to him on the bed in the hotel suite. They had been having nonstop sex for the last three hours. She was breathing hard and fast after their recent bout of sex. He was nowhere done with her and didn't intend to stop taking her body until the morning. But he decided to pause briefly to give her body some rest since she had more or less lost consciousness when she climaxed in his arms a few minutes ago.

But the woman didn't seem to want any rest.

She watched him with her big eyes. Her eyes appeared fascinated by the scars on his torso. There were a few healed knife wounds from his childhood during the time he and Bhargav worked in bad neighborhoods.

Narmada Mohan traced the scars on his chest with her fingers. Her touch was gentle as though she was worried she might hurt him even though the scars were long healed. Her fingers paused, and she looked up at him.

Once again, he was struck by how beautiful and bewitching she was. Something about her drew him to her so strongly that the need he felt for her seemed unstoppable.

"Do you belong to the Mafia?" she asked.

His mouth automatically quirked in amusement at her question. "No."

She smiled. "You know you could pass off as Italian Mafia," she said, tracing his lips with her fingers.

Her smile and touch caused havoc inside him and made his body stir in need. Controlling himself from pulling her under him again, he focused on her words.

He knew she was right. Despite dressing in expensive suits and wearing expensive watches and shoes, he had a rough, muscled body that came from having worked in construction since a young age.

Narmada Mohan didn't ask him what he did for a living because she would have to tell him what she did and who she was in return. He knew she wanted to maintain their anonymity that night.

He watched as she continued to touch his scars. She leaned over and kissed the scar on his cheek.

That simple touch broke his control. The dark passion to possess her once again consumed him.

A shocked gasp escaped her when he flipped her until she was lying beneath him on the bed. Watching her face, he pushed her legs apart. Then gripping her hips to hold her still, he sank deeply into the tight and wet heat of her body. He gritted his teeth at the pleasure he felt while her body adjusted and tightened around him.

Her beautiful eyes glazed with passion, and she clung to him while he tried to purge his dark need for her.

Yash knew he had failed that night.

He wasn't able to purge away his dark need for her. If anything, his hunger had grown fiercer since then. And as a man who thrived on absolute control, he hated his beautiful enemy for the effect she had on him.

She is just a pawn. In two more months, she would have no choice but to watch him marry another woman.

CHAPTER ELEVEN

"Good morning, Mrs. Mohan."

Narmada forced out a smile at Yash Varma's executive assistant as the man exited his boss's office.

"Good morning, Mr. Raman," she greeted the middle-aged man.

Narmada still wondered why unlike most businessmen, Yash Varma had an older executive assistant. During her investigation, she had also found out that Mr. Raman had been working for his boss for close to fifteen years, even before Yash Varma had made it big.

According to the investigative report, Yash Varma had only been fifteen when he began to work in construction with his younger brother. It was his utter ruthlessness and cold calculation and high risks that made him into the man he was now.

But the fact that he still kept the same personal assistant over the years also meant that he chose loyalty over anything.

What else did the man value?

A small shiver racked Narmada's insides at the thought of trying to win over a man like him.

No. I will win over him. I won't let him intimidate or defeat me.

Pushing away her nervousness, she continued to smile at the older man.

"Is Mr. Varma free, Mr. Raman?" she asked.

The man nodded. "Yes, Mrs. Mohan. You can go in."

"Thank you," she said. "And please call me Narmada. We are quite informal here at Genesis."

There was a small smile on the older man's face. "Sure, Narmada."

Continuing to paste a pleasant smile, Narmada went to the chairman's office.

Unlike the previous two times, she made an effort not to barge angrily into the office. Although Yash Varma seemed incapable of feeling anything, she had to be careful not to piss him off.

He wasn't always unfeeling.

Another shiver racked through Narmada's body as she recalled the night in Milan when she had experienced his raw passion and intensity.

He had gotten what he wanted from her willing body that night. But would he want something more?

Oh God. I hope so.

Sucking in a deep breath, she stopped at the door and knocked.

"Come in," the familiar deep voice commanded.

With butterflies exploding in her stomach, Narmada pushed the door open and walked into the large office room.

Yash Varma was typing on his laptop. He threw a cursory glance towards the door, but when he saw who was standing inside his office, he paused the typing momentarily, and his eyes flared.

Tense silence filled the air.

Narmada knew he was probably waiting for her to lash out at him like the last two times when she had barged into his office.

Even though she hated him still and wanted to curse him out loud, she kept her anger and hatred carefully hidden.

"I would like to speak to you... Yash," she said in a polite tone.

She cringed inside at having to use his first name.

Yash Varma didn't say anything. He simply sat back on his thick leather chair while watching her with an unreadable look.

Feeling encouraged, Narmada went closer and stood behind the chair opposite him. She felt slightly more in control, standing and looking down at him rather than sitting down.

With that false sense of courage, she took another deep breath before speaking out her rehearsed speech.

"I know you want to marry my sister-in-law for her twenty-five percent shares, but she doesn't want to marry you. She must have told that to you already."

There was no reaction from him.

Feeling nervous at his lack of reaction or response, she hurried through the rest of her explanation. "Divya is willing to sell her shares to me," she continued. "And... and... I'm willing to sell the shares to you. But..."

Even though she left the sentence hanging, there was not even a spark of interest in his eyes.

Oh God.

The fluttering in her stomach intensified so much that she felt nauseous with nervousness.

But she forged on. "I will sell those shares to you and give you whatever you want... provided... provided... you... you... marry me instead."

This time there was a reaction.

For a split second, there was a flash of surprise in his eyes before going back to a neutral unreadable look.

Why is he not saying anything?

"I-if you marry me," she continued. "I will also help you run Genesis and support any other acquisitions. I would be a good asset for you in business. I-I will make a better wife to you than Divya."

Silence weighed heavily once again.

Slowly, he leaned forward and rested his elbows on top of the table with his fingers interlinked while he watched her. Even though Narmada was standing and he was seated, he looked like a predator playing with his prey. His mouth twisted with a dark smile before he finally spoke.

"Being able to take care of my businesses is not what I'm looking for in a wife, Mrs. Mohan. I hire people for that."

Narmada's cheeks were on fire at his taunt.

But she pushed away the embarrassment. "If... if... it's my father-in-law's business network and contacts... then you can gain those through me as well."

His eyebrow rose. "That's not what I want from a wife either." His eyes swept over her body before landing on her flushed face.

Oh God.

"I... I would make a better match for you than Divya in other aspects too... the night in Milan has already proven we have good physical chemistry between us."

Her cheeks burned even more as she reminded him of their night. No man could fake his arousal those many times. He had been attracted to her that night. He had been demanding and relentless until she shattered in his arms over and over again. Her heart thudded, and her entire body flushed in heat as images from the night flashed into her mind recalling how many times they had passionate sex until dawn.

Yash Varma's eyes flashed darkly as he read her thoughts on her face.

"What else?" he asked in a dangerously rough voice. "I'm sure you thought this through and have a list of advantages of why I should be marrying you rather than Rajesh Mohan's daughter."

Narmada hadn't thought through that much. The thought had occurred to her after two days of non-stop thinking of how to stop her enemy from marrying Divya.

Even though the thought of marrying the man she hated with a passion horrified her, it was the only solution she could come up with.

She took another deep breath. "Unlike other wives, I wouldn't expect much from you," she said. "You can do whatever you want. And I... I will do whatever you want."

His eyes continued to flash dangerously, and his mouth twisted into a small dark smile.

"Whatever I want?" he asked in a tone that sent a shiver up her spine. "Be careful what you promise, *Mrs.* Mohan."

She somehow knew he was using her married name deliberately. Was he trying to convey that she was not a great marriage prospect because she had been married once?

Pushing away those doubts, she put in her case desperately.

"I-I have thought this through," she lied. "I-I will sign whatever pre-nuptial agreement you want with the terms put in."

He didn't say anything. But keeping his gaze locked on her, he got up from his chair.

Her heartbeat thundered loudly in her ears as he walked around the desk until he was standing right behind her. He was so close that she could feel the heat of his body. The subtle expensive cologne he used filled all of her senses.

She wanted to turn, but she controlled the instinct. She didn't want to meet his dark, intense eyes that would strip out the truth from her.

Her breath froze as his deep voice rumbled into her ear. "So despite your hatred, you are willing to let me fuck you again?"

A dark shiver racked her body at his deliberately crude words. She knew he was trying to push her limits to get an angry reaction out of her. But she controlled herself.

"I will demand fidelity from my wife," he continued. "I will also want children. So if you become my wife, you will have to stay faithful to me and bear my children. You will be tied to the man you hate until death pulls us apart."

The thought of being tied to him for eternity was beyond frightening. He would destroy her soul.

Narmada's legs shook under her, and she could barely manage to stand upright.

"I... I don't hate you," she whispered out the lie.

She hated him beyond anything. His deception destroyed her life and took away her self-respect. She didn't think she could ever forgive him for that.

Thick and heavy silence once again followed her statement.

Her breathing came out heavily as she waited for him to respond. She gasped out suddenly when he held her upper arms and whipped her around until she faced him. The firm press of his fingers on her arms heated her body.

He searched her eyes, stripping her to her soul. Whatever he saw in them made his eyes harden and flash darkly. Suddenly, he dropped his hands from her and stepped away. He walked back to his chair and sat in it, his face once again became unreadable.

Narmada felt jittery. "S-so do you agree?" she asked. "I will sign a pre-nuptial document agreeing to all of your terms. Fidelity, children and any other things you want. I will also give you the twenty-five percent shares on our wedding day."

His eyes hooded as she stated her proposal.

"Do you recall our last meeting in this office, Mrs. Mohan?" he asked. "It was just two days ago."

Narmada did remember. But he repeated her words back to her.

"You told me I was the last man you wanted in your life, let alone as your child's father. You also said you wished you had never met me and would be very happy if you didn't see me again."

His mouth twisted into a dark, mocking smile. "That's quite a change of heart in two days' time."

Narmada's face burned in embarrassment as he reminded her of the words she flung at him after the pregnancy test report.

"I-I was emotional at that time and didn't know what I was saying right then," she said. "But over the weekend, I realized that—"

"Stop," he said curtly, cutting her off.

"Save your lies for some other day, Narmada. And even if you weren't lying, it wouldn't make any difference. I have already made up my mind to marry Rajesh Mohan's daughter."

Narmada's cheeks heated in humiliation at his blunt rejection.

She felt a burning need to get away. Dragging her eyes away from his, she hurried out of his office.

She went back to hers. As soon as she stepped inside her office, she shut the door and leaned against it.

Oh God. He rejected me.

Of course, he would reject her. She didn't have anything much to offer that he could easily get from all the women he had slept with.

"Men like Yash Varma know how to differentiate between low-class whores like you and decent women whom they can marry and take to their mothers."

Maybe her father-in-law was right. Maybe Yash Varma did give importance to class status. Maybe he wouldn't want to marry a woman who was a driver's granddaughter.

She didn't know why, but that thought hurt her.

She still hated Yash Varma with a passion, but she never thought he was the kind to give importance to social standing or class status.

Her shoulders hunched in defeat.

But immediately, she straightened them. Anger began to grow inside her.

No, I won't give up! I can't. There is too much at stake.

There was no way she would allow Yash Varma to get away with stealing her company and marry her sister-in-law.

I will find a way.

CHAPTER TWELVE

Yash hated surprises.

He wanted all of his pawns to be completely predictable, which gave him absolute control to move them around according to his needs.

But Narmada Mohan surprised him by not being predictable. Her marriage offer had shocked him.

"Marry me instead."

"I will sign a pre-nuptial document agreeing to all of your terms. Fidelity, children and any other things you want. I will also give you the twenty-five percent shares on our wedding day."

Yash had known right away why she had asked him to marry her.

Although she hated him still, her savior complex was much stronger. She foolishly thought of saving her dead husband's sister from his clutches at the cost of own feelings.

"I don't hate you."

Even though he knew it was a lie, he had searched her eyes to see if there was a speck of truth in her words. And what he saw was her anger, fear and hatred towards him along with her desperation to save the world from him.

It made him furious.

He had barely stopped himself letting go of his control and doing what he had wanted to since the moment he saw her again. He wanted to kiss her and push her over the office desk and make her desire the man she hated.

But he had stopped himself and rejected her offer.

He wouldn't allow his obsession with her to interfere with his goal.

Even though he craved her like a drug, he knew touching her would be a big mistake. He couldn't risk the plan he and his brothers had set into motion. There was too much at stake, along with a burning desire to set a past wrong to right.

But he knew Narmada Mohan would not give up that easily. She would continue to scheme to stop him from marrying her sister-in-law.

Instead of getting angry at her interference, Yash's mouth twisted into a dark smile.

A primal anticipation grew inside him, waiting to see what his beautiful pawn would do next.

CHAPTER THIRTEEN

"What do you mean by you asked him to marry you! Are you insane!"

Narmada was at her home speaking with Supriya in the living room. She had spent many sleepless nights trying to think of how to stop Divya's marriage to Yash Varma, but she still couldn't think of a way.

She was nearly out of her mind and needed all the help she could. So, she decided to tell her friend about it.

But Supriya more or less shouted at her in shock.

Narmada took a deep breath. "I had no choice, Supriya. Marrying him would have meant saving Divya and also having some control over Genesis."

Supriya frowned. "Dammit, Narmada. I can understand why you want to get Genesis back. But that Mohan family has constantly been screwing you over. I don't understand why you feel responsible for all of their problems. Why do *you* have to save your sister-in-law from an unwanted marriage? I know you loved Vaibhav, but after what you went through because of him, I'm not sure if he deserves your loyalty. Even though he was my friend too, I can't forgive him for what he did to you."

Narmada knew her friend was upset and outraged that Vaibhav hid many secrets from her which she discovered only after their marriage.

But Narmada didn't hate her husband. He was her best friend, and she understood why he had to keep things hidden from her.

"I can't abandon them, Supriya. They are... my family too." Although she had only faced insults and aggression from her father-in-law, she felt protective towards her mother-in-law and Divya.

"Fine!" Supriya said in angry resignation.

Narmada knew her friend was still outraged on her behalf and wasn't convinced.

"As I said, it's not just about protecting Divya. I need to take back control of Genesis too. Yash Varma is not willing to sell the shares back to me. By marrying him, I can achieve both targets."

Her friend still didn't look convinced. "Yash Varma is a powerful *and* dangerous man, Narmada. He won't be that easy to manipulate."

A shiver passed through Narmada at the reminder. "Yes, I know that. But I have no other choice right now."

Supriya looked thoughtful. "You know, what I have always found very odd?" she asked.

"What?"

"That Yash Varma personally got involved in taking away your shares. He could have easily hired another man to sleep with you. Why would he risk spending a night with you? Knowing that he would be taking over your company and would be marrying your sister-in-law?"

Narmada's cheeks heated at the reminder of how stupid and gullible she had been to fall for his deception that night in Milan. But over the last few days, even she had wondered about his personal involvement in deceiving her.

"I think it is arrogance," Narmada replied. "He knew I couldn't do anything, even if I were to reveal he had slept with me."

Supriya didn't seem convinced. "Hmm... there is more to it than the arrogance of a powerful man. I feel Yash Varma is strongly drawn to you. I saw him watching you many times during meetings. That man still has a thing for you."

Narmada's cheeks heated. She had felt his intense gaze on her many times too. It was so strong that goosebumps often broke out on her skin.

"That doesn't mean he is willing to marry me," she murmured. "Why would he marry a driver's widowed granddaughter when he could marry an innocent virgin from an upper-class family?"

Supriya frowned. "He said that?"

"My father-in-law thinks that, and I believe even Yash Varma might think that way too."

"No way! Yash Varma might be a ruthless man, but he is in no way a snob. Haven't we read enough articles about him? He spent his childhood in bad neighborhoods in NewYork. He comes from a working-class background too."

Narmada knew that. Yash Varma led a humble life during his childhood until his late teens when he earned his first million. She had also read the article where it was mentioned that his mother worked as a nanny at a doctor's house before earning a teaching degree. His mother still worked as a teacher.

Narmada found his mother's story quite inspiring, and it touched her heart. The fact that Yash Varma gave that information during an interview meant that he wasn't ashamed of his roots or his humble background.

Narmada sighed.

"Fine, he isn't a snob. But he doesn't want to marry me. He made it very clear he wants to marry Divya."

She had recalled their conversation over and over again.

Why did he speak to me about fidelity and children? Why did he play with me until the last moment before rejecting my offer?

He had even held her arms and looked into her face at one point.

Did he see her fear and hatred?

Did that piss him off? Or hurt his ego?

She didn't think he was a man who made decisions based on his anger or a hurt ego. He always looked indifferent and coldly practical.

"I have an idea!" Supriya burst out.

"What?"

"Seduce him!" Supriya said in excitement.

Narmada was stunned. "What!"

"Even though it will be hard to break a ruthless man like Yash Varma... if anyone can do it, it is you, Narmada!"

Narmada was too stunned to process her friend's words right away.

But then slowly and steadily her mind began to spin with thoughts.

He seduced me first, and it cost me my company.

Narmada hated him for that. But she also desired him still. She still felt the buzzing awareness whenever he was around. And sometimes, she still had heated dreams about their night together.

What if he didn't feel as strongly as her?

Even if he felt a fraction of awareness and attraction of what she did, she could work on it and make him want her enough to marry her.

"What do you think?" Supriya asked in excitement.

Narmada took a deep breath. "Okay. I will try to seduce him."

CHAPTER FOURTEEN

"When I grow up, I'm going to marry you."

At Narmada's statement, the handsome boy's mouth quirked. "Is that so?"

"Yes," Narmada said with conviction. "Do you know why I want to marry you?"

The amused smile remained on the boy's handsome face. "No, Maddy. Tell me why."

"Your computer," she said. "I'm going to marry you for the computer in your library."

The boy laughed in amusement.

"So, do you agree to marry me?" she demanded.

The boy grinned. "I guess I have to since you ordered me to marry you."

Narmada was reminded of her first marriage proposal. Even though she was no longer a child, she hoped she would succeed in getting her enemy to accept her marriage proposal.

With a small shudder, Narmada shut down her laptop.

Her heart thudded loudly as she stared at the time on the clock. It was seven twenty, which meant she only had ten more minutes until her next meeting.

Oh God.

Even though she decided to seduce the man she hated, she could barely get herself to act on it. But she knew she couldn't delay it any longer. The phone call she received earlier that day made her decide she couldn't afford to wait any longer.

"Mamma took me shopping today, Narmada. She wants me to buy a dress for the engagement party next month."

Narmada shut her eyes, feeling guilty while listening to her sister-in-law.

"Don't worry, Divya. I have found a way to stop the marriage. Just... just go along with whatever your parents are asking you to do."

Less than two months remained until Divya would be forced to marry Yash Varma, and he would gain complete control of Genesis.

I can't let that happen.

Her hands trembled slightly as she stood up and picked up her laptop from the desk. It wasn't really needed for what she had planned, but she wanted something solid to hold on to when she faced her enemy.

It was dark outside the office window. She glanced at her reflection and smoothed her navy blue business suit. It was far from seductive, but she still drew courage from her power suit.

Taking a deep breath, she went to the chairman's office.

"No thank you. I have made up my mind to marry Rajesh Mohan's daughter."

Words from their last confrontation resonated in her mind. She was still humiliated by his rejection.

What if he rejects me again?

He may even fire me.

Her steps faltered at the last thought. She had always been friendly yet professional at work and encouraged her employees to maintain similar decorum. Even when Vaibhav had been alive, she had behaved professionally with her husband inside the office.

But now, she was going to seduce the chairman of her company inside his office.

Oh God.

She tried not to think of the professionalism or ethical aspect of it. Winning back her company and stopping an unwanted marriage was more important.

The corridors were empty right then. Most employees would have left an hour ago, and the top floor was usually for just the chairman's office and executive meeting rooms. There would be enough privacy.

As expected, Yash Varma's personal assistant had left for the day. But she knew Yash Varma would be in the office. She had seen his car parked in the designated spot when she left home around seven during the evening.

I hope there is no one else with him.

Her heart thudded loudly as she neared the chairman's office.

Deciding to use an element of surprise to keep him off balance, she pushed the door open without knocking.

For a split second, she was disappointed when she didn't find him seated at his desk. She thought he must have left. But she felt his presence inside. Turning her head, she saw that he was standing near the window looking outside at the dark moonless sky.

She felt tongue-tied as she stared at his broad back.

"I don't recall setting up a meeting this evening, Mrs. Mohan," his deep voice drawled while he still faced the other way.

Although she was angry about the daily update meeting with him, she still attended them for professional reasons. But those meetings were always held in the morning in his office.

"I-I didn't come here for a meeting. I came f-for something else."

He turned his head to look at her. Her heart thudded loudly as his eyes slowly swept over her. He took in her clothes, the way her fingers clutched her laptop tightly and then finally her tense face.

His face remained unreadable as he waited.

She reminded herself of the mission. She had to conquer the mind and body of her powerful enemy until he surrendered to her. But even though she was supposed to be the aggressor in their battle, he appeared to be the conqueror with an upper hand.

She stood rooted to the spot near the door while he moved away from the glass wall and sat in his chair. He watched her as though to see what his defeated and powerless enemy would do next.

"And what exactly is that something else?" he asked.

Her voice was once again stuck inside her throat. She couldn't speak and didn't know what to say either. So she forced her trembling legs to slowly walk towards him.

He watched her with his dark, intense eyes as she neared.

She walked around the desk and stopped right next to him. "I'm going to convince you," she whispered finally.

His eyes darkened even more. "Convince me for what?" he asked.

"I... I'm going to convince you to marry me."

His eyes flashed. "And how exactly are you going to do that, Mrs. Mohan?"

Even though he must know what she intended, he wanted her to spell it out

She couldn't say it out loud about wanting to seduce him. So she acted on it. Placing her laptop on the desk, she turned to look at him. He was watching her closely with a dark, intent expression.

The intensity in his eyes made her body tremble. But she still forged on.

Taking a small step closer, she leaned towards him, and then raising her slightly trembling hand, she brushed her fingers against his hard jaw.

His entire body visibly tensed, and his eyes turned darker as he watched her.

She held her breath, bracing herself for his rejection. She expected him to jerk away from her touch or say something harsh that would clearly reject her again.

But she gasped out loud when his hard, muscular arm wrapped around her waist and dragged her close until she fell on his lap.

Suddenly, the power dynamics changed.

Instead of standing over him leading the seduction, she was now looking at him from below while being trapped in his arms. A thick cloak of sexual tension enveloped them while they watched each other.

His jaw was clenched, and his eyes flared in anger. But the heat of his hard, muscular body and the rise and fall of his broad chest indicated he was aroused. She could also feel his hardness against her hip through the layers of clothes.

Her heart pounded inside her chest as he continued to watch her with dark, angry eyes while he held her trapped on his lap.

But despite his anger, his fingers skimmed the skin of her throat softly, making her skin break into goosebumps.

"I will take everything you offer," he said in a deep yet harsh voice. "But that will not change my mind about marriage."

Her cheeks heated at his warning. He was willing to have sex with her, but he would not marry her.

"I won't give you everything," she whispered in reply. "For me to give in completely, you'll have to be my husband first."

His eyes flashed dangerously at her condition of withholding sex until marriage.

She gasped when he suddenly gripped the back of her neck and pulled her up until their mouths were barely an inch apart.

Their hot breaths clashed while their eyes locked together in a heated, dueling gaze.

Her lips tingled in anticipation, but she resisted from closing the distance. She didn't want to make the first move.

Reading her mind, the grip of his fingers tightened behind her neck. He looked angry that she was withholding the pleasure of a kiss.

But she continued to make him wait.

She wanted him to kiss her first as a way to agreeing to their deal. And also to prove that he craved her touch as much as she craved his.

Their breaths grew heavier and faster as they dueled with their eyes and breaths.

Finally, after what seemed like an eternity, he made the first move.

A growl emitted from deep inside his chest before he closed the final inch between their mouths and captured her lips. Hot and wet, his tongue violently thrust past her closed lips and went deep inside to taste her. A moan escaped her throat as pleasure shot through her entire body. She grabbed his head with both hands and kissed him back.

Their kiss was urgent, greedy and full of need. But it also held anger and desperation.

He was angry that he wanted her. And she was desperate to make him want her enough to marry her.

Her body was on fire even as she tried to control her burning desire towards the man who was her enemy. Placing a hand on his broad chest, she pushed him away from her before turning her face to the side.

A growl escaped him when she broke their kiss. The hand at the back of her neck tightened, and he tried to drag her back to him.

"No! Wait!" she said, trying to hold him off.

She had to confirm her terms before it was too late and he took everything from her without any promises.

"Yash! Stop!" she gasped when his mouth was on top of her cheek.

Suddenly, he froze.

Slowly, the pressure of his fingers on the back of her neck eased.

She turned her face towards him and almost gasped at the dark, angry desire she saw on his face.

"D-do you agree to the terms?" she asked.

His eyes flared while his jaw clenched. "You want to seduce me without letting me fuck you fully?"

Her breath caught in her throat when he put it out like that.

"Yes," she whispered.

There was a momentary silence.

"Will you allow me to do everything else?" he asked. His dark voice made her body tremble.

Y-yes," she replied shakily.

He watched her for a few angry, tense moments.

"Take off your jacket and shirt," he growled.

The tone of his order sent shivers up her spine along with tingles into her stomach and in between her legs. She was reminded of the night in Milan when he was the dominant stranger she had spent a passionate night with. She had listened to his orders at that time and was rewarded with unbelievable pleasure.

Even now, her body hummed in anticipation to experience that pleasure again. Her body demanded that she follow his order and allow him to do whatever he wanted.

Slowly, she removed her suit jacket and dropped it down next to the chair. She then pulled up the tank top underneath and dropped it on the jacket. She was only wearing a thin white lacy bra she had specifically purchased for him.

Her chest heaved as her breathing came out faster and heavier. He watched her, but she couldn't read anything from his face. His anger disappeared, and now he looked like a cold, ruthless stranger.

"Remove that piece of cloth too," he ordered.

Her cheeks were on fire, but she reached behind her and unclipped the back of her bra. Slowly and reluctantly, she pulled it away and dropped the soft fabric along with the rest of the clothes.

This time his eyes flared as his burning gaze fell over her bare breasts that showed her arousal through hardened peaks.

Her body heated even more. She was embarrassed that she was sitting half-naked inside an office on top of a man who was fully clothed.

Although she could feel his arousal, she could see the dark angry flush and the tightening of his jaw indicating that he was fighting their attraction.

Suddenly, a heady rush of confidence coursed through her bloodstream. She was beyond thrilled and excited that she was able to control a man like him.

He must have read her thoughts because his eyes flared, and his hand caught the back of her neck again. Threading his fingers into her hair, he dragged her head closer until her lips were barely an inch apart from his.

Their breaths clashed again along with their eyes. Her breathing came out fast and uneven while his was deep and hot. The tips of her aroused breasts brushed against his suit, the friction causing them to tingle.

He didn't kiss her. This time, he waited.

She could neither move away nor get closer because his grip on her hair was strong. Her entire body vibrated in tension and awareness caused by the proximity.

Kiss me!

She mentally begged him to kiss her. But he still didn't move.

The need to kiss became unbearable, and she couldn't wait. She needed to touch him.

Sucking in a deep breath, she parted her lips and used the tip of her tongue to lick his firm, masculine lips. The small gesture made him tense even more.

He let out a deep growl before his mouth crashed on top of hers.

She moaned as his hot mouth devoured hers with an urgency that stole her breath. His tongue entered her mouth and tangled with hers while she gripped his short, thick hair and pulled him closer.

Nothing about the kiss was soft. It was wild, untamed, passionate and explosive.

But the kiss didn't last long.

He dragged his mouth away from hers. She opened her mouth to protest but ended up moaning when his rough stubble scraped against the sensitive skin of her neck.

He kissed her neck and inhaled deeply. "Fuck, I missed your scent. I dreamed of it in the last fifty days."

She was shocked listening to his words. She didn't think he cared enough to keep a count of the exact days since their night in Milan.

Before she could react, once again she gasped and cried out loudly. His mouth slipped lower and latched on to the tip of her breast. She couldn't see him because the grip on her hair remained tight. She was held in place for him to do as he desired. She could only feel him.

His mouth was hot as he used his teeth, tongue and lips on her breasts to drive her insane. She moaned and shifted as hot desire and pleasure flowed through her bloodstream with every pull of his hot mouth.

He groaned deeply and roughly as though tasting her skin gave him equal amounts of pleasure. He switched to her other breast, licking and pulling it into his mouth, using his teeth to scrape against her sensitive skin. He latched on to it, sucking with a pressure that made her body shake. A loud cry escaped her mouth.

The ache inside her body grew with every tug. He released the grip on her hair and instead gripped her hips. His fingers dug into her soft skin at her waist while he ground his hard arousal against her core.

Another dark groan escaped from deep inside his chest. "Give in to me fully," he demanded as he continued to steal her mind. "Let me in."

She badly wanted to give in. She wanted him to strip the rest of her clothes off and take her right then in his office until they both exploded in pleasure.

But she couldn't give in. Not even when her body begged her to.

"No," she gasped out even as she clutched his head closer to her bare chest. "You have to marry me first."

He stilled all of a sudden.

His mouth left her breast, and he drew back until she could see his face. Anger and frustration radiated from him along with his desire. Suddenly, his face turned cold even though his body still radiated heat, and she could feel his hard arousal under her.

The grip on her hips tightened before he lifted her off him and placed her on top of his desk. His dark, furious gaze swept over her half-naked body before he got up from his chair and walked away from her.

The door shut behind him, leaving her alone in his office.

She crossed her trembling arms over her bare chest as she stared at the door for a long time. Her body screamed and continued to tremble with suppressed passion.

How long would it take to break him?

What if he breaks me first and I give in to him as he demanded?

CHAPTER FIFTEEN

"The sale deed is finalized, Yash. The acquisition will be made by Ventura Holdings."

Yash was at his penthouse speaking with his brothers on the phone regarding the long-awaited purchase which was finally going through.

"Good. Have the work start as soon as the rest of the plans are finalized."

"Yes, I've already begun some of the execution," Bhargav replied.

While Yash and Bhargav discussed the rest of the details, there was a significant deafening silence from their youngest brother.

Yash knew Aryan hated the purchase.

Although their childhood home contained many good memories, towards the end, the memory of the event that had happened scarred and shaped the rest of their childhood and also their adulthood—especially Aryan's, who had only been seven at that time.

Aryan had only been seven when he found the body of their father hanging from a ceiling fan.

Yash and Bhargav had also seen their father's body, but they hadn't held the deep grudge against their father for choosing to escape the hardships in life and leaving his wife and three children to fend for themselves.

"Aryan, I want you to join me when I fly out to meet Ma next month."

The last confrontation between Aryan and their mother had been tense. Since then, their mother had not spoken to Aryan much.

"I think it will ruin Ma's vacation, bro. Let's leave it for now."

"No. Ma would want to see you."

Yash knew that their kindhearted and gentle mother could never keep a grudge against anyone, let alone her favorite son. Although their mother loved the three of them equally, Aryan was much closer to her. She felt Aryan was openly affectionate, unlike her other two sons, who barely displayed their emotions.

"Fine. I'll join you," said Aryan.

Yash was planning to fly out before his wedding. Although he knew his mother would be shocked by his choice of bride, he hoped she would understand when he revealed it to her later.

Rajesh Mohan's daughter was far from his choice of bride. But given a choice, he wouldn't have married anyone right then. Not even the woman he was madly obsessed with.

Aryan's voice on the phone cut into his thoughts. "Divya Mohan hasn't yet told her boyfriend or her friend about the impending marriage. Do you think the boyfriend will cause a problem when he finds out?"

"No, he won't," Yash replied.

Divya Mohan's boyfriend came from a modest family background and wasn't the type to have confrontations. Not even to fight for the woman he proclaimed to love.

"What about Narmada Mohan?"

Aryan's question made Yash's jaw clench. "What about her?"

"I don't trust her, bro," Aryan added. "Despite her innocent-looking face, she's way too smart and holds a genuine grudge against you. She's not going to wait and watch quietly. She's already having you followed. She's going to try something soon."

Yash knew that already. The taste and feel of Narmada still lingered on his lips, reminding him of her seduction a few hours ago.

"I'm going to convince you to marry me."

Her words along with the visuals of what had happened in his office, flashed in his mind.

"I won't give you everything. For me to give in completely, you'll have to be my husband first."

Yash was left angry and frustrated by her games. Somehow his beautiful pawn sensed that he wanted her badly enough for her to try to change his mind.

"Don't underestimate the pretty widow, bro," Aryan advised. "It's the innocent-looking ones who carry a bigger punch. I'm having the devil of a time trying to get the attention of our other enemy's daughter."

Yash didn't know enough about the woman Aryan was pursuing. But he did know Narmada should not be underestimated.

"I'll take care of Narmada Mohan. But the two of you need to remember that you only have a couple more months' time than me," Yash warned. "We cannot risk our other two targets being warned by Rajesh Mohan."

When Yash and his brothers made plans, they had known the risks they would run into if one of their enemies decided to warn each other.

"I don't think they will have a clue. They have lost touch with each other. The last time all three of them met was more than three years ago when Rajesh Mohan's son died. There haven't been any phone calls between them since then."

"That's good."

Yash spoke to his brothers for a few more minutes, discussing the details of the rest of the plan and the updates on the progress of things they already set into motion.

When he ended the call, it was well past midnight.

"I'll talk to you both tomorrow," he said.

Putting his phone on the bed, he walked towards the glass wall in his bedroom to look at the night sky. Even though it had been a long day, he was barely tired. In fact, his body was buzzing with restless energy.

"Don't underestimate the pretty widow, bro. It's the innocent-looking ones that carry a bigger punch."

There was a lot of truth to his brother's warning.

When he had made plans to take over Genesis, he had only expected to tackle Narmada Mohan until the takeover. He had not expected her to fight so hard. And he definitely hadn't expected her to use seduction as the means to win her company back.

Despite his angry frustration, a dark thrill of chase ran through him and heated his bloodstream.

Circumstances in his life ensured he never backed away from challenges. He wasn't the kind who thought twice about taking advantage of a weakness in his enemies either.

He always fought to win.

He was going to take up the challenge his beautiful pawn threw at him.

He would let her seduce him, but he would not let her drive him out of his mind enough to risk everything.

CHAPTER SIXTEEN

It was the weekend, but Narmada couldn't visit her grandfather once again. Too many things were hanging by a thread for her to suddenly leave.

"I'm fine, Grandpa. Just a little busy at work."

There was laughter on the phone. "You are always busy, Maddy."

Narmada smiled at her grandfather's use of her childhood pet name.

"I promise I'll come in a few weeks, Grandpa... as soon as things at work settle down."

Narmada hadn't still told her grandfather that the company she built was no longer hers.

"Sure, Maddy. Come only when you can. Definitely don't come until things at work get sorted."

Narmada smiled. She had grown up seeing her grandfather being dedicated to his job and to the people he had worked for. He had always taught her to do the same.

"Oh! I almost forgot why I called had you in the first place, Maddy. I'm going to take up a job soon."

Narmada was surprised. "What job, Grandpa?"

Narmada hoped it wasn't a driving job because even though her grandfather was perfectly fit physically, she wasn't sure if he could get back to working as a driver at the age of seventy-five. It would be too strenuous for him.

"I've been hired to help restore the gardens at the estate."

Narmada was surprised.

Her grandfather had worked at the estate for over three decades before he began working for Rajesh Mohan. She knew her grandfather held a special softness for the place.

Narmada felt happy for him. "That's good, Grandpa. I'm glad they are restoring the estate."

"Yes. I'm glad they are restoring the place too. Anyway, when you come for a visit, I'll take you there."

"Sure, Grandpa." Narmada didn't remember the place much, since it had been well over fifteen years since she had lived there. But she had many good memories of the place.

"All right, Grandpa," she said with a smile. "Goodnight. I'll talk to you soon."

She knew her grandfather preferred to sleep early. After retiring from his job, her grandfather adapted to the small-town village lifestyle very quickly.

Ending the call, Narmada checked her phone messages.

Supriya had left a few messages. But since it was close to eight o'clock and the weekend, Supriya must be busy with her husband and family. Narmada sent a short text letting Supriya know she'd speak to her in the morning.

There was another call from an unknown number with a text message. Looking at the name of the caller, Narmada was very surprised.

She called back immediately.

"Hello, Narmada," a familiar man's voice answered.

"Oh my God, Tanuj! How are you?"

Narmada was shocked that Tanuj finally reached out to her. After Vaibhav's death, Tanuj disappeared completely from her life. Narmada had been trying to reach out to him several times over the last three years, but all her calls and emails went unanswered.

"I'm fine, Narmada. I shifted to London three years ago."

Narmada was surprised but didn't blame him. She understood why Tanuj chose to move away. He wanted to leave behind the place that held painful memories.

"That's very good, Tanuj. I'm happy for you. I'm happy that you reached out to me."

There was a short silence.

"I'm not entirely happy, Narmada. I still feel very guilty."

Narmada's heart sank. "Please don't feel guilty, Tanuj. Whatever happened with Vaibhav wasn't your fault. It was nobody's fault. Vaibhav's decision was entirely his."

There was a shuddering breath on the phone. "But you got blamed for it, Narmada. I know Vaibhav's family blamed you for what happened. I'm really sorry I wasn't there to help you or protect you."

Narmada knew Tanuj's presence would have only added fuel to the fire that Vaibhav's father had created. Although she had taken the major brunt of the accusations, she knew she was strong enough to withstand it.

"That's okay, Tanuj. My father-in-law has never been happy about Vaibhav marrying me. Regardless of the truth, I would have still been blamed."

There was silence again.

"When can I meet you, Tanuj?" Narmada asked urgently. She hoped he didn't disappear again. She had to meet him and speak to him.

"I'm coming there for a visit soon. I'll meet you then."

"Yes. Please come. You are always welcome. I really want to see you again."

"Okay, I'll come," he replied softly. "Bye, Narmada."

The call ended, but Narmada stared at the phone for a very long time.

Her thoughts revolved around the man who carried an immense amount of guilt, which she desperately wanted to help him relieve.

She knew inviting Tanuj to her home would get strong reactions from her in-laws and many. Tanuj was the man Rajesh Mohan and many people believed she had cheated on her husband with, leading to her husband's suicide.

Narmada didn't care what people thought about her. She was determined to do what was right.

But what about Yash Varma?

Her mind once again went to the man who dominated most of her thoughts.

She hated Yash Varma. But the majority of her waking hours—and also during her sleep— were filled with thoughts that revolved around him.

It had been only twenty-four hours since her seduction attempt after which he had left her half-naked on his desk and stormed out of his office.

Since then, she was barely able to get him out of her mind.

"I will demand fidelity from my wife. If you become my wife, you will have to stay faithful to me and bear my children."

A small shiver racked her body, recalling his words from before.

She wasn't his wife. But she was doing her damnedest to get him to agree to marry her.

What would he do if he found out that she would be meeting with Tanuj?

She was sure Yash Varma knew why the chastity clause was put in place. Like everyone, he thought she had cheated on Vaibhav by having an affair with Tanuj.

I will have to keep meeting with Tanuj a secret.

Under no circumstances should Yash Varma know she was going to meet with Tanuj at her home.

CHAPTER SEVENTEEN

Yash was going through the restoration plans made by the architect hired by Bhargav.

Despite her young age, the architect had done an excellent job of recreating the interiors and the exterior.

He stared at the pictures of the garden and recalled the times he and his brothers spent a lot of time either playing games in the lawn area or the orchard area. His parents, especially his father, had also insisted the three of them help with the gardening. When his father wasn't busy running the vast family estate and several businesses, he used to spend a lot of time gardening.

"To plant a garden is to believe in tomorrow."

Yash recalled his father's often repeated words. His father had believed in nurturing things, so the next generations could have a better future. Although his father was a good businessman, he hadn't been a shrewd, selfish one. His father had always thought about how much of a good impact any of his businesses would have on people.

It had also led to his downfall and cost his life.

All through Yash's childhood, he held his father as his role model. But once tragedy struck, Yash became the exact opposite of what his father had been.

His father was a warm, generous and kindhearted businessman that people had adored. But Yash became a cold, ruthless and calculating businessman that people feared.

Despite finding out the truth about his father, too much had already happened for Yash to change.

Even though Yash couldn't bring back his father, he and his brothers were determined to bring back the good memories of their father by bringing justice to his name, and also by gifting their mother the estate where she had lived before being forced to leave.

Yash clenched his jaw as he recalled the devastated face of his mother when she was told her husband killed himself to escape debts and a bad reputation.

Yash frowned as a sudden thought struck him.

Did Narmada feel devastated by her husband's suicide?

Did she really cheat on him? If she hadn't, why would Vaibhav Mohan kill himself?

Yash's gut instinct said she hadn't cheated on her husband.

But then, he felt that way because he didn't like to acknowledge that he obsessively desired a woman who could be a cheat.

Yash knew Narmada and that man she supposedly cheated with hadn't been in touch for three years. After Rajesh Mohan's son's suicide, the man had left the country and settled down in London.

Before meeting Narmada, Yash had done enough groundwork to know she wasn't linked to any other man for the last three years. The woman who had broken apart in his arms on the night in Milan wasn't experienced. The innocence and wonder on her face gave it away.

Yash felt agitated.

Only a day had passed since he had left Narmada half-naked on his office desk, determined not to let her get to his mind. But right then, he felt a strong need to storm into her home and demand the truth.

He picked up the phone and was about to call his driver to ready his car when his phone began ringing. It was Aryan.

"Narmada Mohan has spoken to her lover, bro. I didn't think he was still in the picture."

Yash's clenched his jaw as rage hit him hard. "When?" he growled.

"Three hours ago," Aryan replied. "The man called, and they spoke for a few minutes."

Why the fuck was she speaking with that man again?

"I will take care of Narmada Mohan and that man," Yash told his brother. "You keep your focus on Girish Shetty."

Yash ended the call.

You are a fucking fool.

The dark, angry rage continued to course through him. Yash knew he shouldn't care what Narmada Mohan did or who she spoke and met with. She was no one to him.

She was at most only a bloody pawn.

All his focus should be on the woman he was going to marry. He should be wooing Rajesh Mohan's daughter and make her agree to whatever terms he stated after their marriage. All of his plans would depend on how the other woman would cooperate.

And yet, even though he knew all of that, his gut twisted at the thought of his beautiful pawn reaching out to her old lover.

She doesn't mean anything to you. Get rid of her.

He was going to get rid of her. But in a way that he would stop thinking about her and she would be out of his mind permanently.

He picked up his phone. "Mr. Raman. Have the jet readied. I'm flying to Paris tonight."

The only way to get rid of an attraction towards a beautiful woman was to be with several other beautiful women.

"I want us to put together the integration plan of Ikon Tech in the coming week."

"But Narmada, didn't we cancel our partnership with them?"

Narmada nodded with a smile. "Yes. But it was done for a reason, and we are now following a different strategy of partnering with them."

Narmada's executive team looked confused. But she couldn't yet reveal that Ikon Tech was getting acquired. That information would have to come after having discussed it in the board meeting.

And when the chairman is back from wherever he went.

A week had passed since she last saw Yash Varma. After her failed seduction attempt, she had not seen him in the office. She had only received a brief message from his personal assistant that he was travelling on business.

Considering Yash Varma was more or less a billionaire who ran a huge corporation, it was very likely he travelled often on business. But still, Narmada had a hollow, sinking feeling that he was ignoring her deliberately.

I can't give up.

It was humiliating, but she couldn't afford to give up. She had to try seducing him again. She had to keep trying until he wanted her desperately enough to agree to marry her.

All week she had felt jittery, anxious and confused. She felt a strange urgency to see him again.

But it wasn't just because she had to proceed with her plan. It was also because she was searching through the corridors to hopefully see his darkly handsome face and also checking her email constantly to see if he had reached out to her.

She missed her enemy.

I must be stressed or falling sick. Why else would I miss the man I hate?

Taking a deep breath, she smiled at her executive team. "All right. Let's meet again next week with updates. Thank you, everyone."

As everyone cleared the conference room, she picked up her laptop to follow behind them.

She had deliberately set up the meeting on the top-floor conference room, so she could peek to see if Suresh Raman was seated near the executive assistant's desk. But the older man wasn't there, which meant neither was his boss.

Feeling disappointed again, she headed back to her office. She had just got out of the elevator and was walking towards her office when she felt a strange awareness.

She sensed him before she could even see him.

"Mrs. Mohan," Yash Varma's deep voice rumbled from behind her. "I'd like to speak to you. Right now."

His curt order made her spine stiffen. But choosing not to oppose him, she simply nodded and continued walking towards her office room.

The floor wasn't carpeted, and her heels made a soft clicking sound. But she couldn't hear his footsteps. She could only sense his presence as he walked behind her. He was so close that she could feel the heat of his body and could smell his expensive, musky cologne. A small shiver racked through her which she hoped he didn't see.

She didn't want him to know she had missed him or was pining for him.

They reached her office room, and her executive assistant looked towards her with widened eyes.

"Good morning, Mr. Varma," Pooja greeted with a slightly awed look.

Narmada knew Pooja and many executive assistants didn't get the chance to meet Yash Varma up close. And just like everyone else, Pooja felt awed by his darkly handsome looks.

Yash Varma didn't greet Pooja back. He must have given out one of his cut nods as acknowledgement to the greeting.

Narmada smiled at her assistant. "Pooja, please move my next meeting to later this afternoon. I will be in an urgent meeting with Mr. Varma."

The younger woman nodded. "Sure, Narmada. I will."

Pooja's eyes remained wide as she continued to stare at Yash Varma.

Narmada felt a small ripple of annoyance. Pushing the feeling away, she stepped into her office.

Barely a moment later, the door closed, and there was a soft click of the lock. Before she could turn to face him, she felt strong fingers digging into her waist and pushing her against a wall.

Narmada gasped out.

Yash Varma's tall, broad and muscular form pressed against her back, pinning her to the wall. Her heartbeats raced as the heat of his body enveloped hers while his harsh breaths fell against her ear.

"Did you miss me?" his deep voice rumbled into her ear.

Her body shivered, feeling his hot breath against her sensitive skin. There was an angry edge to his voice which she didn't understand.

"Yes," she replied honestly.

She probably should have acted as though she didn't miss him to make him want her more. But her need for him lowered her defenses.

She heard the harsh inhale of his breath at her honest answer.

"Good," he rasped. "Because I fucking missed you too."

His nose rubbed against her neck, breathing her in as though he missed her scent. She could feel his hard chest rising and falling rapidly like hers as he pressed her against the wall.

Her body trembled in need. She wanted to turn back and look at him, but he kept her pinned to the wall restricting her movements. All she could do was feel him.

His slightly callused fingers brushed over her arms. She had left her suit jacket on her office chair and was wearing a formal white shirt. Her skin broke into goosebumps under the thin material of the shirt.

Suddenly, the heat of his body disappeared, and his fingers dug into her arms as he turned her around to face him.

She gasped at seeing his face. His darkly handsome face looked harsh and tensed with anger and some other emotion she couldn't read.

"What the fuck are you doing to me?" he growled.

Her breath caught in her throat. Despite his anger, the impact of seeing him after a week of missing him hit her like a punch. The need to touch him made her hands tremble.

"The same thing you are doing to me," she whispered.

She raised her hand, and with slightly trembling fingers, she touched his strong jaw. The tips of her fingers tingled with tiny sparks as she traced his hard jaw line.

His eyes closed, and when he opened them again, they were burning with an intensity that trembled her body. He looked as though he were seconds away from ripping away her clothes and taking her against the wall.

She held her breath as conflicting emotions warred inside her.

She wanted him badly enough to allow him to take her against the wall of her office. But she knew the devastating consequences it could have if she gave him what he wanted without the promise of marriage.

His jaw clenched hard, reading her mind easily.

Dropping his hands from her arms, he stepped away from her.

"Dinner. Tonight. I'll send my car." Gritting out those words, he walked away from her.

Narmada clung to the wall behind her, staring at the closed office door even after he left.

Even though she should be celebrating her win of being invited to dinner which indicated his interest to spend time with her, she felt terrified.

She felt as though she was heading towards an unknown precipice without any control over the fall.

***

"Oh my God! He invited you to dinner? That's great news! It means your seduction plan is working!"

Narmada was speaking to Supriya on the phone while getting ready for dinner.

Yash Varma didn't exactly invite her to dinner. He had gritted out the order in anger before storming out of her office.

"I don't know whether or not the plan will work, Supriya. I have less than a month before the wedding date."

"Don't worry, Narmada. Just continue with the plan. He will agree eventually."

Narmada bit her lip in uncertainty. Yash Varma was a ruthless man who wasn't the kind to be easily manipulated. He was always ten steps ahead of her. So, it made her nervous when he seemingly was giving in.

"I'm withholding sex from him. I told him unless he becomes my husband, I will not give in completely."

There was a shocked gasp from Supriya. "My God! And Yash Varma agreed?"

Narmada shivered, recalling the angry, frustrated rage on his face when she put in her condition. "Yes, he agreed."

"Wow. A man like Yash Varma would have many beautiful women lining up to give him what he wants. If he still agreed to your condition and is inviting you to dinner, that's a very good sign. He is truly interested in you, Narmada."

Narmada didn't know if it was his interest or simply a challenge she posed to him. Maybe he wanted to prove to her how easily he could break her. And despite her hatred towards him, she wasn't entirely confident about stopping him mid-seduction when her own body's needs became unbearable.

No. I can't give in to him. There is too much at stake.

The sound of her doorbell cut into her thoughts.

"I think his driver is here to pick me up. I'll talk to you later, Supriya."

"Sure. Be careful. After what he did to you, the least he can do now is treat you to a romantic dinner and pamper you with luxury before marrying you and handing back Genesis."

Despite her nervousness, Narmada smiled at her friend's wishful thinking. "I will be careful. Good night, Supriya."

Ending the call, Narmada shook her head. Yash Varma was far from romantic. She couldn't imagine him pampering her either. The man was way too intense and brutally direct.

A shiver racked her body, recalling his dark, angry frustration.

"What the fuck are you doing to me?" he growled.

She could sense that he still wanted her. But merely wanting her wasn't enough. She wanted to make him want her enough to marry her.

Taking a deep breath, she checked herself in the mirror and smoothed the red dress she wore for the occasion. She left her hair loose. The only additional jewellery she wore was the simple gold bracelet that her grandfather gifted her on her eighteenth birthday.

Satisfied with how she looked, she grabbed her purse before going to the door to answer it.

A middle-aged man dressed in a brown uniform waited outside the doorstep.

"Good evening, Miss. I'm Raju. Mr. Varma sent me here to pick you up."

Narmada forced out a smile. "Thank you for coming to pick me, Mr. Raju. I'm Narmada."

Stepping out, she locked the main door and followed behind the man to a waiting car.

Normally, she would have chosen to drive to whatever restaurant Yash Varma had made dinner reservations. But she didn't want to pick an argument that might anger him. She had to pick her battles and use a lot of restraint. Until he agreed to marry her.

She sat in the backseat and checked her messages while the car drove on. A few minutes later, she put her phone back into her purse and looked up.

"How far is the restaurant?" she asked, hoping the restaurant wasn't too far.

There was surprise in the driver's voice when he answered. "Mr. Varma asked me to bring you to his penthouse, Miss Narmada."

Narmada was shocked.

She had expected to spend a couple of hours in a fancy restaurant before being dropped back home. But discovering that dinner was going to be at Yash Varma's penthouse, her already nervous stomach began to flutter anxiously.

Sucking in a deep breath, she tried to distract herself by having a conversation with the driver.

"Have you worked for Mr. Varma for long, Mr. Raju?" she asked. She could see the older man's reflection in the rearview mirror.

The man smiled. "No, Miss Narmada. Mr. Varma hired me just a month and a half ago."

Narmada was disappointed. She hoped that like Yash Varma's personal assistant, the driver had been a longtime employee who would know something about his boss.

"It's only been a month and a half, but Mr. Varma has been a very generous employer. Along with a very good salary, he has even offered to pay for my younger daughter's engineering college fee."

An unsettling feeling erupted inside Narmada's chest listening to the older man.

Her mind couldn't process that Yash Varma could be generous. In her mind, Yash Varma was the villain who had ruined her life. And she was forced to make the ultimate sacrifice by trying to gain the attention of such a villainous man to make him agree to marry her.

Maybe he has an ulterior motive in helping his driver.

She tried to reassure herself with that thought.

"My grandfather worked as a driver for forty-five years," she said with a smile. "The employer he had worked for thirty years paid for all of my education too."

There was surprise in the older man's face. "Oh. Does your grandfather work even now?"

"No. My grandfather retired three years ago and lives in our village. Even though he loves the village life, he says he misses the family whom he used to work for many years ago."

The older man smiled. "My wife and I plan to go back to the village too as soon as I get my daughter married. Mr. Varma isn't married, but maybe by the time my daughter finishes her education and gets married, Mr. Varma will have a family of his own too."

A strange shiver ran through Narmada at the thought of Yash Varma being married with a family of his own.

All of her focus until then had only been to get him to agree to marry her instead of marrying Divya. She hadn't thought beyond the marriage.

"I also want children. So if you become my wife, you will have to stay faithful to me and bear my children. You will be tied to the man you hate until death pulls us apart."

Her heart thudded as she recalled his words.

If she married him to get back Genesis and save Divya, he would expect her to have his children.

Oh God.

That thought shook her from inside out.

No. Don't think about it right now. Simply focus on the present.

Taking a deep breath, she smiled at the older man. "Have you met Mr. Varma's family?" she asked. "His mother or two younger brothers?"

At her slightly probing question, the older man shook his head. "Not yet, Miss Narmada. I heard they live in America. I hope they visit him soon. Sir lives alone by himself."

She felt slightly disappointed that the older man didn't know much about the family and hadn't even met them. Even the investigators haven't come back with any useful information either.

She contemplated silently on how to bring up the topic of family while having dinner.

While she made plans, the car drove into the underground parking of a tall building in an upscale area in the heart of the city.

As soon as the car stopped, Narmada got out. She thought she would have to go up to the penthouse on her own, but she was glad when the older man accompanied her in the elevator.

"I'll take a cab while going back, Mr. Raju," she said with a smile.

She didn't want to keep the older man up until late at night. Since the dinner was at the penthouse, she had no idea how long it would last.

"Oh no, Miss Narmada. I will drop you back. Whenever it is late in the night, sir asks another driver to fill in the next day so that I can get rest."

Narmada was once again surprised and confused by Yash Varma's considerate behavior.

The elevator stopped on the top floor, and the older man led her to the penthouse. He pressed the button on a digital doorbell with a small screen on top.

The door was answered within a few moments.

Narmada stifled a gasp seeing Yash Varma at the doorway. She had expected a housekeeper or someone else to answer the door. But seeing her enemy's darkly handsome face, looking devastatingly good in a long-sleeved t-shirt and jeans, she felt tongue-tied.

She had only seen him in three-piece business suits. But even in casual wear, unlike most people, he still looked powerful and dangerous.

"Thank you, Mr. Raju," he said.

"It was my pleasure, Mr. Varma. Miss Narmada and I had a pleasant conversation during the ride."

"I see." Yash Varma watched her with an enigmatic look.

Narmada's cheeks heated, hoping he didn't suspect her of trying to dig up information about him through his driver.

"I'll see you later, Miss Narmada," said the older man left before turning to leave.

Narmada was now left alone with her enemy.

Yash Varma's mouth twisted into a dark smile. "Come in, Mrs. Mohan," he ordered.

Narmada felt a strong urge to turn and run away. Somehow, she felt threatened by the man and also the intimacy of having dinner with her enemy at his penthouse.

But resisting the urge, she stepped into his home.

While he led her inside, she only gave the barest of glances to his penthouse. She was too nervous about the evening.

She wondered why he still called her Mrs. Mohan. Was it as a reminder of her past?

Did he mind that she had been married before?

There were too many things that were working against her according to society's standards for an ideal wife of a rich man. She was from a lower working-class background, and she had been married before.

Narmada bit her lip, trying to push away her uncertainty.

She needed to be confident of herself, and she had to convince her enemy that they made a perfect match.

"Are you allergic to anything?" his deep voice asked

Narmada blinked and turned to see him watching her. "What?" she asked.

"There are sea food dishes for dinner," he explained. "Do you have any food allergies?"

Narmada's cheeks burned. They had spent a night together and knew each other intimately. They also knew a lot about their personal lives because they investigated each other. But something basic such as food preferences was still unknown to one another.

"No," she replied. "I don't have any food allergies."

He nodded and led her further inside to the dining area.

The room overlooked the city. Outside the huge window, she could see a large balcony with an outdoor swimming pool to the side. When her eyes fell on the dining table, her stomach fluttered even more in nervousness seeing the intimate setting.

Although the dining room was large and could comfortably seat well over a dozen people, the dining table was relatively smaller with only two seats placed opposite to each other.

Did he not entertain anyone in his home?

"Sit down," he said, pulling out a chair for her.

She did as he instructed and sat down. He took the chair opposite hers.

A middle-aged woman served appetizers and salad onto the plates and disappeared from the room.

"Champagne?" he asked.

Narmada's cheeks heated when she noticed that the champagne was the same brand as the one they had together in Milan.

"N-no, thank you," she said, not wanting to drink any alcohol. "Just plain water."

She needed all her senses. She had to both lure her enemy as well as to keep him at bay.

She already felt unnaturally drawn to him. Even though she knew what he did to her and what he planned, she still enjoyed his kisses and touch. Maybe a little too much.

He didn't say anything when she turned down champagne. He surprisingly poured them both water.

Narmada's eyes fell on his strong hands as he poured water and handed back her glass. He had long fingers with a small dusting of hair and nails that were neatly trimmed. His palms were large enough to do some serious damage to a person if he wished. She recalled their night together in Milan when he could easily pick her up and move around her body to give them both intense pleasure.

A shiver racked her body at the memories, and her breasts peaked behind her red dress.

No! Don't think about that night!

She was there to seduce him, not the other way around. She couldn't afford to recall the pleasure he gave her that night. Her body would once again beg to feel the same.

Taking a deep breath, she focused on her plan to extract information without sounding too nosy.

"Has your family visited you here?" she asked, picking up a fork and beginning to eat.

Despite her nervousness, she found the food delicious.

His mouth twisted. "I'm sure you already have the answer to that from Mr. Raju," he replied.

Her cheeks burned, making it obvious that she had been talking about him to his driver.

"I was just making conversation," she said in a slightly defensive tone.

"I see. And what else have you deducted from such conversations?" he asked.

Did he know about her hiring an investigator? She hoped he didn't.

"Not from conversations," she lied. "I looked up information about you that is available on the internet. It said you grew up in New York with two younger brothers and a mother."

He didn't react. He simply continued to eat while watching her. "What else?" he asked.

"N-nothing much. Everything else was how you got into construction at the age of fifteen and built your real estate empire and diversified it to hospitality and IT sector."

"Fourteen," he said. "I was fourteen when I decided to quit my education and begin working."

"Oh."

She was taken aback by the information.

She and her grandfather were by no means well-off. But she never had to quit her studies to help make money for her family.

"Do you regret it?" she asked. "Quitting school, I mean."

He shrugged. "My mother is a school teacher. She hated that her two older sons quit school to begin earning at a young age. But we did what had to be done to survive at that point. My youngest brother fulfilled her dream in education, though."

Narmada recalled reading that the youngest brother had a Harvard degree, and he joined his older brothers after his graduation to further grow their company.

"What about your father?" she asked. But immediately, she regretted it.

She knew he and his two brothers grew up with just their mother. Either their father died or had abandoned them when they were young.

His eyes flashed. "He died."

He didn't offer any more details. She didn't want to push either, just in case it was a sore point.

"Enough about me, Mrs. Mohan. Why don't you tell me about yourself?" he asked.

A sudden flash of bitterness passed through her.

"You already know enough about me, Mr. Varma. You knew about me even before we met in Milan."

He was silent for a moment.

Did he regret deceiving her? Did he feel any remorse?

He was a ruthless businessman. He most likely didn't care enough to pause and think about how he played with her emotions.

"Yes, I have known about you before. But I want to know more from you directly."

Narmada didn't want to tell him anything. But she knew she had to say enough to win his trust.

"Fine," she said. "There's nothing special to know. My parents died when I was six months old, so I grew up with my grandfather."

Yash Varma didn't say anything. He sipped on his water while he waited for her to speak more.

Feeling oddly encouraged, she continued to speak about her past. "I used to live with my grandfather in a large estate near our village where my grandfather worked as a driver for a family. But we left the estate when my grandfather took up a job in the city for the sake of my education. He became Rajesh Mohan's driver. Vaibhav and I became very good friends since we both loved computers and were of the same age. We created Genesis software together when we were eighteen. But since we didn't have the money to fund our company, we took Vaibhav's father's help, who agreed to invest in his son's venture. A year later, Genesis began to book profits and had expanded into the company it is now."

Yash Varma listened to her calmly. But when she was done talking, there was a strange flash in his eyes.

"Rajesh Mohan only invested a small amount," he said. "The company is now worth several hundred times more."

She nodded. "Yes. At that time, neither Vaibhav nor I had any personal money. My grandfather contributed ten percent of the investment, but he didn't want any shares in return."

Over the years, Narmada had insisted her grandfather take the shares owed to him for the initial investment. But he had always refused.

The dinner conversation came to a halt when the woman who had served them food earlier returned. She served them the main course.

"Thank you, Lakshmibai. We'll serve dessert ourselves. You can leave now."

At Yash Varma's order, the woman nodded. She was just about to leave when Narmada smiled at her.

"The food is wonderful, Lakshmibai," she said. "Thank you so much."

There was a rush of pleasure on the older woman's face. "You are welcome, miss. I hope you enjoy the rest of the meal."

The older woman left with a smile.

Narmada had grown up feeling invisible in Rajesh Mohan's house. Although the employer's son was her best friend, she was repeatedly reminded by the employer that the help and their families were expected to remain low-key.

Most of the servants were never appreciated or acknowledged for their effort to make their employers happy. After she grew up, she always made it a point to appreciate the efforts made by people from all walks of life.

They finished the main course in silence, and dessert was already served into two separate bowls.

"Do you meet your grandfather often?" Yash Varma asked, breaking the short silence.

Narmada was surprised by his question. "I am very close to my grandfather, but I don't see him often since he lives in a village now. I'm hoping to visit him soon when... things settle down."

When I get back the company you stole from me.

And also when I stop the marriage you planned with my sister-in-law.

Narmada didn't say those things aloud. But she did want to ask him about it.

"Why Divya?" Narmada asked, digging into her dessert.

Even though he might not tell her the truth, she couldn't control herself from asking that question. She had to try to find out what his true motives were.

"Why not her?" he responded.

Anger and annoyance rose inside her at his offhand answer.

"You are rich, handsome and powerful. Why would you choose to marry Rajesh Mohan's daughter when you are worth several hundred times more than him? You have never even met Divya before proposing the alliance. And she isn't your kind."

His eyes hooded as he watched her face. Narmada knew she wasn't able to hide her anger completely from him.

His mouth twisted into a small smile. "Most powerful men deliberately choose women who are simple, meek and pose no challenge to them. Powerful men want to be made to feel powerful both inside and outside the bedroom."

Narmada's cheeks heated at his sexist explanation. "That maybe true, but you are not like those men," she said. "You thrive on challenges."

His eyes flashed.

She knew she was right in her analysis.

She had constantly dreamed of the night in Milan, enough to begin analyzing it hundreds of times. He had been the dominant one each time they had sex, but whenever she touched him or wanted to be on the top driving their lovemaking, it had driven him mad with lust. He definitely didn't like passive partners in bed or outside.

"Come here."

Narmada's heart leaped at his soft command.

They were finished with dinner, so she couldn't pretend to be still eating. She didn't want to refuse him, especially when her purpose for agreeing to dinner was to seduce him.

With her heart beating loudly in her chest, she got up from her chair and went towards him.

She gasped when he caught her hand and pulled her until she was sitting on his lap. She could barely catch her breath when he dragged her head closer and caught her mouth in a deep, carnal kiss.

A loud moan escaped her as heat exploded inside her. She dug her fingers into his short, thick hair and kissed him back. Their mouths clashed in a swirling heat of lips, teeth and tongues.

She couldn't get enough of his addicting taste or what he made her feel.

But before she could deepen their kiss even more, a small gasp escaped her.

He stood up, and his arms tightened around her while he carried her somewhere. Once again his mouth fell on top of hers, and they continued to kiss passionately and greedily.

But their mouths parted again when he lowered her on something soft.

She blinked slightly when she realized they were in his bedroom, and he had lowered her on his bed. Seeing the room, her heart began to thud uncertainly.

He watched her closely. "Take off your dress," he commanded.

Swallowing a little because her mouth had suddenly turned dry, she did as he ordered. She pulled up her red dress.

"Everything," he added.

Her cheeks heated as she slowly reached behind her and unclasped her bra and let it fall, baring her breasts to him.

The heat of his gaze made her stomach quiver and breasts peak in arousal.

His eyes blazed as they swept over her nearly naked body. It wasn't the first time he was seeing her naked, but there was something about the way he looked at her right then.

There was darkness, madness and a strange possessiveness.

Her heart pounded so hard inside her chest that she almost didn't hear his next order.

"Take it off," he barked.

She didn't understand at first. The only item of clothing she was wearing was her panties. But his eyes were on her left hand, where her fingers were digging into the soft bedding. His face had suddenly hardened, and there was a dark look that bordered on angry possessiveness in his eyes.

"What?" she asked, feeling confused.

"The wedding ring," he gritted. "Take it off."

Immediately, her fingers curled protectively over her wedding ring. She had never taken it off before. It reminded her of her best friend and the promises she had made to him.

She bit her lip and stared at the ruthless man who was watching her with a dark, pissed-off look. His eyes turned even darker when he took in the way her fingers had curled protectively over her wedding ring.

"Remove it, Narmada," he ordered again.

Slowly, she uncurled her fingers.

She didn't want to argue with him on the matter. Although she cherished the memories of her marriage to her best friend, she understood that Yash

Varma didn't want any reminders of another man in his bedroom.

A strange thrill ran through her at his possessiveness.

Once again a heady feeling coursed through her at being wanted and desired by a dominant and typically cold, ruthless man like him.

Slowly, she slipped off the ring from her finger and placed it carefully on the nightstand next to the bed.

His eyes immediately flashed with satisfaction and also a dark madness that made her unconsciously move back. But he didn't let her escape.

He caught her leg and dragged her closer, making her gasp. Before she could say anything, her mouth was captured in a deep, passionate and possessive kiss that resonated deep inside her.

She moaned and kissed him back.

She savored the heavy press of his hard, muscular body lying on top of hers, but she also desperately wanted to feel the heat of his skin without the thin layer of cloth in between. She slipped her hands under his t-shirt and soaked in the feeling of his hot skin like an addict.

A deep groan rasped out from him as she ran her palms over his bare chest.

Suddenly, his mouth left hers and he moved away. She opened her mouth to protest, only to stare at him in awe as he shrugged off his t-shirt and bared his beautifully sculpted body.

Her lips began tingling in anticipation of his passionate kisses. But he shocked her by not kissing her on the lips. Instead, his mouth enclosed over the hardened peak of her aroused breast.

She cried out loudly as pleasure shot through her body, making her shudder. She clutched his head as he sucked hard, driving her out of her mind with the pleasure overload.

The heat of his mouth was everywhere on her skin. He bit, licked and sucked her skin with an urgency that rivaled certain madness. He moved down lower. Before she could catch her breath, with one hard tug, he pushed aside the thin scrap of silk she had purchased for him. And then, he kissed her core.

"Yash!" she screamed as her body shook and trembled.

His name on her lips made his movements more aggressive. He licked her, tasted her essence and thrust his tongue deep into her repeatedly. He did to her with his tongue what she didn't allow him to do with his hard arousal. He possessed her.

She shattered hard.

She was barely in her senses when she felt him moving on top of her. He caught the hair at the back of her head and kissed her deeply until she tasted herself on his lips.

Her body shook as need rose inside her again.

His mouth parted from hers, and her eyes met with his stormy, dark ones on his harsh face. She moaned when his hardness rammed against her quivering core.

"Let me in," he growled.

The raw, harshness in his voice made her stomach tremble hard. A burning need in her body grew uncontrollable, begging her to give into him. But her mind refused to surrender. She couldn't let him take her completely without facing the consequences.

She somehow clung to her resolve. "I can't," she gasped out. "You have to marry me first."

He looked furious. But he didn't move away from her. Pushing her legs wider, he rammed his hard arousal against her soft core once again. She gasped out loud even as her body softened and yielded.

Despite the thick material of his jeans, she could feel the hard length and heat of his arousal.

She clutched his hair as he groaned and grunted into her neck as he continued to ram his hardness against her soft core. The force of it was so hard, it was as though he was determined to tear through the cloth barrier and push deep inside her.

A loud cry tore out of her mouth as her body shattered again.

He caught her cry with his mouth in a deep, possessive kiss while she shook in his arms again and again. Pleasure sizzled through her core and radiated to all of her nerve endings. She clung to him wanting to feel him as close to her as possible.

She didn't know how much time had passed, but slowly, after what appeared to be a long time, she gained back her senses.

She opened her eyes, only to see the harsh and tense face of the man who gave her immense pleasure, but didn't find a release of his own. Wanting to give him the same pleasure, she moved her hand to his jeans.

But he stopped her. "No," he bit out.

"B-but you didn't... and I want to—"

He rolled away from her. "Go home, Narmada."

"What? But I can help you," she said, trying to move towards him.

"Don't," he ordered. "If you touch me now, I won't be responsible for my actions. I will be inside you, and you won't be allowed to go home until morning."

Her heart thudded, and she held her breath at his harshly uttered warning.

Knowing her weak mind wouldn't be able to withstand him anymore, she got up from his bed on shaky legs. She hurriedly put on her bra and slipped into her dress.

The heat of his gaze grew intense when she went to the nightstand and put her wedding ring back on.

"I... I'll see you tomorrow," she whispered before more or less running out from his bedroom.

But as she exited his penthouse, she wondered who had seduced whom that night.

CHAPTER NINETEEN

Yash watched the security cameras with his jaw clenched while Narmada Mohan took the elevator and then went down to the underground parking.

He had already notified his driver to start the car and wait for her in front of the elevator.

As soon as she exited the elevator, there was a look of surprise on her face. She then smiled at the older man while he held the door open for her. She got into the car, and soon the car drove away.

Yash shut off the security camera and let out a vicious curse.

He was still painfully hard, and his body ached while it screamed for release.

He was tempted to follow behind Narmada in another car, and go to her house and drag her back into his arms. He wanted to push her on the nearest flat surface, and watch her face while he sank deeply into her.

"You have to marry me first."

He let out a growl of frustration. "Fuck!"

He was horny as hell, but he knew there would be no outlet for him that night. And just like in the last two months, he would have to relieve his pain inside the shower cubicle with the image of his beautiful pawn in mind.

But jerking off didn't bring him any satisfaction except for a temporary physical release.

A week ago, he had foolishly planned to sleep with another beautiful woman to get over the burning need he had for Narmada. But it only ended in a disaster. He was hardly aroused, and even with the veil of darkness where he could imagine the woman he was going to fuck was his beautiful pawn, he still couldn't get himself to act on it.

His ex-lover had tried everything possible to get him aroused, but it only left him cold and annoyed. He left her place within an hour, angry and frustrated like he had been since two damn months.

He hadn't bothered to go to his other ex-lovers, knowing none of them could satisfy him either.

And so, his dangerous obsession with Narmada Mohan continued to grow without any obstruction.

He constantly wanted to be close to her.

But it wasn't just because he desired her. His obsession was to see the sweetness of her smiles and feel the taste of her and capture her pleasured sighs as he touched every part of her.

He wanted to possess not just her body but also her mind. He wanted to smash through the barriers she held against him.

"Fuck!" he growled again.

In a bloody month, he was supposed to marry Rajesh Mohan's daughter. But he had barely spoken or reached out to her again. Instead, he was panting like a horny dog behind his soon-to-be bride's sister-in-law.

All of the well-laid plans would depend on how much he could control his obsession towards Narmada. And he was risking it all.

He sucked in a harsh breath and let cold, determination fill him.

He knew what he had to do next. It would change the course of his and Narmada's future, but it was the only thing he would do.

He was going to woo his future bride.

CHAPTER TWENTY

"Ikon Tech will now be a part of Genesis. Fortune Group has acquired it."

There was an excited buzz as Narmada declared the acquisition news to her employees.

She was holding an all-hands meeting. Yash Varma was standing right behind her along with a few other board members. Even though it was a Fortune Group acquisition, he had wanted her to make the announcement.

The buzz continued to grow.

"That's such great news!" most of the employees remarked.

Narmada smiled. "Yes. This will add a lot of value to our company. And our teams have already put together an integration plan."

Narmada presented the high-level details on the timelines and how the acquisition would impact the shares' value. There were a few questions and concerns from the employees which she cleared.

She smiled at everyone. "Thank you all for your continued support. Let's work together and welcome our new co-workers from Ikon Tech."

The meeting finished in high spirits, and all the employees headed back to their offices.

Narmada headed back to hers as well. But while she walked, she could sense Yash Varma's presence behind her.

It was hard trying not to make any eye contact with him when others were around.

She was worried that if she saw him, she would end up blushing and making it obvious that something was going on between the current chairman of Genesis and CEO.

Just as she entered her office, Supriya followed her inside and shut the door.

"All right. Spill. What happened?" Supriya demanded.

Narmada sat down on her chair and smiled at her friend. "Fortune Group acquired Ikon Tech last month, and I made the announcement after the legalities were completed."

But her friend rolled her eyes. "You know very well I meant what happened in the penthouse between you and Yash Varma?"

Narmada suppressed a small shiver at the memories from two nights ago.

"Nothing much," she said. "We had dinner at his penthouse, and once again I told him if he wants me, he would have to marry me."

Supriya frowned. "That's it? I'm sure something more must have happened. Yash Varma was watching you as though he was only a few moments away from throwing you over his shoulder and carrying you away to do some unspeakably hot and passionate things."

Another small shiver racked through Narmada because she knew there was some truth to what her friend was saying. It had barely been two days since the dinner at the penthouse ended hot and heavily yet in an unfulfilled manner.

Since then, Narmada hadn't spoken to Yash alone. The brief moments earlier that morning while he instructed her about the all-hands meeting were in the presence of others.

Narmada bit her lip. "I'm planning to invite him to my home for dinner this weekend," she said. "I feel I'm getting close to making him agree. I just need to do a little more for the last push."

Narmada thought her friend would cheer her on. But Supriya looked worried.

"You should be careful, Narmada. Yash Varma is quite dangerous. Not because I think he would force you physically. I feel he is dangerous because he is capable of breaking your heart."

Supriya continued to look concerned. "I've seen how lonely, sad and vulnerable you were because of Vaibhav. You deserve happiness in your life, but not with Yash Varma. The man is cold-hearted and ruthless. Even though he might make you deliriously satisfied in bed, he will leave your heart aching and empty."

Narmada fell silent as she listened to her friend. She knew there was a lot of truth to what Supriya was saying. Each time Narmada had been with Yash Varma, despite her hatred and the reminder of what he did, a part of her still felt a strange connection to him and was drawn to him. It was her loneliness imagining that connection.

What she felt for her enemy wasn't just physical desire. She was beginning to see something beyond ruthlessness in him. Having talked to his driver and discovering the compassionate and generous side of her enemy muddled her mind further.

Narmada forced out a reassuring smile. "Don't worry, Supriya," she said. "I will be careful. I am not going to fall in love with him. All I want is to get him to agree to marry me instead of Divya."

Even as she said those words to her friend, a warning inside her mind wondered if it was too late. Was she falling for her enemy?

***

Narmada stepped into her home with a lingering frown.

All day, she was disturbed by the terrifying thought.

Am I falling for Yash Varma?

Even though she had told her friend she wasn't going to fall for him, the question constantly ran through her mind.

Only a month remained for the wedding, and Divya's parents were already planning the event.

Although Narmada promised Divya she would stop the wedding, Narmada felt a strange anxiousness and uncertainty creeping through her.

What if I fail?

She pushed away the thought. It had barely been two days since her enemy had proven he wanted her and desired her as much as she did. All she needed to do was continue to build on it.

She would have to plan another intimate dinner with him. This time, she decided to invite him to her place and cook the meal. Although she wasn't that good of a cook due to a lack of experience, she hoped the effort would be appreciated by the man she wanted to impress.

I would have to ask grandfather for his recipes.

Her grandfather was a great cook. People always appreciated his cooking. All she needed to do was take a few of her grandfather's recipes that were relatively simple and cook a meal for Yash Varma.

She was virtually planning her menu and dinner setting when the doorbell rang, surprising her.

Oh God!

Was it him?

She hadn't seen Yash Varma after that morning's all-hands meeting. After her conversation with Supriya, she had deliberately kept away from him. She had even cancelled the daily meeting she had with him.

Was he pissed off with her for avoiding him?

Taking a deep breath, she went to her living room and answered the door.

It wasn't her enemy who was standing outside her door. It was a familiar handsome man.

"Tanuj!" Narmada remarked in shock.

The man she hadn't seen after her husband's death looked at her with a sad smile. "Hello, Narmada. Can I come in?"

Pushing away the shock, Narmada hurriedly stepped aside. "Yes, of course. Come on in."

As soon as Tanuj stepped in, Narmada shut the door and led him into her living room.

"What would you like?" she asked. "Soft drink, juice or something hot?"

"Nothing, Narmada. I'm fine."

Narmada waited until he was seated on the sofa. "I'll be right back with some water," she said and went into the kitchen.

She filled up two glassed of chilled water from the fridge. When she carried the glasses on a small tray to the living room, Tanuj wasn't on the sofa.

He was standing near the wall staring at one of the photos of him, Vaibhav and her. Tanuj was a part of many photos she had on the wall.

Narmada placed the water glasses and the tray on the coffee table and joined Tanuj near the wall.

He turned to her. "I'm unable to forget, Narmada," he said softly.

Narmada's heart ached at seeing the deep misery on his face. She held his hand. "It's not your fault, Tanuj. Vaibhav loved us both. I'm sure he knew you didn't deliberately try to hurt him."

"Maybe," he whispered. "But the final ultimatum had pushed him to the edge. He felt too torn and cornered."

"Both of us didn't expect that to happen, Tanuj. We didn't think he would take the extreme step. Please don't blame yourself."

Tanuj was silent.

"Come, sit down," she said. "Tell me about how you've been in London."

He sat on the sofa, and she took the seat across him.

"I'm doing, fine, Narmada. I... I... even met someone in London."

Narmada smiled. "Oh! That's great! I'm so happy for you."

Tanuj nodded. "But I'm unable to commit... because of the past. I feel guilty and as though I don't deserve happiness or a second chance."

Narmada frowned. "Don't ever say that, Tanuj. Of course, you deserve happiness and love once again in your life. Vaibhav would have wanted his loved ones to be happy."

He was silent.

Narmada wanted to cheer Tanuj. And being in the house with pictures of Vaibhav seemed to make him sad.

"Let's go out for dinner," she suggested. "We can catch up at a restaurant."

Luckily, he nodded.

Narmada smiled at him. "Give me five minutes. I'll be right back."

She hurried into the bedroom to change. She pulled out a simple cotton dress and changed into it. Even though it was evening, because of summer, it was still quite warm outside. She skipped makeup and just put on some pale pink lipstick.

She grabbed her purse and was about to step out of the bedroom when her phone rang.

It was Divya.

Narmada knew a call with Divya would take a while. She didn't want to keep Tanuj waiting. But at the same time, she couldn't afford not to answer Divya's call.

She decided to answer the call and let Divya know she would call her back in a few hours.

But as soon as Narmada picked up the call, Divya's panic-ridden voice came through.

"Narmada! Oh God! You need to help me!"

Narmada frowned in concern. "What happened, Divya? Are you okay? Is everyone all right?"

"He's here, Narmada! Oh God, what do I do?"

Narmada was surprised. She wondered if Divya's boyfriend had gone to her in-laws' house to speak with them. Although it would be entirely out-of-character for the mild-mannered Rahul, Narmada was glad that Rahul was fighting for his love.

"Is your father angry with Rahul?" Narmada asked.

"No! Not Rahul. Yash Varma is here!"

Narmada froze. "What?"

"H-he came here a few minutes ago, saying he made dinner reservations for the two of us. My father ordered me to get ready. I-I came into the room, but I don't know what to do! Help me, Narmada. I can't go to dinner with Yash Varma."

Narmada felt as though her breath had been knocked off her chest. She also felt a sharp pain at the thought of Yash Varma taking Divya out for dinner.

Nothing has changed. He still wants to marry Divya.

Narmada had foolishly thought that something special was happening between her and her enemy. The special connection and attraction she felt two nights ago in his penthouse was only in her imagination.

She inhaled a deep breath. "Get ready and go out with him, Divya."

"What!"

"Your father will not let you reject the dinner invitation. The best option is to go with Yash Varma and once again let him know how you feel."

"I can't, Narmada! Rahul will never forgive me if I do that."

"I will speak with Rahul. And besides, I will come to the same restaurant as you are. Just let me know where he's taking you."

"Please come soon then! I'll find out and send you the details of the restaurant right away."

Divya appeared to have calmed down a little.

Ending the call, Narmada stared blankly into the mirror.

"Most powerful men deliberately choose women who are simple, meek and pose very less or no challenge to them. The men want to be made to feel powerful both inside and outside the bedroom."

Narmada had thought those words hadn't applied to him. But now, she found out in a terrible way that Yash Varma wanted a simple, meek wife. Not someone who constantly teased and challenged him.

And all he felt for her was lust and nothing more.

Pushing away the pain, she took another deep breath.

This changes nothing. I will still stop the marriage.

She decided to change her dress. This time, she changed into a dress that had a deeper cleavage and was shorter in length. It was her old dress from her college days she had worn during parties or when she and Vaibhav went to nightclubs with friends.

She spent an additional five minutes reapplying her makeup, highlighting her eyes with glittering eye shadow and dark eyeliner. She put on bright red lipstick, drawing the focus on her fuller bottom lip. Feeling satisfied, she stepped out of the bedroom and went to the living room.

"Sorry for the delay," she said.

Tanuj almost did a double-take when he saw her.

Narmada fought a blush. "I've made reservations in a more formal restaurant. I hope you don't mind."

"Not at all," he replied. "Do I need to wear something more formal?" he asked.

Narmada smiled at him. "No. You look perfect."

Tanuj looked quite handsome. She recalled the time he used to receive many marriage proposals from women. Narmada used to tease him often about that. Tanuj had classic good looks that made most women think of him as husband material.

Unlike Yash Varma who looks ruthless and dangerous. No sane woman would think of him as an ideal boyfriend or husband.

Stop thinking about that man! He doesn't deserve it.

"So where are we going?" Tanuj asked, cutting into her thoughts.

Before she could reply, Narmada's phone beeped, indicating a message. She quickly opened the screen and saw the name of the restaurant.

She looked up from her phone and smiled at Tanuj. "It's not that far. I hope you like five-star restaurants with Italian food."

***

"I didn't know you liked five-star restaurants with Italian food. I remember Vaibhav used to pick small restaurants when the three of us dined together because you enjoyed authentic and spicy food."

At Tanuj's remark, Narmada laughed. "I still enjoy smaller family-style restaurants," she replied as she handed over the car to the valet. "Tonight will be an exception."

They walked towards an exclusive restaurant inside a five-star hotel.

"Good evening, madam and sir," a woman greeted. "Do you have reservations for tonight?"

Narmada smiled at the hostess. "No. But we are here to surprise our friend. Mr. Yash Varma. We'd like to keep our visit a surprise, but my sister already knows we are coming. It's her... fiancé' we will be surprising. You see, it's his birthday."

"Oh. That's wonderful, madam. Then please go in. They are booked at a private corner table overlooking the lake."

Narmada pasted a wide smile. "Thank you so much."

While they were being led, Tanuj watched her curiously. Narmada felt guilty about dragging him into the drama. "Sorry," she whispered. "Divya needs help. I'll tell you about it later."

Tanuj looked surprised. "Divya? Vaibhav's sister?"

"Yes."

Tanuj nodded. "Not a problem."

As soon as they turned to a private corner overlooking the lake, Narmada's eyes clashed with her enemy. Yash Varma's eyes flared at seeing her.

Although her stomach fluttered with a combination of nervousness and anger, her steps didn't falter as she went closer.

Ignoring her enemy, she pasted a smile on her face. "Oh hi, Divya. What a pleasant surprise."

Divya looked nervous and worried. "Y-yes, a very pleasant surprise."

Narmada continued to smile. "Do you remember Tanuj, Divya?" she asked.

"Yes, of course. We met a few times. My brother spoke about him many times as well. How are you, Tanuj?"

Tanuj looked surprised. "I'm good, Divya. I'm glad to see you again."

Narmada sensed a change in Tanuj's voice. She knew Divya looked a lot like her brother. Divya must have reminded Tanuj of Vaibhav. Narmada hoped Tanuj would get closure if he sees that Divya didn't hold a grudge against him for Vaibhav's death.

Narmada was determined to make it happen.

"Do you mind if we join you?" Narmada asked Divya with a wide smile. "It'll be great for us to catch up."

Divya nodded. "I-I don't mind. Yes, y-you should definitely join us."

Narmada was proud of her sister-in-law. Despite being nervous, Divya understood the plan and played along.

"That's great!" Narmada sat next to Divya, and Tanuj took the seat next to Yash Varma.

Ignoring the burning stare of the man opposite to her, Narmada forced out another smile. "Tanuj, this is Yash Varma, the man Divya's parents have arranged her marriage with."

There was an awkward exchange of greetings. It was only Tanuj who greeted while Yash Varma was silent.

Although Narmada didn't look at her enemy, she continued to feel his burning gaze on her.

But despite the cold and heavy silence of her enemy, surprisingly easy conversation flowed between Tanuj and Divya.

Tanuj asked how Divya was faring in her job search, and he gave her some advice since he was in a similar field.

Narmada smiled at Divya. "Did you know that Vaibhav advised you to take biomedical sciences because of Tanuj?"

Divya was surprised. "Oh. That's so awesome."

As conversation continued, food and drink orders were placed.

Divya placed her order. When it was Narmada's turn, Yash Varma cut in.

"Get champagne for Mrs. Mohan," he told the waiter. His intense eyes met with Narmada's. "I remember you enjoying champagne on a certain occasion, Mrs. Mohan."

Narmada's heart jolted, and she was immediately angry at his deliberate taunt.

"My taste has evolved since then, Mr. Varma. I only pretended to like it, even though I find it distasteful."

Yash Varma's eyes flashed at her deliberate taunt. But he didn't react in any way. His voice remained deep and even when he ordered his drink and food.

Divya and Tanuj continued to converse. But Narmada couldn't sit through it calmly.

The dark, burning intensity of Yash Varma's gaze combined with her angry nervousness and hurt jealousy made her feel suffocated.

"Excuse me," she said, getting up from her chair. "I'll be right back."

She walked away from the table and went towards the restrooms. As soon as she went in, she leaned against the granite counter in front of the mirrored wall.

Her eyes prickled slightly. Immediately, she blinked rapidly with anger.

Stop feeling hurt and jealous. He doesn't deserve it.

The door to the restroom suddenly burst open. When she looked up into the mirror, she gasped.

Standing behind her was Yash Varma. And he appeared quite pissed off.

"Why the fuck are you with him again?" he barked out.

Narmada was shocked by the question.

She expected him to ask why she had intruded into his romantic dinner with Divya. She didn't think he would notice, let alone ask her about the man accompanying her.

"I don't want you to ever meet him," he ordered. "I want him gone as soon as the dinner is done."

Immediately, Narmada felt defensive.

"Why do you care who I am with?" she demanded. "And who are you to tell me not to meet someone?"

She gasped again when he stepped closer.

She didn't turn. But her heart thudded as he moved closer. His hard chest met with her back as he placed his hands on both sides of her, trapping her against the granite counter.

Their eyes clashed in the mirror.

She watched as he bent his head until his mouth was at her ear level.

"You are quite surprising, Mrs. Mohan," he taunted in a dangerously calm tone. "You insist that I marry you, and yet you show up with your past lover. Does he know you let me fuck you two months ago? And also two nights ago when you let me fuck you with my tongue until you broke in my arms calling out my name?"

Anger shot through her at his deliberate crude, taunting words. Turning towards him, she slapped him hard.

His eyes flashed dangerously, but he didn't react. She raised her hand to slap him again, but the second time, he caught her hand and dragged her closer.

"I hate you!" she screamed.

His eyes flashed. "I'm not going to let you go back to him," he growled. "You are mine."

He covered her mouth with his.

She was shocked, angry and instantly aroused as his tongue violently thrust deep into her mouth and kissed her. He kissed her cruelly and possessively until she responded. Moaning angrily, she caught his hair and yanked him closer to both hurt him and also to kiss him back.

She didn't know how long the kiss lasted. It eased some of the burning inside her heart.

He was the one to pull away.

Their harsh breaths were loud inside the restroom as they stared at each other. He watched her with a violent emotion in his eyes.

She was shocked seeing his anger and another emotion he did not hide.

Jealousy.

"If you let him touch you again," he growled. "I will break both his hands before ruining him completely. If you want me to marry you, stick to the bloody fidelity condition. You don't touch any other man but me."

With that warning, he walked out of the restroom.

Narmada was shocked. Her heart thudded as she tried to analyze what had just happened.

Yash Varma still wanted her. He was even jealous thinking she was with Tanuj.

Strangely, hope took root again in her heart. There were still chances to go ahead with her plan.

Taking a deep breath, she turned back to the mirror to straighten herself before returning to the table. She was shocked seeing her swollen lips and her completely smeared red lipstick.

Oh God.

If Divya or Tanuj or anyone saw her right then, there would be no doubt in their minds that she had been kissing someone passionately.

Pulling out a tissue, she wiped away her smeared lipstick. And then, she adjusted her hair which had turned messy after her enemy dug his fingers into it while kissing.

She splashed cold water on her lips to reduce the redness. Feeling slightly better, she threw the used tissue into the trash and walked out of the restroom.

The food and drinks had arrived. Divya watched her curiously and so did Tanuj.

Narmada forced out a smile. "I'm starving," she said and slid into the seat next to Divya.

Lighthearted conversation continued. Even though Narmada joined the conversation, she made it a point not to look at the man responsible for her lips to feel swollen and tingle.

"You are mine."

"If you want me to marry you, stick to the bloody fidelity condition. You don't touch any other man but me."

Yash Varma's possessive words inflamed by his jealousy resonated in her mind in a loop.

Finally, the dinner came to an end.

Although it barely lasted a couple of hours, it felt long and torturous. The four of them went to the entrance and waited for the cars to be brought in by the valets.

Meanwhile, Narmada murmured a goodbye and hugged Divya. "I'll speak to you later," she said softly. "Don't worry."

Divya didn't look as panicked as before and nodded. She looked at Tanuj. "Thank you so much for your advice, Tanuj."

Tanuj smiled. "You are welcome. Don't hesitate to reach out to me for anything."

Narmada sneaked in a glance at Yash. Surprisingly, he wasn't looking angry about Divya speaking to Tanuj or even wanting to keep in touch.

All of his attention was on her.

Feeling confused, Narmada looked away from his piercing gaze. "Our car is here. Good night, Divya... and Yash," she said before hurriedly getting into her car.

Tanuj got in. As soon as he wore his seatbelt, Narmada began to drive back home.

"Thank you for bringing me to dinner," he said. "It was nice meeting Vaibhav's sister. He loved his sister a lot. He used to often tell me to guide her."

Narmada smiled. "I know."

There was a brief momentary silence.

"Who exactly is Yash Varma?" Tanuj asked. "And why was he watching me as though he was ready to beat the crap out of me?"

Narmada fought the blush in her cheeks. "He... uh... is a rich businessman. Vaibhav's parents are keen to get Divya married to him."

"Hmm... are you sure it's Divya he is interested in? He barely acknowledged her through the dinner. He was busy watching you while you were trying hard not to look at him."

The heat in Narmada's cheeks intensified. "I think you might have misread the situation."

There was a short laugh. "I didn't imagine the attraction between the two of you, Narmada. It was obvious to me."

Narmada didn't know what to say. She didn't want to unload her problems on Tanuj. Because he would soon piece everything together, and he would feel guilty if he found out about the chastity clause or why it was put in place.

"I wonder what Yash Varma would do if he knew the truth," Tanuj remarked.

Narmada was surprised.

Tanuj laughed sadly. "I know what everyone thought, Narmada. They thought I was your lover."

He turned towards her. "Even though the truth was that I was Vaibhav's."

***

Narmada remained silent through the car ride.

She knew she couldn't rake up the past that would lead to feeling hurt and bitter. But Tanuj wanted to talk, and she let him.

"I loved Vaibhav so much," he said with a slightly shaking voice. "But I also used to hate him for being such a coward."

Narmada's heart ached at the anger and pain in Vaibhav's voice. Narmada hadn't known the truth about her husband until after her honeymoon. In fact, even Vaibhav hadn't known it himself.

"I can't hide it anymore, Narmada."

"Hide what? Please tell me, Vaibhav. I'm your best friend."

"I love you. But I'm not attracted to you. Not just to you... but to any woman."

Narmada had been stunned by the revelation at that time. Her world had shifted on its axis because of the truth. And she had to carry that secret all through her marriage and even after Vaibhav's death.

But she hadn't been the only one impacted by the truth.

A year after their marriage, Vaibhav fell in love with Tanuj, but they couldn't be together because of Rajesh Mohan's harsh orthodox convictions. It further led to Vaibhav's depression.

Tanuj wanted Vaibhav to come out in the open with their secret. He wanted to be acknowledged in public as Vaibhav's partner. Narmada had supported her husband and his lover fully. She was more than willing to divorce so that the couple could be together. She had even suggested they move out of the country. But Vaibhav couldn't take the step.

A heated argument with Tanuj giving Vaibhav the ultimatum led to their final breakup. Two hours after the breakup, Vaibhav crashed his car. The reports stated that the accident had been self-inflicted.

Narmada had gone into shock at that time. Vaibhav had called her earlier from the car, angry and upset. She tried to calm him down and told him she would speak with Tanuj and sort things out.

She had even mentally laid out the plans to convince Vaibhav to leave the country and run the operations of Genesis from abroad. But thirty minutes after the phone call, she had received another call about the accident.

"It is my fault, Narmada," Tanuj said in a broken voice. "I never expected him to take such an extreme step. We had broken up many times before, but we always got back because we knew we still loved each other."

Narmada couldn't remain silent any longer. "No one expected Vaibhav to take the extreme step, Tanuj. I've known Vaibhav since we were ten years old. He did threaten self-harm at times, but he apologized later. Please don't blame yourself."

Tanuj was silent.

They reached Narmada's home. Tanuj got out of the car, but shook his head.

"I'll get going, Narmada."

"Please stay for a while, Tanuj."

"No. Although I'm glad I met you and Divya, it's too painful for me to go down the memory lane."

Narmada nodded in understanding. "All right. But please keep in touch."

"I will," he promised. "I always valued your friendship. Had it not been for you, I don't think I would have had the chance to cherish those years I had with Vaibhav. Thank you for everything."

Narmada's eyes prickled with tears. "You are welcome," she said and hugged Tanuj.

They pulled away, and Narmada accompanied Tanuj to his car. But just before he got in, he looked at her with a small smile.

"It isn't just attraction Yash Varma has towards you, Narmada. It's more. Much more." His eyes softened. "I recognize it because that's how I used to feel about Vaibhav. It's a deep longing combined with angry desire and obsessive love."

Narmada held her breath at Tanuj's words.

"I hope the two of you get things resolved soon. Because if Yash Varma marries anyone but you, it would end in a disaster."

CHAPTER TWENTY-ONE

"I don't know if I'll succeed in this, Supriya."

The next morning, Narmada was on the phone with her friend. She was speaking while driving towards her grandfather's village.

"Of course, you will!" Supriya's voice sounded loud and firm on the car speakers.

"I thought so too, until Divya's call last night. Why would he ask Divya out for dinner if my so-called seduction was working?"

Supriya let out a frustrated breath. "I know your confidence is low right now. And it isn't just because of Yash Varma. You met with Tanuj, so memories of what happened are affecting you as well. I still remember how you looked when you came back from your honeymoon. You had looked shocked and broken. When it came to Vaibhav, of course you couldn't succeed in seducing him during your honeymoon because he wasn't attracted to women. But we can safely say Yash Varma prefers women, especially you."

A shiver passed through Narmada as she recalled the previous night and Yash Varma's possessive kiss. Her lips still tingled with the kiss.

"He might be attracted to me, but that still doesn't mean he'll ditch his original plans and marry me instead."

"Then ask him what his intentions are. If you lay it out in the open, he will be forced to commit and answer."

Narmada knew it wouldn't be as straightforward. The man she was trying to seduce was ruthless and also a master manipulator. He would easily evade the question and continue to keep her in a sexual haze with seduction without making any final promises.

"Maybe I'll try when I get back to the city," Narmada told her friend.

"All right. Give my regards to your grandfather and call me as soon as you get back."

"I will."

The call ended, and Narmada stared at the road ahead.

She decided to visit the village because she missed her grandfather a lot. And she also wanted to get away from home and have some time to think.

Her mind was too messed up.

She still couldn't get over the pain she felt when Divya called her and said Yash Varma was taking Divya out for dinner to woo her.

"You are mine."

"If you let him touch you again, I will break both his hands before ruining him completely."

He had been jealous of Tanuj even though he had no right to be possessive. By taking Divya out, he made it obvious where his inclinations lay.

When did he begin to mean so much to me?

What began as a desperate attempt to win back her company and stop the marriage became something more. She had started to fall for her enemy.

No! I don't love him!

Her mind was truly messed up and needed sorting.

Taking a deep breath, Narmada pushed the thoughts of her enemy away from her mind.

She reached the village mid-morning. As soon as she saw her grandfather's small tiled-roof house, her heart felt lighter. With a small smile, she parked her car under a huge tree and got out with her carry bag.

As usual, the door was open.

"Grandpa!" she called out.

She passed through the small open sit-out and went around the courtyard to the other side of the house where the kitchen was. She peeped into the backyard to see if her grandfather was working in his garden.

"Grandpa!"

A woman was drying clothes in the backyard. Narmada smiled at the woman who helped with cleaning and cooking for her grandfather.

"Oh hi, Kamala. Is grandfather home?"

"No, madam. He is at Vardhaman estate."

"Oh. I'll go there then."

Placing her carry bag in the spare bedroom, Narmada went back to her car and drove towards the estate, where her grandfather was working as the head gardener to oversee the restoration project.

Narmada had spent her first ten years of childhood at the estate. Even though her grandfather had worked as one of the drivers for the family, Narmada and her grandfather were never made to feel that the family living in the mansion was above them in any way.

The family was rich with royal bloodlines while she was their driver's orphaned granddaughter. And yet, when she played with the family's children, not once did the family care that she belonged to a different class. The family had treated her as an equal.

Unlike Rajesh Mohan.

When her grandfather began to work for the Rajesh Mohan, she thought his family would be the same way. Although she became close to Vaibhav, Rajesh Mohan hated it and constantly yelled at her for overstepping her limits and playing with his son. She and Vaibhav had to meet in secret when the older man wasn't around.

Vardhaman estate was about thirty minutes away. The tall, dense trees on either side of the road indicated she was nearing the estate. A few moments later, the mansion came into view.

Narmada was still shocked by how old it looked now with the peeling paint and climbing weeds all over it. Nearly two decades ago, it was the most beautiful place she had seen with bright white paint and several huge majestic marble pillars. The interiors had resembled to that of a palace.

But now, one part of the mansion was nearly black where the fire accident in the family wing had occurred, killing the entire family. Narmada's heart still ached at the loss. She had been only ten when she found out that the family died in the fire that started due to faulty wiring in the mansion. She had felt devastated as did her grandfather. But as a child, she was eventually able to adapt and move on. Friendship with Vaibhav had helped a lot too. But she knew it was hard for her grandfather even now to get over the loss.

Her grandfather couldn't even visit the estate until recently. After the family's deaths, the entire estate had been seized by the government since the family had been in huge debt and owned large amount in loans to several banks. But now, since it was purchased by a private company, her grandfather was able to access it as an employee. She hoped that whichever company had bought the estate would restore it to its formal glory.

A smile broke out on her face when she saw that a small part of outside was cleared up, and there was a freshly planted garden. She knew her grandfather would be around.

Parking the car outside the mansion, she went in search of her grandfather.

She found him right away at the side of the mansion. He was wearing a wide-brimmed hat and instructing workers to plant the rose bushes.

Her grandfather looked up, and when he saw her, a bright smile covered his face. "Maddy! What a surprise."

Narmada ran and hugged her grandfather. "I missed you so much, Grandpa."

Her grandfather laughed. "I'm glad you did."

Smiling, she looked around the mansion. "Looks like you will be busy for quite a while," she remarked. The place was huge, and it would take several months to restore it to its previous state.

Her grandfather smiled. "Oh, I'll definitely be busy. But I love it so much. I told the landscape architect how it used to be before. Although I can't remember exactly, I'm trying to give as many suggestions as I can."

Two decades was a long time. Although Narmada didn't remember much since she had only been ten years old when she left, she knew her grandfather would have a better memory despite his age since he had worked in the estate for thirty years.

"Will the company that purchased it run it as a hotel?" she asked.

The estate was a five-hour drive away from the city, but it would be a wonderful weekend getaway for family or couples or even corporate stays.

"I'm not sure, Maddy. For now, we were told to restore it the way it used to look."

"Hmm... that's good. Have they opened the mansion as well?" She wanted to check inside. She used to spend a lot of time in the impressive library of the mansion.

"Not yet," her grandfather replied. "But the restoration work will begin inside too in a few days."

Narmada was glad. She also recalled the beautiful antiques and large portraits and paintings inside. Hopefully, none of them were damaged or stolen.

"Will you be here for a while, Grandpa? I can bring lunch here."

"No need, Maddy. We can go home now. Saturdays and Sundays are my days off, but I came here today after remembering that Mr. Vardhaman had a vegetable garden planted on this side as well."

Narmada laughed. She knew how close and affectionate her grandfather had been to the Vardhaman family, especially to Ashok Vardhaman, who had been passionate about gardening. Ashok Vardhaman had always treated her grandfather like a father figure instead of just his driver. Having known

Ashok Vardhaman since he was as a little boy, it was particularly hard for her grandfather to cope with the loss.

"The fruit orchards need to be replanted too. Do you remember the mango orchard, Maddy?"

Narmada did remember. She had loved the mango orchard in particular. Although she was bad at climbing trees, she hung around the orchard during the season, hoping someone would pluck some mangoes for her.

"Yes, Grandpa. I don't think I ever ate such mangoes again." She led her grandfather to her car.

Her grandfather laughed. "Oh. Mr. Vardhaman had the best fruit trees. He used to collect the best seeds from all over the country and some from abroad too."

Narmada wasn't surprised. She recalled that the fruits used to be the juiciest and the sweetest she had ever tasted.

Smiling at the memories, Narmada drove back to the village. On the way, she stopped the car when her grandfather wanted to purchase fish.

"You better give me the biggest catch," her grandfather said to the fish vendor. "My granddaughter is visiting me."

The fish vendor gladly did as asked and gave them a huge fish.

Narmada laughed. "Grandpa, it's just the two of us."

"You can take some home tomorrow when you leave, Maddy."

Narmada's heart melted. She knew her grandfather loved to pamper her. The two of them were the only family to each other.

Most of the time, she selfishly wished her grandfather would agree to move in with her in the city. She wouldn't miss him then and could take care of him as well. But she also knew she couldn't do that because her grandfather liked living in the village and had his own circle of friends and distant relatives.

And she couldn't move to the village because of her work.

Maybe soon, I will succeed in convincing him to move to the city.

"I'll bring the fish inside," she said when they reached her grandfather's place.

Narmada followed her grandfather into the kitchen. Although her grandfather had help, Narmada wanted to assist.

Her grandfather cooked while she helped with the prep work like cutting vegetables and handing whatever he needed during cooking. Even though she had seen him cook hundreds of times, she hadn't picked up much of the cooking process. Her interests had always lay elsewhere in computers and technology. Cooking seemed like a lot of work.

But she loved to assist her grandfather because it meant getting to spend time with him.

"Mmm... it's wonderful as always, Grandpa!" she said, tasting a small spoonful. She smiled at him. "Why don't you freshen up? I'll set up the table and dishes."

She knew her grandfather freshened up before lunch, especially if he returned from outdoors. She went to freshen up as well, wanting to get rid of the smell of fish curry from her clothes and hair. Taking a quick shower, she wore another cotton dress. She left her hair free to dry.

Her grandfather hadn't returned from his bath. Meanwhile, she set up the dishes with two plates on the small table overlooking the central courtyard. She was just filling buttermilk into an earthen tumbler when there was a knock on the door.

"The door is open, Kamala!" she called out.

She wondered if her grandfather's help had forgotten something. But Kamala wouldn't usually knock. Wondering if it was one of the neighbors who might have got a whiff of the delicious fish curry, she went to answer it.

Smiling, she opened the door about to ask the neighbor to join for lunch.

But her smile died immediately.

Standing outside her grandfather's house, looking larger-than-life and devastatingly handsome was Yash Varma.

***

Narmada continued to stare in shock. Meanwhile, Yash Varma's eyes swept over her before he watched her with his usual unreadable look.

"I want to talk to you," he said, breaking the silence.

Narmada snapped out of her shock and glared at him. "How did you find out I was here?" she demanded.

"Does it matter?"

His calm voice made her angry. "Yes, it matters! And you can leave because I don't want to talk to you."

"I'm not leaving until we speak, Narmada."

Narmada was about to yell at the maddening man when her grandfather's voice cut in from behind.

"Who is it, Maddy?" her grandfather asked.

Narmada panicked.

She couldn't introduce Yash Varma without having to reveal that she lost her company. It would only worry her grandfather.

Before she could react and say it was no one and shut the door, her grandfather came near the door.

"Oh hello," her grandfather greeted.

Yash Varma's gaze moved away from Narmada to look at her grandfather. "Hello, Mr. Rao. I've come to meet Narmada."

Narmada's mind became blank.

She turned to see her grandfather watching Yash Varma curiously. In his three-piece-suit, Yash Varma looked completely out of place in the village.

"H-he is my employee, Grandpa. He came to ask me about an important work-related question."

Narmada's cheeks heated at the lie. Yash Varma hardly looked like he worked under someone.

Her grandfather smiled. "Oh, I see. Please come in and join us for lunch. Maddy and I made some really good fish curry."

Narmada was about to open her mouth to find a reason to refuse, but Yash Varma replied before she could.

"Thank you, Mr. Rao. I love fish curry."

Narmada was stunned. She stared at Yash Varma while he watched her.

"Maybe we can talk about our critical issue after lunch, Mrs. Mohan," he said with a neutral look. "The long drive here has made me quite hungry."

Narmada wanted to shout at the ruthless man who was manipulating the current situation like everything else he did. But she had no choice. Feeling angry and helpless, she let him in.

As he stepped in, his eyes swept around her grandfather's small home and then landed back on her, especially her simple clothing.

Narmada didn't care if he judged her. She was proud of who she was. Throwing him a glare, she turned away and walked towards the small dining table where her grandfather was setting up an additional plate.

The three of them sat with her grandfather on one side, and she and Yash Varma facing each other on opposite sides.

"You haven't introduced me properly to your friend, Maddy."

Narmada almost shook her head. Yash Varma was hardly her friend. He was a lying, deceptive and ruthless shark who ruined her life while also making her fall in love with him.

No! I don't love him.

"This is Yash Varma, Grandpa."

Her grandfather looked at her enemy for a few moments before slowly smiling. "Yash Varma. A very nice name."

"Thank you, Mr. Rao." Yash Varma's voice was deep and polite.

Narmada served food for the three of them. As she sat back, she briefly stared at the man in front of her. Yash Varma lived in a penthouse and had a personal cook who catered to his champagne lifestyle. She wondered how he would manage to eat authentic food using his hands.

But the man shocked her as always.

With smooth movements, he expertly removed the bones from the fish and ate the spicy dish without even flinching or reaching for the water glass.

"So, Yash. Where are you from?" Narmada heard her grandfather asking.

"I grew up in New York, Mr. Rao."

"Hmm. I've never been to that place. Although I know a doctor and his family who had settled in New York."

"I see."

Narmada's grandfather smiled. "For someone who grew up in New York, you seem quite comfortable with spicy food."

There was a flash of amusement in Yash Varma's eyes. "My mother often cooks spicy dishes, Mr. Rao. Fish curry is one of her special dishes. And she makes it in an earthen pot like you do."

Narmada was surprised. She had served the curry in a different dish, and yet he could catch the subtle flavor one could get only if it was cooked in an earthen pot.

Narmada's grandfather smiled. "I see."

Her grandfather then looked at her. "Vardhaman estate had a spice garden too, Maddy. I'll start working on it next week. Although the place might be used as a hotel, the spice garden can still be used to prepare meals. You should bring your employees to the estate once it's restored."

Narmada's face burned. The employees at Genesis were no longer hers, thanks to the man eating with casual ease in front of her.

"I will, Grandpa."

Her grandfather looked at Yash Varma and smiled. "Our village was famous for the Vardhaman estate. It featured as one of the best royal mansions across the country. The family died in a fire and the estate was seized by the government. But now, a company has purchased it and began the restoration process."

Yash Varma nodded. "I see," he said politely.

Narmada wanted the lunch to end soon, just so she could send away the man in front of her. Once again, he was causing havoc inside her heart.

Strangely, his presence at her grandfather's place felt entirely natural and she had a sense that her grandfather took an instant liking to her enemy.

"My Maddy wanted to marry the Vardhaman family's eldest son. She had even told him she was going to marry him no matter what."

Narmada almost choked on a fish bone. "Grandpa!" she exclaimed.

Her face burned as her grandfather spoke of her childhood foolishness, especially to Yash Varma of all the people.

Her enemy's mouth twisted into a small smile. "Interesting. How old were you, Mrs. Mohan, when you made your first marriage proposal?"

Oh God!

The blasted man was mocking her. It was obvious he was reminded of the time she had proposed to him. In fact, until two days ago, she had been doing everything possible to get him to agree to marry her.

"I think Maddy was only nine or ten when she proposed to the boy. She had proposed because the mansion had an impressive library with a computer. She was fascinated by the computer and spent a lot of time on it even at that tender age."

"Was the proposal accepted?" Yash Varma asked.

Narmada's grandfather chuckled. "Yes, the boy had to accept. My Maddy is quite the force of nature if she makes up her mind about something."

Hardly!

She had been trying to seduce the man in front of her, but she was hardly successful.

Oh God.

Everything sounded so surreal. Narmada couldn't believe she was having lunch at her grandfather's place with Yash Varma joining them.

Soon, the lunch came to an end. For dessert, they had the slightly sweetened buttermilk which would cool down the spicy food they just ate. There were fresh fruits as well.

As soon as they were done, Narmada cleared the dishes with the help of her grandfather.

"I'm going to talk to Mr. Varma, Grandpa," she said.

"Oh yes. Go ahead, Maddy. I'll probably take a nap." Her grandfather smiled. "It's been very nice meeting you, Yash."

"Likewise, Mr. Rao."

"Do visit us again. Hopefully by then, the Vardhaman estate will be functioning for visitors."

"Of course."

Narmada highly doubted if Yash Varma would come to her grandfather's village again. She was sure he had come with an ulterior motive and to play more mind games with her.

"See you later, Grandpa."

Narmada led her enemy to the back of the house, where there would be privacy.

She stopped under a shaded tree and turned to him. "Why are you here?" she demanded. "Shouldn't you be trying to woo your bride?"

His eyes flared at her taunting words. Narmada held her breath when he took an angry step towards her.

"You win," he gritted out. "I'm going to marry you."

Narmada stared at him in shock. "What?" she whispered.

His jaw was clenched while his eyes continued to flash. "You weren't a part of my plan. But I can't fucking breathe without you."

Narmada continued to stare at him. A part of her told her she should be rejoicing at her victory. But all she could do was stare at him in shock.

He looked into her eyes. "I don't care about your reasons for marrying me," he said. "I want to make you mine. Let's get married next week."

Narmada's heart thudded as she felt a strange combination of thrill and fear. Until then, Yash Varma had only been her enemy and lover. But now, he wanted to become her husband.

She stared at his darkly handsome and ruthless face that had captivated her from the moment their eyes met. Two months had passed, but the intensity of her feelings only grew from fascination to hate and then to love.

What would it be like to have him as her husband and to be tied to him for eternity?

"Say yes, Narmada," he demanded, his voice deep and husky with suppressed desire and emotion.

Taking a deep breath, she replied. "Yes."

CHAPTER TWENTY-TWO

"I have asked Narmada Mohan to marry me, and she has accepted my proposal."

There was a stunned silence on the phone when Yash made the announcement to his brothers on a video call.

It was Yash's youngest brother who reacted first as expected.

"What! Have you gone crazy!" Aryan exploded. "Narmada Mohan hates you!"

Yash knew his brother was speaking the truth.

But Yash also knew there was more than just hate that Narmada felt towards him. He knew she felt the same undeniable pull and connection towards him like he did towards her.

"I want her," he replied. "I know this wasn't a part of the plan. But I'll make the rest of our plans aren't impacted by my decision."

Aryan looked angry and shocked while Bhargav seemed calmer.

Yash looked at his middle brother. "I want Ma to attend the wedding. I'm going to fly to New York and bring her here."

"What about Rajesh Mohan?" Aryan demanded. "The man is planning a wedding soon. He will be super pissed to know you dumped his daughter and chose his widowed daughter-in-law whom he hates."

Yash knew that already. "There's nothing he can do."

Yash knew he was taking a huge risk in marrying Narmada and not Rajesh Mohan's daughter as planned.

But he could no longer fight what he felt. He not only wanted Narmada, he needed her in his life. He loved her.

"I'll join you," said Bhargav. "We should all fly to New York and meet with Ma."

Yash knew it was a good idea. Although they spoke to their mother often, she would be beyond thrilled to have her sons visit her in person.

"I'll ask Mr. Raman to arrange the jet for tonight." Yash looked at his youngest brother. "Aryan, I want you to join us as well."

Aryan looked angry, but he nodded.

Yash called his personal assistant. But even as Yash made arrangements to fly to New York, he already missed the woman he would be marrying next week.

"Mr. Raman. I would like you to arrange for a florist as well. Send flowers each day with a note." He gave instructions of what exactly he wanted to send each day to Narmada's office and to her home.

He wanted his beautiful pawn to miss him as much as he would miss her.

CHAPTER TWENTY-THREE

Twenty-four hours later, the Fortune Group jet landed at a private airport in New York.

Yash and his brothers were seated in a tinted SUV driving through the familiar neighborhood. Two SUVs with their armed, personal guards followed discreetly behind them.

"I just received a message from the security that Ma is back home," said Aryan.

Their mother had gone out earlier that morning to the farmer's market to pick up groceries. Although she could well afford to have them delivered to her home, their mother always preferred to pick them up each week.

"Let's not discuss the past with Ma," Bhargav suggested, keeping his eyes on the road while he drove the car. "She would easily guess why all three of us have been away for so long."

Yash knew his brother was right. Their mother did not have an aggressive or vengeful bone in her body. Discussing the topic about the past would make her realize that her three sons were seeking revenge for a past wrong, which would only make her upset.

"I'm going to tell Ma about Narmada," Yash told his brothers. "I'm going to say that we met at a conference, and I recognized her." Although he had arranged for their paths to cross, it would be partially the truth that he saw Narmada at a conference in Milan.

Aryan frowned. "Ma might freak out thinking that Narmada Mohan knows the truth about us."

"She won't freak out," Yash replied. "Ma trusts them, especially Shankar Rao."

Aryan's jaw clenched, but he nodded.

Unlike the cold ruthlessness of Yash and Bharagav, Aryan had always been a hot head. Aryan got the job done using his charms most of the time. But when things went wrong, he would easily erupt.

Yash knew his youngest brother wasn't happy with the sudden turn of things. Aryan didn't trust Narmada or her motives.

Although Yash already knew Narmada had ulterior motives, he wanted his youngest brother to make peace with the fact that Narmada would soon become a part of their family.

Soon Bhargav drove the car into a gated community for seniors and stopped in front of a small house with a big yard. Even though all three Varma brothers were more than capable to keep their mother in the lap of luxury, their mother continued to work part-time as a school teacher and preferred to live independently.

Yash got out of the car and looked at some of the cameras placed discreetly outside the house. He wasn't entirely happy that his mother didn't want a full-time security guard, but the cameras attached to the home's automated system made the house slightly secure.

"Ma must be in the garden," Yash remarked.

Choosing not to ring the doorbell, he and his brothers went towards the side door that led to the backyard. He knew his mother spent her time in the garden during weekend mornings.

He was right. He saw his mother digging up the soil in the garden.

"Hello, Ma," Yash greeted.

His mother turned, and there was a radiant smile on her face seeing her three sons.

"Oh my God!" she shouted with happiness. "It's going to snow today in the middle of summer. My ever-busy sons are all here to visit me at the same time."

Yash felt an ache in his chest, seeing his mother looking so happy. She had always put her sons' happiness and well-being over hers. Even though she hadn't seen the three of them for nearly two months, she never demanded they come to visit her.

His mother stood up and hugged Yash. She pulled Bhargav closer too. Aryan looked at their mother tentatively. Yash knew Aryan felt their mother was angry with him because of their last confrontation.

"What are you waiting for?" Parvathi Varma asked her youngest born. "Come join the group hug."

Yash smiled as Aryan smiled and joined the group hug. Their tiny mother could barely be seen surrounded by her tall sons.

The group hug would look odd to those who associated the Varma brothers as ruthless businessmen. But the brothers had always done anything to keep their mother smiling.

And Parvathi Varma loved hugging her sons. She kissed them on their cheeks before they parted.

"Whew! It's a warm summer day. Are you boys thirsty? Let's go inside. I'll pour us all some ice cold lemonade. I just picked up the brightest green lemons from the farmers market."

Yash smiled at his mother's excitement.

The four of them went inside to their mother's small, cheerful kitchen.

The three brothers sat on the kitchen bar stools while their mother washed her hands and pulled out a jug of chilled lemonade and poured it into glasses.

"You should not be working alone in the garden in such hot sun, Ma," Aryan said, taking a glass. "I think you should get help to stay with you... or simply move in one of us like we always wanted."

Parvathi Varma laughed. "Don't be silly. I was just gardening."

"It's too hot, Ma," Aryan insisted. "You even walked to the farmers market this morning. You can call them and tell them to deliver the produce at the doorstep."

Yash knew what his mother would say even before Aryan finished speaking.

Parvathi Varma waved her hand dismissively at her youngest son. "I'm fine. Your father taught me how to pick the best fruits and vegetables. I don't think any delivered or packaged ones can match up to the ones I hand pick."

Aryan sighed with exasperation.

Parvathi Varma grinned. "Come on, boys. Stop worrying constantly about me. I'm fine. Cheer up! Show me your sweet little smiles."

Yash smiled. At around six feet two inches, he or his brothers were hardly little. But his mother as usual spoke to them as though they were kids.

"What would you boys like to eat?" she asked.

The rest of the afternoon was spent in their mother's kitchen where she made them an elaborate home-cooked meal. His mother enjoyed cooking, especially when it was to feed her sons who she felt didn't eat well due to their hectic work schedules.

"How was your trip, Ma?" Aryan asked about her recent cruise trip.

While Yash and Bhargav spoke to her often, Aryan hadn't spoken to her recently.

Their mother smiled. "It was quite thrilling as well as relaxing. This time, I want you boys to join me. Hopefully, with some special girls accompanying you three."

Yash and his brothers briefly exchanged glances. Yash knew it wasn't a coincidence that their mother spoke about someone special joining them. Their mother had always been highly intuitive.

As they sat down to have their meal, Yash's thoughts ran back to the woman he was going to marry in a few days. The thought of Narmada joining his family during meals or vacations felt right. The love and closeness that Narmada and her grandfather shared showed that she would easily adapt to being a part of his family as well.

Yash waited until the meal was done before he made the announcement. His brothers gave him privacy to speak with their mother alone.

"I met someone I want to marry, Ma," he said. "I want you to attend the wedding next week."

His mother was shocked at first. But slowly, she looked excited. "Oh my God! That's great! Who is she?"

Yash smiled. "You will like her, Ma," he said.

His mother's smile widened. "Like her? I'm sure I will love any woman who has managed to capture my eldest son's heart."

Yash laughed. His mother had tried to set him up many times with several eligible women, only for him to have ignored those women.

"Do you love her, son?" his mother asked with a hint of anxiousness.

Yash knew his mother was worried about how the childhood trauma had shaped his and also his brothers' views when it came to love or relationships. Despite their gentle mother's influence and the values she tried to instill, he and his brothers grew up with the single-minded focus of achieving success without any softer emotions.

"Yes, Ma. I love her."

His mother's eyes shone with happiness. "I can't wait to meet her and welcome her to our family, son."

Yash's mouth twisted into a smile as a primal thrill of anticipation shot through him.

In less than a week, Narmada Mohan would become his wife. His beautiful pawn would have no choice but to surrender and become completely his.

CHAPTER TWENTY-FOUR

It was her wedding day.

"You look so beautiful, Narmada! You are going to knock Yash Varma off his feet!"

Narmada was in a long designer bridal dress with jewellery that Yash Varma had custom-made for her.

Only a week had passed since Yash Varma had proposed to her. Since then, everything had been moving very fast. Within a blink of an eye, it was soon her wedding day.

"Are you nervous?" Supriya asked.

Narmada nodded with a small smile. "A little." Everything felt too surreal.

Supriya held her hand and squeezed in reassurance. "Don't be nervous. Just enjoy the wedding. Your first wedding was inside the courthouse. I'm so glad this one isn't."

Although a court wedding could have sufficed, Narmada was surprised that Yash Varma insisted on having a proper wedding ceremony with rituals.

The wedding was being held in a private resort with only a handful of guests in attendance.

"Did you receive the pre-nuptial document yet?" Supriya asked.

Narmada shook her head. It was odd that she hadn't received any document to sign. Neither had any lawyer contacted her so far.

Supriya laughed in delight. "Oh. It really must be true love for Yash Varma. The man is a billionaire. If he screws up, you'll be entitled to half his fortune!"

Narmada felt her heart clench in a strange way. "Maybe there will be a post-nuptial document."

"I highly doubt it! The man is crazy about you. Anyone can see that! Especially after seeing those flowers he sent to your office!"

Narmada's cheeks heated as she recalled the huge bouquets of exotic flowers that arrived at her office each day.

She hadn't seen him or spoken to him since she accepted his marriage proposal. He was in New York most of the week and had flown back only the previous day. But even while he was gone, he made his presence felt by sending a note with the flowers.

The note was brief with a countdown of the days left for their wedding. The last note arrived the previous morning.

Tomorrow you will be mine.

Narmada's heart thudded with nervous anticipation.

"It isn't just attraction Yash Varma has towards you, Narmada. It's more. Much more. It's a deep longing combined with angry desire and an obsessive love."

Narmada recalled Tanuj's words. Although she didn't think Yash Varma loved her, she knew he desired her intensely.

Taking a deep breath, she checked her phone for more messages. One particular message made her heart much lighter.

A knock on the door dragged her gaze away from the phone.

Supriya opened the door and saw a young boy who must be the priest's assistant.

"The priest has asked me to inform that the ceremony will begin in five minutes."

Supriya nodded. "Sure. The bride is ready. We'll be there in a minute." Shutting the door, Supriya turned with a smile. "Ready?"

Narmada took a deep breath. "Yes."

They stepped out of the dressing room and went towards the main garden area, where the ceremony would be held. Narmada's stomach fluttered hard in nervousness, and she continued to take deep breaths.

You have been waiting for this day.

She had to do a lot to win the attention of a ruthless man like Yash Varma. She had not only succeeded in getting his attention, she had made him want her enough to marry her.

And now, it is the day of reckoning.

She sucked in another nervous breath.

A decorated dais came into view. There was a small group of people, including the priest on the dais. But Narmada's eyes fell only on the bridegroom.

In a dark royal blue ethnic suit, Yash Varma looked breathtakingly handsome and larger-than-life. His dark, intense eyes were locked on her as he watched her walking towards the dais.

Narmada's heart thudded so loudly in her ears that it almost drowned out the sounds of the ceremony. The last conversation she had with Yash Varma outside her grandfather's house resonated loudly in her mind.

"You win," he gritted out. "I'm going to marry you."

His jaw was clenched while his eyes continued to flash. "You weren't a part of my plan. But I can't fucking breathe without you."

He looked into her eyes. "I don't care about your reasons for marrying me," he said. "I want to make you mine."

Taking a deep breath, Narmada reached the dais. But instead of taking the steps leading up to the ceremony, she took a few steps further and stood in front of it.

Everyone looked puzzled, including her friend. "Narmada?" Supriya asked in confusion.

Narmada briefly saw a grey-haired older woman and two men standing on the dais. Ignoring them and everyone else, Narmada kept her eyes locked on Yash Varma who was watching her with his usual unreadable look.

"Did you really think I would marry you?" she asked softly.

There was a shocked gasp from Supriya.

"You deceived me," Narmada continued. "You preyed on my loneliness and stole the company I built. You also threatened the people I care about. You are the last man I would ever marry because I hate you."

There was no change in Yash Varma's face. He continued to watch her silently while people around him were shocked and angry.

"Divya married her boyfriend this morning like I had planned," Narmada said. "She just sent me a message that they are on their way to London. There is nothing you can do to her. Do whatever you want now. I don't care."

With that, she dragged her eyes away from Yash Varma's intense gaze and turned away. Supriya looked shell-shocked.

"Let's go," Narmada told her friend softly and walked away from the dais.

The shocked, angry conversations on the dais grew louder.

Biting her trembling lips, Narmada continued to walk away.

She went towards the hired car that was parked outside. She had hired a car with a driver rather than use hers or Supriya's because she knew neither she nor Supriya would be in a state to drive back home.

The driver looked shocked seeing her back so quickly and also without a bridegroom.

"Let's head back," she instructed the man.

The man nodded. As soon as she and Supriya got in and the car started, Supriya burst out.

"My God, Narmada! What did you just do! You not only rejected Yash Varma in front of his family and others, you even challenged him to come after you!"

Narmada's stomach still trembled hard with the shock and adrenaline rush.

"What happened?" Supriya asked. "I thought you were going to marry him for the sake of Genesis. Now he will never give it to you or let you work there!"

Narmada felt a deep ache in her heart at the thought of never walking the corridors of the company she built.

"I never had the intention of marrying Yash Varma," she said quietly. "My first priority was to save Divya from the unwanted marriage. Two weeks ago, Divya's boyfriend got a job offer abroad after which they both applied for a visa. I asked them to get married today. And they did. They got married today at a court wedding and took a flight to London."

There was a stunned silence.

Narmada took a deep breath. "Sorry I didn't tell you about my final plan," she said.

Supriya blinked. "Don't be sorry! Believe me, I laud your bravery to stand up to a ruthless, powerful man. But I'm worried about what he would do to you. And... and... it was obvious that Yash Varma fell in love with you. It wouldn't have been a marriage of convenience."

Another deep ache tugged Narmada's heart which she ignored.

"It doesn't matter how he feels. It's done now, and I don't regret what I did."

The ride back home was silent. Narmada closed her eyes briefly and rested her head on the seat.

She had spent the last two months in many sleepless nights. She had not only been worried about her company and Divya, she was also constantly fighting the battle not to fall in love with her enemy.

The ache in her heart indicated she had lost that battle badly.

***

An hour later, the car stopped at Narmada's house.

173

"Are you sure you want me to leave?" Supriya asked with a worried frown.

Narmada nodded. "I'm fine, Supriya. You should go home. I'm going to catch up on some sleep and work on the transition documents."

Supriya didn't look too convinced. "All right. But call me if you need me."

"Yes, I will."

Narmada waved her friend goodbye with a small smile. But as soon as she shut the door, the tears that she had controlled until then burst out.

She walked into her bedroom and lay on her bed while silent tears of heartache continued to flow from her eyes.

What is wrong with me?

I should be happy that I won and got what I had intended all along.

But she wasn't happy. Her heart ached, and tears continued to flow.

She desperately tried to remind herself of all the things Yash Varma had done to her, which should make her loathe him.

But she couldn't get herself to hate him.

She hated that she cared about him. She hated that she didn't feel lonely in his company. She hated that her enemy had also made her feel the warmth of his love along with strong desire. She hated that it hurt her when she hurt him.

And she also missed him.

She would no longer get to see him or speak with him anymore. The very thought of it sent an empty ache inside her heart.

Narmada closed her eyes as silent tears continued to stream from her eyes.

She knew she wouldn't be able to get over her heartache any time soon. Maybe ever.

CHAPTER TWENTY-FIVE

It was late evening when Yash returned alone to his penthouse.

He was still wearing an ethnic suit as he hadn't changed out of his wedding clothes. He had just dropped his mother at Bhargav's penthouse.

Even though his mother hadn't said a word to him, Yash knew she was quite upset and hurt. His gentle mother would never condone the route that her three sons had resorted to bring justice to a past wrong.

"There is always a price for revenge."

Yash remembered his father's words from childhood. The price Yash had to pay for revenge was love. He would eventually win the game of revenge, but he lost the biggest battle of his life by losing the woman who held his heart.

"How could you let that woman do that to you!" Aryan asked in outrage. "You risked everything, only for her to deceive you."

"She might risk the rest of our plans now," Bhargav added.

Yash knew his brothers were shocked and angry about Narmada rejecting him at the wedding.

But he wasn't.

Even though his heart felt as though it was ripped out of his chest, he wasn't shocked or angry. He had expected her not to go through with the wedding.

Narmada loved her grandfather more than anyone in the world. The fact that she hadn't invited her grandfather to the wedding ceremony made it obvious how she felt about marrying the man she hated.

But despite Narmada's obvious hatred, Yash had foolishly hoped she felt something other than hatred for him.

You are a damn fucking fool.

He had fallen in love with the woman he had deceived as a part of his revenge.

Clenching his jaw, he dialed a number. Things were already set into motion and at a critical stage which he needed to monitor closely. Even though he wasn't in the mindset, he knew it was his responsibility to finish what he started.

The phone was answered in two rings.

"Did Rajesh Mohan find out?" Yash asked his younger brother.

Rajesh Mohan would have found out about his daughter's disappearance.

There was silence. Yash knew his brother was still angry and outraged about what Narmada did. But like him, Aryan was also focused on their plan.

"Yes, he found out," Aryan replied. "He's now super pissed and shit scared."

Yash wasn't surprised. "Being angry and scared is a dangerous combination. I want you to increase the security around Narmada's house. Make sure there is someone tailing Rajesh Mohan at all times."

There was a long silence. Yash knew Aryan wasn't happy about offering Narmada additional protection.

Yash frowned. "Aryan, did you get what I just said? I don't want Narmada's security compromised in any way."

There was a sigh. "Yes, big bro. I completely understand. I also understand that despite what that woman did to you this morning, you still love her." There was a small chuckle. "I'm glad. Because you will love my wedding gift to you. Enjoy, bro."

Yash didn't want to play whatever game his younger brother was trying to get him to play. He focused only on what was important right then.

"I want the additional security reaching Narmada's home within two hours."

With that order, Yash ended the call.

He knew both his brothers would never go against any of his direct orders. Regardless of how they felt about Narmada, they would offer her protection.

Letting out a sigh, Yash rubbed the back of his neck.

He was tempted to drink himself to oblivion to forget about the woman he loved and lost. But he needed all of his senses in case an emergency arose.

He wondered if he could get cameras installed in Narmada's house. She would hate him even more if she found out he was tracking her movements. But right then, her safety was more critical to him than anything else.

He decided to call Bhargav and make plans about the installation of cameras the next day. But first, he wanted to change out of the wedding clothes.

He stepped into his bedroom. He didn't turn on the lights because he preferred the darkness right then. Only faint lighting came in from the night sky with city lights outside. He took a couple of steps towards his closet area when he suddenly stopped.

Immediately, his mind and body became alert.

He wondered if he was imagining things. His heart began to race as the subtle fragrance of roses that was unique to the woman he loved filled his senses.

With his heart continuing to beat faster, he reached for the light switch and turned it on.

"Fuck."

He wanted to kill Aryan right then.

"You will love my wedding gift to you. Enjoy, bro."

But even as he was furious with his younger brother's recklessness, a part of him was fiercely glad.

Lying on his bed, sleeping peacefully and still in her complete bridal attire—was Narmada.

CHAPTER TWENTY-SIX

Narmada woke up from what felt like a deep fog.

A dull headache throbbed at her temples. Her eyes felt dry and swollen, making it difficult to open them, but somehow, she managed to do so, only to be confused.

Instead of her small bedroom window to the side, she saw a familiar massive floor-to-ceiling glass wall. And sitting in front of the wall on a large cushioned leather chair was Yash Varma.

Narmada sucked in a painful breath. She was dreaming once again about the man she both loved and hated.

When will I stop dreaming about you?

Her heart ached as she stared at his devastatingly handsome face as he watched her with an intense, brooding look. He was wearing the same clothes he had worn for the wedding.

Although she had rejected him, her heart ached with longing as he looked at him.

"How are you feeling?" he asked.

The deep, rough masculine voice sent a small shiver through her body, making her skin break into goosebumps. It sounded so real that the dull throbbing in her head grew.

She shut her eyes, and images of a recent memory rushed in.

She opened her eyes to realize she was still in her wedding clothes and had been sleeping curled up on her bed.

She could hear the sound of the doorbell ringing. She wanted to ignore it, but she couldn't. She knew it might be her mother-in-law who must be worried about Divya's sudden absence.

Forcing herself to get out of the bed, she walked towards the door. And then, taking a deep breath, she opened it.

But the person outside wasn't Divya's mother or anyone she had met anytime. He was a tall, handsome stranger who looked very familiar. Before she could speak, a fog appeared in front of her face.

And then, there was darkness.

Narmada opened her eyes and stared at Yash Varma.

Suddenly, she realized she wasn't dreaming. She also realized why the man who had rang the bell at her home looked so familiar.

Anger shot through her, and she sat up hurriedly

"How dare you have me kidnapped by your brother!" she shouted.

Immediately, she began coughing because her dry and scratchy throat turned even drier.

Yash Varma didn't respond to her angry accusation. He got up from the chair and walked towards her.

Despite her anger, her heart thudded in fear.

"My God, Narmada! What did you just do! You not only rejected Yash Varma in front of his family and others, you even challenged him to come after you!"

She froze as he stood next to the bed. But when he leaned towards her with an outstretched hand, she flinched back.

His eyes flared. "I'm not going to hurt you, Narmada."

She didn't know whether to believe him. She was the woman who had rejected him publicly at their wedding. He would feel justified to hurt her.

His jaw clenched when he saw the fear on her face. "I'm not going to touch you. Not unless you ask me to."

Some of her fear dissipated because of her anger at his arrogant statement.

Before she could say she would never ask him to touch her, he picked up something from the nightstand and handed it to her.

"Drink some water," he ordered calmly.

She wanted to reject his help, but her throat was too dry. Grudgingly, she accepted the glass of water and drank. As soon as her throat felt a little better, she put the glass back on the nightstand.

And then, ignoring her lingering fear, she got up from the bed and glared at him.

She didn't want to be seated while he loomed over her. But even as she stood, she still had to look up since he was quite tall.

"Why am I here?" she demanded.

His eyes swept over her face. "You've been crying," he said.

She was taken aback by his response. And the tone of his voice indicated that he cared.

Taking an angry breath, she pushed away his concern and focused on her anger. "I asked you why am I here!"

"Tell me why you were crying?" he asked. "I thought you would be happy to get your revenge on me."

She hated how he could read her so easily.

"I was crying because I lost Genesis to a ruthless bastard like you. Not because of anything else."

His face remained unreadable, but she could see it in his dark, intense eyes that her reply affected him.

"Now answer me," she demanded. "Why did you bring me here?"

"For your safety."

She had expected him to threaten. But his answer shocked her.

"My safety? To keep me safe from whom? You are the only person who has a grudge against me."

He didn't say anything. He picked up a set of folded clothes near the foot of the bed and handed it to her. "You can change into these," he said.

"What? No! I want to go back to my house!"

"You can't right now."

Anger shot through her again. The anxiety, the hurt, and the confused feelings she held during the last two months boiled over.

She slapped him.

The force of the slap was hard enough to leave a pale mark on his tanned skin, but he didn't flinch. His eyes flared dangerously, and his jaw clenched while he continued to watch her.

"I deserved the slap for what I had done to you," he said calmly. "But I won't let you go."

A shiver ran through her body at his words, but she was too angry to care.

"Let me go!" she shouted.

"When it is safe, I will," he repeated once again in the same tone. "Until then, you'll be my guest."

Before she could react, he turned and walked out of the bedroom, closing the door behind him.

She ran towards the bedroom door and tried to pull it open. But it was too late. It was locked.

Frustrated, she shouted loudly again. "Let me go!"

***

An hour later, Narmada was fuming.

I hate him!

She was seated by the glass wall with a view on the same cushioned leather chair where Yash Varma had sat earlier when she woke up.

She was still trapped inside his bedroom.

Even though she hadn't wanted to, she showered and changed into the clothes he handed to her. She was wearing the cotton nightshirt and pants that had tags attached to them earlier indicating they were purchased recently. They fit her perfectly which also meant they were purchased specifically for her.

Her face burned. It wasn't entirely due to anger. She felt angrily embarrassed that her enemy knew her intimately enough to guess her sizes correctly.

She took a deep breath.

She felt angry, hurt and confused. She didn't mind the anger, but it was the hurt and confusion that bothered her.

She was hurt because she had fallen in love with her enemy. She was confused because her enemy continued to manipulate her and deceive her.

He is lying about my safety. He wants to keep me here to prove he still has power over me.

Narmada continued to fume.

She might love him, but she will not allow him to manipulate her emotionally.

Even as she braced herself for his return, her heart began thumping hard when she heard the soft click of the lock before the bedroom door opened.

Yash Varma stepped into the bedroom, holding a file in his hands.

Narmada hated herself for noticing he had showered and changed as well from the wedding clothes. He wore a t-shirt and track pants. Despite how she felt, her stomach flipped, looking at his wet hair combed back using his fingers.

Stop it!

A voice inside her shouted at her for noticing him and letting his presence affect her.

Taking a deep breath, she dragged her gaze away from him and stared outside at the night view. But she continued to feel the strong awareness of his presence.

Suddenly, she was also reminded that it was supposed to be their wedding night, and she was completely alone with him inside his bedroom.

A small shiver racked her.

"I'm not going to touch you. Not unless you ask me to."

She believed his words. She knew he wouldn't force himself on her. But she also knew he didn't have to. All he had to do was kiss her, and her body would melt and she would give in to him.

No! I won't be that weak.

Even as she decided not to give in to him, her heart thudded loudly inside her chest. Awareness and tension grew stronger and stronger as he came closer to her.

Her stomach quivered at the subtle smell of his body wash and cologne as she felt him lean toward her.

A blue folder was placed next to her on the armrest of the cushioned leather chair.

"This is for you," he said. "I was going to give this to you this afternoon."

Narmada wanted to ignore the folder, but she was curious about what it could possibly contain.

Was it a lawsuit against her?

Post-nuptial document?

Ignoring him by not looking towards him, she opened the file.

Her eyes slowly widened in shock when she began to read the contents.

Yash Varma had transferred the thirty-five percent shares he had taken from her back into her name. He had also included an additional forty-five percent shares that he had bought from the share holders and also from Divya. The total shares on her name were now eighty percent, making her the undisputed majority shareholder and owner of Genesis.

Happiness, relief and gratitude coursed through her.

But she forced herself to push aside the gratitude.

Why should I be grateful to him for returning what he had stolen from me using deception?

She looked at him. "I will pay you for the additional forty-five percent shares."

"That's not needed," he said. "I returned what was yours and the rest is a gift."

She raised her chin. "I don't want to accept gifts from you."

Something flashed in his eyes, even though his face remained unmoved.

"When can I return home?" she asked.

There was silence.

Anger built inside her again. "You can't keep me here, Yash. I'm not going to sleep with you or marry you just because you returned my shares.

You have to let me go!"

There was another heavy silence.

"Rajesh Mohan knows about his daughter's disappearance and that she spoke to you last."

Narmada was taken aback by his reply.

She looked at him and frowned in confusion. "So?"

"He'll want to hurt you," he said. "He feels it's because of you, he has lost the chance to make me his son-in-law. He now owes a lot of money to dangerous people who will be out for his blood."

Narmada was stunned. "What?"

"He made a lot of risky investments and took out loans that will be due in a few months."

Narmada knew Yash Varma was speaking the truth. Her father-in-law was stupidly arrogant enough to make high-risk shady deals with dangerous people.

Oh God.

A shiver ran through her.

Her father-in-law hated her already. But if he blamed her for his disaster, he was capable of harming her.

She took a deep breath. "Thank you for letting me know," she said. "I-I'll be careful and make sure I don't speak with him unless there is someone with me."

Yash Varma read the fear on her face.

"It's not safe to be alone at your home. Until Rajesh Mohan is in jail, which he will soon be, it's safer for you to stay here."

She knew he was right, but she didn't want to stay with him. Not when her body, mind and heart were constantly at war.

"I will stay with Supriya," she said.

"No. That's not advisable. Rajesh Mohan knows you might go there."

Narmada once again knew he was right. And by going to Supriya's house, she might be risking her friend and dragging her friend into the mess.

Narmada felt cornered. She couldn't think of a place where she could go and be safe. She didn't want to risk her grandfather either.

Yash Varma watched her calmly while she struggled to think of a better option.

"Just stay here for a few days," he said.

She had no other choice than to agree. "Fine. I-I'll stay here," she said. "But I'm not going to sleep with you."

His eyes flashed. "I didn't ask you to."

Her cheeks heated.

Is he only keeping me safe out of responsibility?

Maybe he can't wait to throw out the woman who ditched him once it is safe to leave.

She felt hurt by that thought.

His voice cut into her confusing thoughts.

"Dinner is ready," he said. "The cook has made a special meal for us tonight. Come out and join me if you want to. Or you can call the cook on the intercom and have a tray delivered into the room."

He waited for a few moments for her to respond. When she didn't, he turned away and walked out of his bedroom.

She felt a strong urge to call him back. She wanted to tell him she didn't want to be alone.

But she resisted the urge. Her feelings were too raw and confusing right then.

But one thought shook her.

I don't want him to think of me as his unwanted responsibility. I want him to love me and miss me as I love him and miss him.

CHAPTER TWENTY-SEVEN

The next morning, Narmada stepped out of the shower to see the smiling woman who had come into the bedroom to deliver a suitcase and a laptop bag.

"Good morning, madam. Would you like me to bring your breakfast?"

The suitcase looked familiar, and Narmada recognized her laptop bag.

"No. I'll join... Yash for breakfast."

"Oh, that's very good, madam. I'll set up the breakfast on the table right away."

As soon as the older woman left, Narmada opened the suitcase and was relieved to see her clothes packed into it.

She quickly changed into her clothes and felt much better.

But she hesitated to step out of the bedroom. She wondered if it was too soon to face Yash Varma.

The previous night, despite badly wanting to join him for dinner, she had decided to stay back. She had her dinner in the bedroom. The special meal was delicious, but it left a hollow feeling inside her stomach. She felt lonely and dejected.

I can't keep hiding in the room.

Taking a deep breath, she went out of the master bedroom.

As she walked out, she took in the spacious interiors of the penthouse decorated in rich, dark colors of browns that contrasted well with the white marble flooring. The penthouse decor suited the owner.

It wasn't the first time she was in the penthouse. She had visited the place a few weeks ago for dinner. But at that time, she had been too nervous and busy with an agenda to notice much about the penthouse. All of her focus had been on the man she had wanted to seduce.

Suddenly her cheeks heated as memories flashed into her mind of what had happened in the master bedroom during that night.

Pushing away those torrid memories, she focused on her current agenda.

To seek answers.

She went to the dining area, but the breakfast wasn't served at the dining table. It was served outside on the spacious balcony by the pool.

"Please begin with your tea, madam. I'll bring the rest of the breakfast out."

Narmada smiled at the cook. "Thank you, Lakshmibai."

She sat down and picked up the cup where the cook had just poured a hot cup of tea. The first sip felt divine, and it somewhat calmed her mind.

The view outside looked beautiful in the morning as well. She was admiring it when her neck began to prickle.

She didn't need to turn because she felt his presence. A faint, subtle scent of his cologne wafted in the air as he came around the table and took the chair opposite to her.

Once again, he looked devastatingly handsome.

He was wearing a form-fitting t-shirt and jeans like the last time. The t-shirt showed off his impressive, toned muscular body.

"Would you like another cup of tea?" he asked, running his eyes over her face.

She had showered and changed into her cotton dress, but she knew she looked tired and exhausted because she had been up the entire night.

"Yes, please," she murmured.

He poured her a cup before placing the tea kettle back. He picked up another kettle and poured black coffee into his cup. She wasn't surprised that he didn't add sugar or milk to it. The bitter taste didn't seem to bother him.

"I want to call Divya and my grandfather," she said. "I need a phone."

His expression didn't change at her demand. "Your phone is already with you. The charger should be in your suitcase."

Her face heated in embarrassment. She hadn't looked through her suitcase because she was in a hurry to get out of the bedroom and talk to him.

She was about to ask him about what happened to her father-in-law when the cook returned with the breakfast.

A delicious-looking spread that also smelled divine was placed on the table.

Narmada smiled. "Thank you, Lakshmibai."

The cook smiled cheerfully. "You are welcome, madam."

The older woman served the breakfast onto their plates and left.

But Narmada couldn't enjoy the delicious meal without first asking the question that had bothered her for a very long time.

"What did my father-in-law do to you?" she asked.

Yash Varma paused for a moment before resuming eating his breakfast. "What makes you think he did something?"

She frowned at his deflection. "It is obvious you are targeting him. And it is also obvious you deliberately let him make risky investments without the intention of bailing him out. Why? What did he do to you?"

She couldn't think of a reason how a man who grew up in New York could possibly be connected to a man who had always lived in India.

There was silence.

Narmada thought he would ignore her question, but he looked at her with an expression that made her hold her breath. There was dark hatred in his eyes.

"Rajesh Mohan was responsible for my father's death."

Narmada was stunned.

How can Rajesh Mohan be responsible for his father's death?

Before she could ask, Yash Varma got up from his chair. "Let me know if you want anything else brought from your home or elsewhere."

She nodded.

When he left, a lonely and heavy feeling crept into her heart again.

She returned to the room and kept her phone for charging. But she didn't wait until it was fully charged. As soon as her phone turned on, she checked for messages from Divya.

The last message from Divya was asking to call back on a certain number. Hoping everything was fine, Narmada called the number Divya had messaged.

"Hello?" Divya's voice was husky.

Narmada realized it was too early in London. "Sorry, did I wake you up?"

"Oh no, it's okay. I've been waiting for your call for a while. I was worried about what my father said to you. I'm sure he knows by now that I got married and escaped to London."

Narmada didn't want to tell Divya about the threat her father-in-law posed. Divya would feel guilty and worried.

"I haven't spoken to your parents yet, Divya. But I will soon. How are you and Rahul doing?"

Divya let out a sigh of relief. "We are doing well, Narmada. That job Rahul got a month ago was truly a godsend. They not only expedited his visa process, they even helped with mine. They even gave us an apartment to stay for three months until we find one of our own."

"That's good, Divya. I'm so glad. But don't hesitate to let me know if you need money."

"Oh no. Whatever you sent is more than enough. And besides, the company that Rahul is working for is paying quite well. It is supposedly a subsidiary to one of the biggest real estate companies in the United States."

"That's very good. Are you meeting with Tanuj again?"

"Oh, yes. He received us at the airport last night and took us to his home for dinner. He dropped us here and said he'll meet me this evening to help me apply for jobs in the company where he works."

Narmada was glad things were working out well for Divya. "Keep me posted, Divya. Go back to sleep. I'll speak to you later."

Narmada ended the call, hoping Divya could go back to sleep.

A dull headache throbbed inside her temples, reminding her that she hadn't slept well the previous night as well. But ignoring it, she pulled her phone from the charger and called her grandfather next.

A strange feeling nagged at her. She felt as though she were in a daze and couldn't figure out something.

Hoping her grandfather hadn't left to work at the Vardhaman estate, and speaking to him would calm her mind, she dialed his number.

Her grandfather answered within the first ring. "Maddy? Where are you? And how are you doing?"

Narmada was taken aback when her normally cheerful grandfather sounded extremely worried.

"I'm fine, Grandpa. I... I'm home. How are you? Are you at work right now?"

There was silence on the line.

"I was there yesterday at the wedding, Maddy. I saw what happened."

Narmada was shocked. "What?"

She had deliberately not let her grandfather know about the wedding she had no intention of going ahead with. But she never expected her grandfather to attend and see the spectacle that took place.

There was a sigh. "Yash had invited me, Maddy."

Oh no.

Narmada closed her eyes. The fact that Yash invited her grandfather when she hadn't must be shocking to her grandfather.

"Grandpa, whatever you saw yesterday... I had to do it. I will explain it to you soon. Please don't worry about me."

She felt helpless that she wasn't able to tell her grandfather about the danger her father-in-law posed and also what Yash Varma's revenge had cost her.

There was another sigh. "I already know most of what happened, Maddy. Yash told me about it two days ago. He told me about how you lost your company and his role in it. Everything."

Narmada was speechless. Yash told her grandfather that he had deceived her and took away her company?

Why didn't her grandfather call her and ask her about it? Something wasn't adding up.

Narmada took a deep breath. "Yash Varma deceived me, Grandpa. I didn't call you to the wedding because I didn't intend to go ahead with it. I-I can't forgive him."

There was a momentary silence.

"Maddy, haven't you met his mother? Did you not figure out who Yash is? I knew who he was the moment I saw him when he came to the village to meet you."

Narmada's head throbbed harder.

Once again, she felt as though something enormously significant was close to being revealed, but she couldn't quite figure it out.

"N-no, Grandpa. I haven't seen Yash Varma's mother." She had barely glanced at the wedding guests. All her focus had been on the man she was going to reject at that time.

"Maddy... Yash Varma is Yashwanth Vardhaman. The boy you proposed marriage to when you were ten years old. He is the oldest son of Ashok and Parvathi Vardhaman. Yash and his two brothers returned to punish the people who made the world believe Ashok Vardhaman died by suicide to escape debts."

CHAPTER TWENTY-EIGHT

Yash was speaking to Aryan and Bhargav on the phone about the current situation. Things were falling rapidly into place.

"Rajesh Mohan has gone into hiding," Aryan said with disgust. "And the coward left his defenseless wife behind."

"I expected him to do that," Yash replied. "Tighten the security around his house. Make sure his wife is safe and protected."

"We have ten armed men guarding the bastard's house. None of the goons would dare approach the place."

Although Yash wasn't happy about Rajesh Mohan's escape, he was glad the bastard's wife was going to be safe.

"What about the other two?" Yash asked. "Have they been warned in any way?"

"No, bro. They haven't a clue. But it wouldn't be long."

Yash knew Aryan was right. The fact that their one enemy was in deep trouble would reach their other two enemies soon. "How far are we from our targets?" he asked.

"I would say a month at most," Bhargav replied.

There was a frustrated sigh from Aryan. "I would need a slightly longer time for mine. My target is a tough nut to crack."

Yash was silent.

He and his brothers held the bloodlust to bring justice to what was done to their father. The people responsible would be soon be punished. But even though he and his brothers were close to their goal, the hollow feeling inside his heart didn't disappear.

When everything was accomplished and he returned back to his old life, he would have to live with a deep void in his heart.

"Look for Rajesh Mohan at his friend's guest house," he instructed. "He won't be able to hide anywhere beyond a day or two. He's going to get more desperate and try something."

Yash was about to add more instructions when he heard a knock on the bedroom door.

He was inside a guest bedroom because Narmada was staying in the master bedroom.

Although a part of him had initially cursed Aryan for kidnapping Narmada and placing her in his penthouse, he was now fiercely glad about the situation.

He didn't want to leave Narmada unprotected anywhere other than his penthouse.

A soft knock repeated on the door again.

"Come in," he said, expecting it to be his housekeeper or cook to give him updates about Narmada.

But when the door opened, he saw Narmada's shocked face.

"I'll call back later," he told his brothers before ending the call.

He looked her shocked face while she stared at him with wide eyes.

"Y-you are Yashwanth Vardhaman," she whispered.

Yash knew she must have spoken to her grandfather and discovered the truth.

A week ago, he had taken a huge risk going to the village to propose to Narmada. He had known that there was high possibility that her grandfather would somehow recognize him.

Yash didn't look a lot like his late father. But there was enough resemblance to both his parents that someone who had lived with the family for decades would know right away.

Yash had known that Narmada's grandfather recognized him.

Two days before the wedding, Yash went back to the village and spoke to her grandfather again, telling him the truth, and also seeking his forgiveness for what he had done to the older man's granddaughter. The older man had nodded silently in understanding.

Yash continued to look at Narmada's shocked face. "Yes," he replied to her question.

Slowly, she came closer to him. Her eyes searched his face as though trying to look for the hints that would prove he was the person he was claiming to be.

"The cheek scar," she said softly. "I caused it when I asked you to pluck a mango for me from the biggest tree. You fell and scratched your cheek on a branch."

"Yes," he replied again.

It had happened when he was twelve. She had only been ten at that time. He was home for the summer holidays from his boarding school in the city.

She bit her lip as she continued to stare at him. "Tell me what happened," she pleaded softly. "When my grandfather told me you and your family died in a fire accident, I-I was shocked and devastated. I thought it was the truth."

Yash knew Narmada had only been ten years old and hardly at the age where she could understand or comprehend what was happening. In fact, her grandfather had kept her sheltered. Her grandfather didn't even let her know that the owner of the mansion's body was found hanging inside his room.

Yash stared at Narmada's shocked and confused face.

Right from the time he had met her again in Milan, he could see the hints of the curious and mischievous girl she had been during their childhood. It was because of that connection that he was unable to keep away from her.

He was fascinated by her because of what she had achieved in life with her intelligence and grit. Her beauty had only added to his fascination and led to his obsession. He fell in love with the girl she had been and the woman she had become.

Narmada had always been her destiny.

Unable to control himself, he cupped her soft cheek.

Her eyes closed shut. When she opened them again, there was hurt and confusion. "Tell me the truth, Yash. Please, tell me everything."

CHAPTER TWENTY-NINE

Narmada was too shocked to discover that the man who had deceived her and yet stolen her heart was the boy who she used to adore during her childhood.

She had loved his whole family, especially his parents, who were among the kindest and most generous people.

"Please tell me the truth, Yash," she pleaded again.

The darkly handsome face which had been haunting her dreams was now filled with a different darkness at her question.

His hand fell from her cheek, and she immediately missed his touch.

"Aryan discovered our father's body hanging from the bedroom ceiling," he said.

Narmada was shocked.

She couldn't imagine the handsome, ever-smiling Ashok Vardhaman in such a state.

Yash's jaw clenched. "For the longest time, my brothers and I thought that our father died by suicide. I was angry with him for leaving my mother and brothers to fend for ourselves."

Narmada's heart went out to his family, who had been very close and affectionate.

"But four months ago, my mother revealed to us that my father wouldn't have killed himself, and that it was my father's close friends and acquaintance who were involved in his death."

Oh God.

Narmada didn't know what to say. It must have been truly devastating to find out that their loved one was murdered.

"One of my father's close friends was Rajesh Mohan. He was my father's childhood friend."

Narmada recalled seeing Rajesh Mohan visiting the Vardhaman estate a few times. But he hadn't been the kind to smile or engage in conversations with the help.

"Rajesh Mohan and another childhood friend made my father invest a lot of money on a project that would provide affordable housing to thousands of poor people living in the city. But instead of using the money for the project, my father's friends reused the money in their own investments. They even collected money from the poor people as advances before the houses were built. My father had initially planned to invest what he had, but his two friends convinced him to borrow huge amounts in loans from the bank."

A sick feeling of dread sat heavily inside Narmada's stomach. She could imagine what must have happened when the people demanded their houses and the banks demanded payback to the huge loans.

"My father was shocked. But according to my mother, he had only been badly disappointed. He was finding a way to repay the banks and also do justice for the people who were swindled by his two friends and partners. But the day before he was supposed to file for a case, he was found hanging from the ceiling."

"I'm so sorry," Narmada whispered, shocked by the tragedy that struck a beautiful family because of a few people's greed.

Yash looked out of the window. "It was your grandfather who helped us out. There was information about our lives being in danger because they didn't want my mother or us children to take up the case. Soon after I lit fire to my father's mortal remains, barely two hours later, your grandfather drove us to the airport and we flew to New York. Meanwhile, your grandfather set fire to the family wing in the mansion and staged our deaths."

Narmada was stunned.

She could only imagine what a harrowing experience he and his family had to go through—from living in a large estate to suddenly running for their lives, and having to fend for themselves in an unknown country.

She could understand his rage, not just on behalf of his father, but also for what his mother and younger brothers had gone through because of the tragedy.

Yash turned to look at her. "You weren't meant to be a part of my plan," he said softly. "I was supposed to marry Rajesh Mohan's daughter and have him make reckless investments making him go through the same things that he did to my father."

Narmada's heart thudded when she heard his plan. "Then why did you come after me? You wanted to ruin me so I won't be able to help them?"

The look in his eyes reminded her of their night in Milan when she caught him watching her. The instant connection and the strong pull she felt towards him now made sense. Her subconscious must have recognized him.

"At first, I didn't recognize you," he said. "I didn't know you had married Rajesh Mohan's son. But when I found out later who you were, I was drawn towards you."

She held her breath at the intense burning desire she saw in his eyes. "I tried hard to stay away. I was only supposed to watch from far as I executed my revenge plan through you. But I wanted you."

A strange memory clicked into her mind. "T-that man who tried to flirt with me... was hired to seduce me."

His jaw clenched. "Yes."

Oh God.

His gaze locked on hers, letting her see everything he felt.

"I know you hate me for what I did," he said. "I don't expect you to stop hating me anytime soon. But I want you to know I regret hurting you, and there is nothing in the world I wouldn't do to atone for the hurt I caused you."

Her heart clenched at his words.

She did hate him even as she was falling in love with him. But it was hard to hold on to that hate.

Feeling overwhelmed by the shocking revelations and what she felt towards him, she couldn't tell him right away that she didn't hate him.

He searched her face again. But when he saw uncertainty in her eyes, his face turned unreadable again.

"It'll only be a few more days until your life goes back to normal," he said softly. "Until then, if you are not comfortable, I can leave the penthouse and stay elsewhere."

Everything inside her rebelled at the thought of him leaving. "No. You don't have to go."

He nodded.

Feeling confused, she turned away and was about to leave. But a gasp escaped her when he caught her hand and pulled her close.

"Yes, I hired a man to seduce you," he said. "But I wouldn't have let another man touch you."

The dark torment she saw in his eyes made her hold her breath.

He watched her while roughly uttered words poured out of him. "I know you hate me and would never forgive me, but I still want a chance to have you in my life."

"Why?" she whispered.

Her heart nearly stopped at the look on his face.

"Because I love you, Narmada."

Even though she could read the truth in his eyes, she was still stunned by his declaration. She had known that he desired her, and they felt a strong connection, but she never expected him to feel anything beyond an obsession.

"I... I..." She stared at his eyes, feeling lost in the intensity of his emotions.

There was anger, torment, desire and a need so strong in his eyes that her body shook with the intensity.

She had always thought love was a calm emotion that brought peace. But loving Yash Varma was like loving a storm. He made her feel alive while sweeping her away in a cocktail of emotions.

"I feel the same way about you," she confessed. "I love you."

There was a flash of disbelief in his eyes.

She knew it would be hard for him to believe her, considering it had been barely a day since she rejected him at their wedding.

They hurt each other with their games of deception. But despite the hurt, something beautiful and powerful was born that they both wanted to hold on to.

She placed her palm on his hard jaw line. "I still think you are a ruthless man who deceived me," she said. "But I couldn't stop myself from falling in love with you."

His eyes closed shut for a moment. When he opened them, some of the darkness disappeared.

His voice was rough with emotion. "I don't deserve your love or forgiveness, but I promise I'll never hurt you again."

Her heart thudded. She pulled his head down towards her and kissed him softly on his lips. "I love you, Yash," she whispered.

It was like unleashing a storm.

His fingers dug into her hips, and dragged her closer before fusing their mouths together. He kissed her hard and deep, like he was never letting her go. She kissed him back equally desperately, letting him feel her anger, pain, desire and love.

She gasped as he swung her up and carried her towards the bed.

Their tongues tangled, and she clutched his hair while trying to draw the taste and essence of him. Every inch of her body burned with need.

Their joining was unrestrained and desperate.

Days and weeks and months of dancing around each other without giving in completely led to an explosion.

Her back hit the mattress, and there was a sound of cloth ripping before both their clothes disappeared. The dark look in his eyes while he watched her rivaled a certain madness that resonated deep inside her.

Her fingers dug into his hard muscles, pulling him closer while he held her thighs apart, preparing her for their joining. She didn't want to wait. She wanted him and needed him urgently.

But he made her wait."Tell me you want me," he growled.

"I want you."

Before she could finish her sentence completely, she gasped out loud as he thrust deep into her, going all the way inside.

She cried out, her back arching at the intense feeling that was a combination of pain and pleasure. He stilled momentarily, his chest rising and falling rapidly while staring into her eyes.

"Don't stop," she begged.

And so he didn't. Fisting his hand into her hair at the back of her head, he held her in place. He took her body like he took over her heart—like a force of nature—dark, desperate and relentless.

She cried out as her body trembled and shook. Her nails dug into his biceps at his deep thrusts which she began to crave as much as her next breath.

His body vibrated in tension. "I'm never going to let you go," he rasped.

At his next hard thrust, she shattered.

Her release was so hard, it shook her body violently. She screamed and clung to him as heat ripped through her lower stomach and reached all over her body.

His release was equally violent, joining her in the explosion. Throwing his head back, he roared out his release, the powerful cords on his neck straining with the fury of the explosion.

As their hearts slammed together against their chests, her eyes filled up with tears at the intensity of their joining. For the first time in her life, she felt she was right where she belonged, with the man who filled her heart.

CHAPTER THIRTY

Narmada woke up to the hot press of lips against her throat.

Her skin broke out in goosebumps even as she moaned softly. The moan wasn't entirely due to pleasure, but was also because every inch of her body was sore.

"Good morning," Yash Varma's voice rumbled deeply.

A shiver racked her body at his voice and touch. Slowly, she opened her eyes and saw that it was morning.

They had been making love continuously for nearly twenty-four hours. They only took two brief breaks for lunch and an early dinner which they ended up not finishing.

Making love with Yash Varma was truly like being caught in a storm.

Sometimes, their joining was rough and desperate, and sometimes it was slow and teasing. But no matter what, it was a thrilling and unpredictable experience that she couldn't get enough of.

Right then, the lovemaking was veering towards slow and teasing.

Moaning softly, she held his head while he kissed her throat.

Her body once again felt the need to feel close to him again. "Yash," she whispered.

The single word was enough to convey what she wanted and needed.

He raised his head and cupped her face, holding her captive with his gaze. The dark heat in his eyes indicated his intense desire while he slowly slid into her.

It burned as she was too raw and sensitive inside due to their constant lovemaking. But she craved the feeling of him being inside her.

Her breath hitched as she stared into his eyes while he moved in and out of her at a slow, leisurely pace. The deep intensity in his hooded eyes along with the soft stroking of his thumb on her cheeks, added to her pleasure.

When her release came, something warm and beautiful filled her heart along with his essence. She clutched his shoulders, holding him as his body shook on top of hers, joining her in the pleasure.

Much later, he raised his head from the crook of her neck and stared at her. "You look so damn beautiful," he said, rubbing his thumb gently against her swollen lips.

She laughed softly and rubbed her fingers on the rough, stubble on his cheek. "You look quite handsome too, Mr. Varma."

He broke into a grin.

The sexy grin fluttered her stomach. The darkly handsome face transformed from harsh lines to utterly charming when he flashed his teeth.

Her heart beat in anticipation, hoping to see him similarly relaxed with his guard down in the future.

But what is in their future?

He had told her about his reasons for deceiving her, and she believed him when he told her he regretted hurting her.

They even declared their love to each other. But was it enough?

She to open up to him and wanted him to open up to her in return. But a small part of her was still cautious and wanted to guard her heart out of habit. The things she had gone through in her life had made her cautious.

Her thoughts splintered when he rolled them until she half lay on top of him. Letting out a sigh of content, she rested her cheek against his broad shoulder.

She smiled. "I still can't believe you are Yashwanth," she said. "I used to have a huge crush on you."

There was a deep chuckle. "I knew that."

She was surprised. "You did?"

"Yes. You were only ten, but I was older."

She laughed. "Not that old! You are only two years older than me!"

"Yes. But I knew about your crush."

Even though it happened nearly twenty years ago, she was embarrassed by how she used to follow him everywhere and dote on him whenever he was home during his school holidays. He and his brother younger studied at a boarding school in the city.

"You also wanted to marry me for the computer in the library," he reminded. "You spent a lot of time sneaking into the library, trying to use it." He sounded amused.

It was true. She was curious to know how a small box could contain more information than the entire library.

She let out another sigh. "I cried a lot when I heard about the fire. I missed you specially. I used to tell Vaibhav about you. One of the reasons why Vaibhav and I became close was because he was very understanding."

Yash was silent. His hand stroked her bare hip in a leisurely manner. The rough pad of his thumb rubbed against her sensitive skin, causing her to shiver in pleasure.

"Tell me more about Vaibhav Mohan," he said.

Although his voice sounded casual, she could sense the underlying tension in him. She wasn't wearing her wedding ring. At some point in the night, she had taken it off. She knew it bothered him.

"Vaibhav was very sweet and kindhearted," she said. "He didn't have many friends and liked to play by himself. And like me, he was fascinated by technology."

She didn't want to tell about Vaibhav's anxiety which was the major cause of him not having any friends apart from her. It wasn't her secret to tell, and she didn't want to disrespect her best friend's memory. She also didn't want to reveal that Tanuj had been Vaibhav's lover.

"Vaibhav and I were eighteen when we created the first prototype of Genesis software. We were equal partners. When Vaibhav suggested we should become partners in real life too, I accepted because I wanted to marry my best friend."

"How did Rajesh Mohan take the news?"

Narmada recalled him having a huge meltdown. "He didn't like it. But Vaibhav and I had eloped and got married before breaking the news to his family. They had no choice but to accept our marriage. Vaibhav threatened to walk out of the house otherwise."

It was one of the rare times when Vaibhav had stood up to his father, and she had been very proud of him.

Taking a deep breath, she pulled away slightly to look at Yash. The relaxed look on his face was gone. It was obvious he didn't like hearing about Vaibhav. She knew revealing the truth about Vaibhav and Tanuj would ease his jealousy. But she didn't want to reveal that secret either which wasn't hers to tell.

"I loved Vaibhav," she said softly. "I will always love him and cherish our memories together since he was my best friend before he became my husband."

Yash's eyes flashed, but he gave a curt nod in understanding.

Narmada placed her palm on his tensed jaw. "But Vaibhav is gone now and I love you," she said.

The tension in his jaw slowly eased.

"I didn't cheat on Vaibhav with Tanuj or anyone," she continued. "Yes, Vaibhav killed himself, but it was because of circumstances he felt were beyond his control."

He was silent and didn't demand that she explain more.

Narmada knew he believed her. Her heart melted that his love held that kind of trust.

"I love you," she whispered again and kissed him softly on his chest, where his heart beat strongly.

Suddenly, the need for him rose inside her again.

She began to place small kisses on his chest and used her tongue and teeth to taste him. He tasted of pure masculine heaven.

His harsh breaths indicated he enjoyed her kisses. His fingers dug into her hair as she continued to kiss the hard muscles on his chest and abdomen. She then slid below.

He had always driven her crazy by tasting her intimately and teasing her until she begged him before bursting apart. But she had never driven him to the edge in a similar way. He hadn't let her.

She knew he was ruthless and dominant when it came to the bedroom. He liked to be in charge and drive the pleasure. But right then, she was determined to give him back the pleasure.

Her stomach trembled in both excited anticipation as well as nervousness. He was the only man she had been with, and she didn't have the experience to pleasure a man.

But she let her need for him drive her actions.

She placed a kiss on his hard arousal, and then ran her tongue over the velvety skin, tasting him intimately. She then took him into her mouth and continued to taste his essence.

Harsh groans escaped his throat and his fingers tightened in her hair as he unconsciously guided her movements. But just when she thought he would lose control, he let out a harsh groan and pushed her away.

She thought he didn't like what she did, but the look on his face indicated otherwise. He looked close to losing control.

"I want you," he rasped and was about to pull her under him.

But she resisted by moving away.

His eyes flashed dangerously. Before he could drag her again, she sat on top of him. Her heart thumped crazily, and her body screamed with need as they both watched her taking him inside her.

A rough groan escaped his throat while her eyes closed shut at the incredible feeling.

But she forced her eyes open again, wanting to see him. She began to move. The movements were slightly awkward due to inexperience, but each time she took him inside her, pleasure burst through her body.

His face was harsh with passion and need. He looked like the ruthless stranger she had been drawn to many months ago. But she now knew her ruthless enemy was also the man who filled her heart and soul.

"I love you," she whispered.

His eyes blazed at her words. His fingers gripped her hips tightly and slammed inside her.

She cried out with pleasure.

"Say it again," he ordered.

"I love you."

He continued to slam inside her while she continued to declare her love over and over again.

The pleasure grew and grew until a tidal wave crashed over her, making her scream her love for him.

She clung to him, holding on to him like an anchor while she was blown apart in the fury of their desire.

"I love you," she whispered one more time.

His body shuddered. His arms gripped her, and he rolled their bodies until he was lying on top of her.

She blinked her heavy-lidded eyes open to see his face. His fiercely intense eyes were now tender as he watched her. The ruthlessness and possessiveness were completely gone from them.

He cupped her face and kissed her forehead gently.

Her heart expanded when she saw his smile.

He then rolled away from her suddenly. And then, getting down the bed, he scooped her into his arms.

"Yash!" She gasped as he carried her.

"Shower and breakfast," he stated. "I'm sure you must be hungry."

She barely had dinner the previous night when they were carried away by desire. She was starving.

"It's okay," she said. But her stomach chose right then to rumble in protest.

Her cheeks heated while he laughed in amusement.

He kissed her tenderly on her lips. "I promise a quick shower and a feast for breakfast," he said.

A few minutes later, he broke the first promise.

CHAPTER THIRTY-ONE

"This is the most delicious feast, Lakshmibai! Thank you so much."

At Narmada's praise, the older woman smiled in pleasure. "You are welcome, madam."

Yash sat back lazily, continuing to watch Narmada. "We won't need your help to serve us dinner, Lakshmibai. You can take off for the rest of the day today as well."

"Oh, sure, Mr. Varma."

There was a knowing smile on Lakshmibai's face as she looked at Narmada and left.

Narmada's face heated with a blush. "Yash! How could you make it so obvious!"

He poured a cup of black coffee for himself and then poured another cup and added sugar and milk before handing the second cup to her.

He smiled in amusement. "I'm sure if she came into the penthouse, she would know. The two of us are not exactly quiet."

Oh God!

The sounds that echoed from inside the master bathroom a while ago resonated in her mind.

She wanted to hide her face in embarrassment. He was right. Their lovemaking was quite noisy.

He laughed. "Don't worry. We'll have the penthouse to ourselves until tomorrow morning."

Even as she blushed and her body was quite sore, her heart thudded with anticipation.

She was about to say something when her phone received a message. It was from Divya, letting her know that she had met Tanuj again, and he was helping her prepare for an interview that would be held next week.

Deciding to reply later to Divya's message, she looked up from her phone. Yash was watching her with a small smile

Narmada's stomach fluttered at the look on his face. She pushed the feeling aside, mostly because she needed time for her sore body to heal, and also because she wanted to ask him something important.

"That was Divya," she said. "She sent me a message from London. Her boyfriend... I mean Divya's husband got a job in London. Divya is applying for jobs too, and Tanuj is helping her."

He didn't say anything and didn't seem surprised either. Once again, a strange feeling nagged at her.

"W-would you have married Divya if I hadn't intervened?" she asked.

"Yes." There was no hesitation in his reply.

Her heart ached at his reply. But she understood the strong need for his revenge and justice that drove him to do certain things. She would do anything for her grandfather too.

"Were you planning to propose to Divya the day you took her out for dinner?"

He watched her face. She couldn't hide the hurt she felt at his actions.

"No," he replied. "I invited her to dinner to break off the alliance."

She was shocked. "What?"

"I didn't need to go ahead with the marriage because Rajesh Mohan had already made many risky investments that would trap him. I invited his daughter to break off the alliance and also to help her."

She was confused as well as shocked. "What do you mean you wanted to help her? Help her with what? She—"

Suddenly, she broke off as things clicked into place inside her mind.

She recalled the conversation she had with Divya the previous morning.

"That job which Rahul got a month ago was truly a godsend. They not only expedited his visa process, they even helped with mine. They even gave us an apartment to stay in for the first three months until we find one of our own."

"Whatever money you sent is more than enough. And besides the company that Rahul is working for is paying quite well. They are into real estate and construction and a subsidiary of one of the biggest real estate companies in the United States."

Narmada stared at Yash as he continued to look at her with a small smile.

"My God," she whispered. "Rahul is working for a company that is a subsidiary of Fortune Group."

"Yes."

Yash got Divya's boyfriend a job and helped them leave the country.

"I love you, Narmada."

She believed him when he said those words to her. But now, knowing how a ruthless man like him had helped his enemy's daughter, made her heart fill with love. She was proud to love a man like him.

She got up from the chair and sat on his lap. His eyes flashed as he watched her while she held his face.

She kissed him. "Thank you for helping Divya," she whispered against his lips.

He gripped the back of her head and deepened the kiss until she clung to him. When they broke apart to breathe air into their lungs, he smiled. It was a darkly amused smile.

"I'm glad you crashed my dinner at the restaurant that night," he said in a rough tone that fluttered her stomach. "That's when I knew you felt something for me other than hate, and it wasn't just me wanting you."

"But you didn't still agree to marry me," she reminded.

His mouth twisted. "I had already decided to marry you the night you left the penthouse after dinner."

She stared in shock.

Oh God. If only I had known the truth earlier.

"Too much was at risk, Narmada," he replied as he read her mind.

Her face fell. "But...but if I had known the truth... I wouldn't have... I'm sure your mother and brothers hate me for rejecting you that way."

"My brothers will get over it," he stated. "And my mother understands why you rejected me at the wedding."

Narmada wasn't so sure. The Vardhamans had been a close-knit family who were protective about each other.

He cupped her cheek. "Hey," he said softly. "Don't worry. My mother used to love you before. She'll love you again now."

The worry inside her heart eased at his reassuring words.

After breakfast, they went inside. Although their desire continued to blaze through them, he carried her to the bed and sat against the headboard and simply held her across his lap.

She loved the sweet side of him as much as she reveled in his dark passion.

She wanted to know more. She wanted to know everything about him and what had made him into the man he was.

"Tell me what happened when you left the estate," she asked softly.

There was a flash of darkness in his eyes. She knew his family was in deep mourning when they were forced to leave and fend for themselves.

"We had no money when we left for New York. The tickets were sponsored by a kind-hearted family friend. Even though my mother legally wasn't obliged to, she chose to give away her money, jewellery and assets she had inherited from her side of the family. She wanted to compensate the people who were impacted by the housing project my father began."

Narmada recalled the conversation with her grandfather the previous day. Her grandfather had tried to help the Vardhamans by offering his savings before they left for New York.

But Yash's mother hadn't accepted it.

"Parvathi Vardhaman refused to take my money and asked me to take care of you and move to the city where you would have better opportunities in education."

Narmada was moved by Yash's mother's selfless gesture. Ashok Vardhaman and his wife had always thought about helping others even if it cost suffering to their own family.

"My mother worked as a nanny and housekeeper during the initial years. My brothers and I used to help her as much as we could because she was also studying part-time to get her teaching degree. And once she got the degree, she was able to teach in schools that paid a slightly decent salary. But unfortunately for her, the day she became a teacher, Bhargav and I quit school."

He spoke in a matter-of-fact tone without wanting any sympathy. But Narmada's heart went out to him as he spoke of the struggles his family went through living in a bad neighborhood because that's all they could afford at the time. He and his brother had quit school and began working in construction sites by faking their age.

Narmada was amazed by the sheer grit he had at such a young age to succeed.

"Aryan wanted to join when Bhargav and I began taking up bigger contracting projects. But we told him to finish his education like our mother wanted for all three of us."

Yash and his brother began to purchase rundown houses in bad neighborhoods and renovated them and sold them for a profit. Soon, they were able to save to buy bigger houses in slightly better neighborhoods and continued to take on more projects.

"Mr. Raman used to work for my father in the trust board. He contacted me and wanted to work for me. He saw the potential in the company we had just started."

Narmada was surprised. She didn't know Mr. Raman used to work for the Vardhamans before.

"We began to diversify our business and expanded it rapidly while taking many calculated risks. At twenty, I felt there was nothing much to lose. And my family was my biggest support."

Narmada felt proud of him and his family at how each of them had a significant role to play in their success, especially his mother.

"My mother always kept us grounded. But no matter how much my brothers and I had loved our father during our childhood, the three of us blamed him for leaving my mother and us to fend for ourselves. Four months ago, it was on my mother's birthday when Aryan called our father a coward. My mother lost her cool for the first time. She told us the truth about the circumstances of his death and how she believed it wasn't a suicide, but a murder. Because she felt the threat was going to extend to us, she chose to leave with us rather than bring out truth and justice"

Narmada's heart ached for the woman who had to carry the truth about her husband's death for so many years even though she knew her sons thought their father left them deliberately.

"We are yet to find the truth of what happened exactly on that day. But we know who are responsible."

Narmada tightened her arms around Yash and rested her cheek against his chest, hoping to give him comfort even as he sought justice and closure.

They sat in silence.

But the momentary silence was shattered when Yash's phone began ringing.

It was mid-afternoon on a Sunday. But having run a company for many years herself, Narmada knew it could be a work-related call too. She hoped the call would be brief.

The muscles on the chest shifted as Yash reached out for his phone.

"Yes, Aryan?" he asked.

Narmada felt Yash's body tense while he heard his brother speaking.

"I'll be on my way there. You and Bhargav handle the situation until then."

Narmada's heart thudded as she stared at Yash. His face was tense and angry.

A dark feeling of dread began inside her as he looked at her in silence. "What happened, Yash?"

His jaw clenched even as he spoke calmly. "Rajesh Mohan escaped last night. Our investigative team tracked him and found him at the Vardhaman estate. Your grandfather is with him."

CHAPTER THIRTY-TWO

Four hours later, Narmada's hands trembled on her lap while she sat next to Yash. He was driving them to the Vardhaman estate.

"The police armed security is outside the mansion monitoring the situation closely. Your grandfather is safe."

Narmada wasn't able to relax. The fact that her grandfather was inside the mansion with a possible murderer made her extremely worried.

"My father-in-law is angry with me, Yash," she said. "He knows he can hurt me through my grandfather."

Yash turned to look at her briefly. "Rajesh Mohan doesn't know the truth about who I am. He won't harm me. Let me handle the situation. You can remain inside the car and listen in. It's not safe for you to join me inside."

Yash had wanted her to stay back in the penthouse. He even threatened to lock her inside for her safety. But she insisted on coming. She said if he didn't allow her to come, she would never forgive him.

Although he eventually gave in and let her join him, Narmada knew he wasn't happy she was risking her safety.

"I can't just stay in the car, Yash. I have to speak to my grandfather. I need to see he's okay."

"All right." Yash's voice was calm, but his clenched jaw indicated otherwise.

They reached the mansion. Several uniformed police officers and security were waiting outside the mansion.

Yash's brothers were standing outside with them.

"Rajesh Mohan is armed," said one of the brothers. Narmada knew it must be Bhargav because she had briefly seen Aryan when he had come to her house a few days ago.

Namrada's heart thudded in fear. "D-did he shoot my grandfather?" she asked.

Bhargav shook his head. "No. Your grandfather is fine."

She felt slightly relieved even though there was still danger of her grandfather being hurt.

"Has he spoken again?" Yash asked.

Bhargav nodded. "He wants to speak with Narmada."

Narmada knew her father-in-law wanted to hurt her. He was only using her grandfather to get to her.

She looked at Yash. "Please, let me speak with him. I-I can reason with him."

Yash looked torn. "He has a fucking gun, Narmada. I can't risk your safety."

"I know," she whispered. "But I can't let you go in alone either. He wants me."

Yash clenched his jaw.

Bhargav looked at his brother. "There's a sniper team at the back. Aryan is monitoring from there. If you can somehow distract Rajesh Mohan, we should be able to take him down."

Yash finally relented. "All right. I'll go in with Narmada. But if anything goes wrong, take him out. Don't hesitate to give out the order."

Namrada bit her lip. She knew the Varma brothers needed Rajesh Mohan alive. Her father-in-law was one of the few people who knew the truth about what had happened with Ashok Vardhaman. Killing him would possibly mean losing the truth. Yash was going to risk losing the truth because of her.

Yash looked at her. "Let's go," he said softly.

With her heart thudding, she followed Yash into the mansion.

The place was nearly barren inside. They walked towards the family wing, which was destroyed by the fire. The walls were nearly black along the corridor.

Yash stopped outside a room and caught her face. Watching her with a torn look, he kissed her hard on her trembling lips. "Just stay calm," he advised softly.

She nodded even as fear gripped her.

They walked to the end of the corridor and went into a large room. At first, all she could see was blackened walls and half-burnt furniture.

But when her eyes fell to the corner of the large room, she saw her grandfather seated on a chair. A man with disheveled clothes and hair stood next to him pointing a gun.

Her grandfather looked calm when he saw her. But Rajesh Mohan's eyes flared when he saw her with Yash.

"So it is true," Rajesh Mohan seethed with anger. "You helped my daughter run away so you could have Yash Varma all to yourself."

Narmada slowly went closer. "Divya loves another man, Papa. She begged me to help her, and she is very happy right now. Please put down the gun. It's not my grandfather's fault."

Rajesh Mohan's eyes flared even more. "You are a lying whore. You deliberately sabotaged my daughter's alliance because you wanted to trap another rich man. Just like you trapped my son!"

"Please call Divya," she begged. "Ask your daughter the truth. She threatened to kill herself if she was forced into an unwanted marriage. She begged me to help her."

The manic look in Rajesh Mohan's eyes grew. "Stop using it as an excuse. I know you are a gold digger. You even married my son for money even though you knew he preferred men and not women."

Narmada was shocked. "You knew your son was gay?" she whispered.

"Yes. I found out the truth when he began an affair with that other man."

"You mean Tanuj? The man you accused me of having an affair with?" she asked. "You knew Tanuj was Vaibhav's lover and not mine, and yet you put the chastity clause?"

There was no remorse on her father-in-law's face. "You are a gold-digging whore, and you proved it by sleeping with a stranger in Italy. You also proved it by sleeping with the man promised to your own sister-in-law!"

Yash took a step forward. "That's enough," he said in a dangerously calm tone. "Put down the gun, Mr. Mohan."

Rajesh Mohan looked outraged. "This whore is responsible for everything! Because of her, I am a hunted man with people out for my blood! If she didn't spread her legs for you, I wouldn't have been a dead man walking!"

Narmada's heart thudded at the hatred evident in Rajesh Mohan's eyes.

"You are wrong," Yash said in a dangerously calm tone. "You are being punished for the things you brought on yourself. Unlike the owner of this mansion."

Shocked silence followed.

Rajesh Mohan looked stunned. Slowly, the older man's eyes widened as he stared at Yash. For the first time, there was terror in his eyes.

"A-ashok..." he whispered.

"Yes, I am Ashok Vardhaman's son."

"B-but how? You died in a fire..."

Narmada's heart thudded harder as Rajesh Mohan slowly turned to look at her grandfather. "You lied, saying the Vardhaman family died in fire. You saved them!" The expression was murderous. "You came to work for me as my driver only to ensure I would never find out the truth!"

Narmada knew her father-in-law was pushed to the edge with the new revelation. He was waving the gun dangerously at her grandfather.

Even as her legs trembled in fear, she took a deep breath and spoke.

"Yes, I trapped Yash Varma deliberately."

At her statement, Rajesh Mohan whipped his head towards her.

"I deliberately seduced him so he would marry me and give back Genesis. My plan worked. Two days ago, after I helped Divya elope, Yash gave back my shares of Genesis along with Divya's shares and more."

Rage flashed in Rajesh Mohan's eyes. "You gold-digging whore!" he roared out and swung the gun towards her.

Narmada braced herself for the pain of a gunshot. But when the loud sound of gunshot went off, she was pushed down. Yash's heavy body covered her to protect her.

Several more shots were fired. Narmada turned her face and saw in shock as her father-in-law was flinching hard as his back was being ridden with bullets.

Suddenly there was silence when the gunfire stopped. Only Yash's heavy, labored breaths were loud next to her ear. Several uniformed policemen surrounded the prone body of her father-in-law.

Narmada was relieved when a few of the policemen helped her grandfather. Her grandfather looked unhurt even though he seemed slightly shaken.

Just when relief hit her, she suddenly noticed hot liquid seeping into her t-shirt. Her heart nearly stopped, and her body was paralyzed in horror as understanding dawned.

She watched in shock as Bhargav and Aryan came rushing towards her. They held Yash and pulled his heavy weight away from the top of her.

Her t-shirt was completely soaked with blood. But it wasn't her blood.

"Yash!" she screamed. "Oh my God! Yash!"

Yash was shot by the bullet that was aimed at her.

CHAPTER THIRTY-THREE

One month later...

"Wow, Narmada! You look absolutely radiant!"

Narmada smiled at her friend. "I think you are biased."

Narmada knew she looked like how a woman would look if she hadn't slept well for nearly a month and had also lost a lot of weight in the process.

Supriya shook her head. "I'm serious! Yes, you do look a bit thinner, but your face is definitely glowing. A very happy glow!"

Narmada laughed. Her friend was right. Despite the harrowing last month, the last three days were spent in excited happiness. She was also excited about the coming days and the future.

"That beautiful jewellery is also adding to your glow."

Narmada smiled and ran her fingers gently over the antique jewellery set which was a part of Vardhaman family heirloom. "Yes, the jewellery is beautiful."

The Varma brothers had acquired all the Vardhaman family heirlooms that were seized.

The beautiful set that Narmada was wearing was gifted to her by Parvathi Vardhaman.

"It was meant for the eldest daughter-in-law. I want you to have it."

Narmada smiled.

Yash had been right. Parvathi Vardhaman did not have a grudge against the woman who had rejected her son right before the wedding. The older woman was in fact happy that Narmada was able to stand up against Yash's often ruthless behavior.

Supriya grinned. "I'm glad you agreed to marry with a ceremony rather than elope again."

Narmada laughed. She was embarrassed about having another wedding ceremony barely a month after she walked away from the previous one. Yash wasn't too happy about the ceremony either and wanted to elope by getting married in a courthouse.

"Let's marry now," he growled.

Despite her son's impatience, Parvathi Vardhaman wanted her eldest son to marry with a proper wedding ceremony. Narmada's grandfather agreed to that as well.

Yash had grudgingly agreed.

Supriya looked excited. "I think it is time. They must have sent someone to fetch the bride."

Supriya was right. Someone knocked on the door.

Narmada felt quite a bit of déjà vu. But unlike a month ago, she went to the door and answered it.

She was surprised to see the man standing outside.

"Wow," the handsome man said with a smile.

It was Aryan, Yash's youngest brother.

Narmada smiled back. "Hello, Aryan."

Aryan's charming smile grew. "Bro wanted me to make sure his bride hasn't escaped from the wedding again."

Narmada's cheeks heated as she laughed. "Tell him I'm still here," she said.

Aryan grinned.

Narmada was amazed by how only a few days could make a huge difference in how Aryan felt about her. Aryan was very protective about his family. He hadn't trusted her because he blamed her for making his brother fall in love with her which put most of their plans in danger. Aryan had also blamed her for Yash getting shot by a bullet meant for her.

Narmada still recalled the terrible day when Yash was shot.

"Yash!" she screamed. Terror gripped her as she saw one of Yash's brothers removing his shirt and pressing it on top of Yash's bullet wound to stop the flow of blood.

There was so much blood that the sight of it made her shudder.

Yash watched her even as he struggled to keep his eyes open. "I'm fine, Narmada," he said. His rough, deep voice sounded slurred. "Take your grandfather and leave with Bhargav. I'll come and see you once everything gets sorted."

The brother who held the shirt on the bullet wound glared at her. It was Aryan.

She didn't care about anything right then apart from staying by Yash. She refused to budge when Yash's other brother Bhargav came to take her away. "It's only a flesh wound," he said. "My brother will be fine."

"Are you all mad! I'm not leaving Yash's side! I'm never leaving his side. Don't you dare ask me to leave him!"

She had stayed by Yash's side as the ambulance took him to the hospital. Like Bhargav had said, it was a flesh wound that did not pierce any vital organs. But because Yash lost a lot of blood, he was kept in the hospital for a week.

Yash asked her to go home since his brothers could take care of him during the nights. He wanted her to rest. But she had refused again.

Even when they discharged him from the hospital, she went along with him to his penthouse and stayed until he was fully recovered and out of danger.

Three days ago, Yash proposed to her again.

"Marry me," he demanded.

"Yes," she replied instantly.

Life was too short and unpredictable. She almost lost the man she loved. There was no way she would take any chances to be apart from him.

As soon as she agreed to the proposal, much to her shock, Yash kissed her passionately before sending her away from his penthouse.

"Three days, and you will be mine forever," he vowed.

Before she could completely catch her breath, arrangements were made for their wedding to be held at the Vardhaman estate. Although the mansion was still being restored, the ceremony was being held in the gardens, a part of which had been beautifully restored. It was doubly special because Narmada's grandfather had worked hard in restoring that garden area.

"Bro asked me to give this to you." Aryan sounded amused as he handed her a white envelope.

"Thank you." She took the envelope. It was light in weight which meant there must be a note or a letter.

Aryan smiled. "Welcome to the family, sis. See you soon." He smiled charmingly at Supriya as well before leaving.

As soon as the door closed, Supriya sighed. "My goodness. How can all three brothers be so shockingly hot? The Varma genes are definitely quite yummy."

Laughing at Supriya's statement, Narmada opened the envelope. There was a small folded paper along with a picture.

She opened the paper and read the bold, masculine and neat scrawl. Her cheeks heated.

Can't wait to make you mine forever. I'm sending you the picture of your wedding gift.

She saw the picture and realized that it was the old computer that used to be at the Vardhaman library.

She burst out laughing.

"What is it?" Supriya asked.

Narmada showed the picture. "I proposed to Yash when I was ten saying I wanted to marry him because of this."

Supriya smiled and let out a sigh. "I never thought I would say this. But damn, Yash Varma can be so sweet and romantic."

Narmada grinned. She was discovering it herself as well. And she couldn't wait to discover more for the rest of her life.

The sounds of trumpets and drums from the outside indicated the ceremony had begun.

As though on cue, there was another knock on the door. This time it was her grandfather. He was wearing simple traditional clothing with a head turban.

"You look beautiful, Maddy," her grandfather said with a smile.

Narmada hugged her grandfather and laughed. "Thank you, Grandpa. You look quite smart too."

Narmada's eyes suddenly turned moist. A month passed by, but she was still shaken up by how close she had been to losing her grandfather. Rajesh Mohan had threatened to shoot him. Her grandfather was the only family she had, and she would do anything to protect him and keep him happy.

While she stayed by Yash in the hospital, her grandfather had been her rock. He comforted her by telling her things would be fine.

"Hey," he said, patting her gently on her back. "No crying. Remember, you are a big girl now."

Narmada laughed as he repeated the words he often said during her childhood.

Her grandfather smiled. "I'm so happy you will be a part of the Vardhaman family. I couldn't have picked a more loving and generous-hearted family."

Narmada agreed with her grandfather.

Yash's mother was a beautiful, generous woman who accepted her wholeheartedly. And although Yash's brothers were treading the path of deception and revenge similar to that of their oldest brother, which Narmada didn't wholeheartedly agree with, both Bhargav and Aryan were protective of her. They considered her a part of their family.

"Come on," said Supriya with excitement. "The ceremony is going to start."

With a smile, Narmada curled her arm around her grandfather's arm and went to the ceremony where she knew Yash would be impatiently waiting.

This time, she took time to admire the beautifully decorated wedding venue. It was an intimate wedding, but almost everyone she cared about was attending the wedding.

Narmada couldn't see Yash as a large piece of cloth kept him hidden from her view.

Yash's two brothers waited by the wedding dais. Tanuj was seated in the front row with his boyfriend. Mr. Raman was seated next to him. Narmada felt a small, painful tug seeing Divya and her mother who were in mourning but decided to attend the wedding.

To the outside world, the cause of Rajesh Mohan's death was listed as a heart attack. Yash and his brothers didn't want the other two men who knew the truth about their father's death to be warned in any way.

Narmada hoped the truth would come out soon and there would be some closure for the Vardhaman family.

"You look beautiful."

Narmada saw the smiling face of Parvathi Vardhaman. The older woman smiled and kissed Narmada on the forehead. "You better sit next to my son soon," she said. "He is making the priests nervous with his impatience."

Laughing and blushing, Narmada joined the ceremony that would tie her to the man she loved.

Epilogue

One day later...

Milan, Italy.

"Madam, champagne from a gentleman admirer."

Narmada was seated by herself at a table in a crowded upscale bar lounge. She looked at the waiter.

"Oh. Tell the gentleman I don't accept drinks from strangers because I had a bad experience once."

The waiter looked surprised, but he nodded before leaving. Narmada pressed her lips together, suppressing a laugh as she watched the waiter taking the unopened bottle of champagne back to the table, where the gentleman admirer was seated.

The darkly, handsome man hardly looked like a gentleman. His eyes smoldered at her when the waiter told him what she had said.

Narmada shivered in anticipation as he gave a short, curt nod to the waiter before getting up from the chair and coming towards her. His strides were aggressive and powerful and that of a conqueror.

But Narmada was determined not to let her ruthless enemy win so easily again. Her heart thudded in anticipation.

"I thought you enjoyed drinking champagne, Mrs. Varma," the man's deep voice rumbled as he took the chair opposite her.

His familiar deep, sexy voice made her shiver deliciously from inside.

Narmada kept her face carefully blank and shrugged her shoulders in a deliberately casual way. "I'm a little bored of champagne. I want to try something new. Something more exciting and adventurous."

The handsome man's dark, intense eyes flashed. "Is that so?" he asked.

"Yes," she said. "You know what I think would be exciting and adventurous?"

"What?"

"Spending a passionate night with a handsome stranger in a faraway country."

The handsome man's dark, intense eyes narrowed dangerously. His eyes fell pointedly on her huge wedding ring that contained the Vardhaman family crest embedded with rubies and diamonds.

"I'm married. But I don't mind having a little fun. Although I must warn you that my husband is quite jealous and possessive."

A rough growl came out from the handsome man. "Let's go," he bit out.

Narmada's heart thudded. "Where to?" she asked.

"My room upstairs," he ordered.

Before she could agree or refuse, he caught her hand and yanked her up. Then placing his large palm against her back, he hurried her outside the bar lounge.

Narmada's stomach fluttered. She had to run to keep up with his long strides. They took the elevator to the top floor and walked through the corridor to the corner room.

The man swiped the key card and pushed the door open to a familiar suite.

Before Narmada could admire the view outside of the suite, her back was pushed against the hotel room wall, and she was trapped when the man caged her using both his arms.

"Finally," he said with a rough growl. "And that wasn't how it was supposed to go. You were supposed to accept the champagne."

Narmada laughed even as her heart thudded with excited anticipation. She stared at the handsome face. Raising her hand, she traced the familiar features. She ran her fingers over the strong jaw, the bold and sharp nose and the firm, masculine lips. She also traced the thin scar on his cheekbone.

His eyes flashed with heat and desire and most importantly love.

She gasped when he dragged her closer and swung her up in his arms to carry her towards the bedroom.

"Yash! Put me down right now! Your stitches might come open again!"

But the maddening man didn't listen. He carried her all the way to the bedroom and lowered her on the bed. His dark, intense eyes flashed before his mouth captured hers in a passionate kiss.

She moaned, her arms curling automatically around his shoulders to pull him closer. But at the rough tug on her dress, she gasped and pushed at his shoulders.

"Yash, wait! You'll tear the dress. Let me change first."

"I don't care," he growled. "We'll buy another dress. Or better still, you can be naked the entire honeymoon."

She laughed breathlessly. But when his mouth met with hers again, she forgot all about her dress. All she wanted and cared about was being with the man she loved.

Their joining was passionate and desperate. Thirty days of being apart made their hunger fiercer.

"I love you," she gasped, holding him close as he slammed into her.

Her declaration of love made him lose control even more, and he joined their bodies with an intensity that shook her from inside out.

She shattered, screaming out his name while he followed her soon after.

She didn't know how long they lay joined together and wrapped around each other. Even though her body ached and she was wet and sticky, she felt blissfully happy.

Slowly, Yash raised his head from the crook of her neck. And then, cupping her cheek, he stared at her.

"What?" she asked softly.

"I can't believe you are finally mine," he said in a rough tone that sent a warm zing into her heart and also set fire to her body again.

"Yes, I am ours," she whispered. "And you are mine."

His eyes turned darker with emotion. "I love you," he rasped out softly before he brushed his lips over her forehead and cheek.

Her heart melted. He wasn't the kind of man who showed or demonstrated affection easily. Circumstances in life had made him hard and ruthless.

But she didn't need to hear romantic or sweet words from him. His every look and every gesture spoke of his love towards her.

Raising her hand, she gently touched the healing scar on his shoulder where he had willingly taken the bullet meant for her. He had even covered her body with his, protecting her from harm while risking his own life.

The ruthless man who had come into her life like a dark storm of destruction was also the man who loved her, cherished her and protected her. He brought passion, love and happiness into her life.

She stared into his eyes. "I love you too," she said softly.

And then, she kissed the man who was her forever.

The End.

Author's Note

Thank you for choosing *Wicked Deception*.

I hope you enjoyed reading Yash and Narmada's passionate love story and were able to escape into their happily-ever-after.

The Varma saga continues in Wicked Lies and Wicked Trap. Do not miss the passionate love stories of Bhargav and Aryan.

Thank you.

MV Kasi

Email: manyavkasi@gmail.com

FB/Instagram: @mvkasi

Twitter: @author_mvkasi

M.v. Kasi's Book List

WICKED TRAP
WICKED LIES
WICKED DECEPTION
WILD IN LOVE
CRASH IN LOVE
DEVIL'S LOVE
DEVIL'S DESIRE
DEVIL'S KISS
UNTIL YOU
ACCIDENTAL HUSBAND
THE PROMISE
THAT SAME OLD LOVE
THE HOLIDAY AFFAIR
MISSION SUPERSTAR
UNTIL FOREVER
BOUND BY HATRED
THE CAPTIVE
SOULLESS
RUTHLESS
BREATHLESS

Short Stories (20-Minute Reads)
HIS CAPTIVE BRIDE
RECKLESS LOVE
THE ROYAL WEDDING
THE PROPOSAL
BOUND BY FOREVER
BILLIONAIRE ESCORT